Robert K. Swisher Jr. has been a ranch foreman and a mountain guide. He knows the outdoors and western history, and has successfully combined these interests in stories, poems and novels.

THE LONELY COWBOY

by

Robert K. Swisher Jr.

Text copyright © 2019 Robert K. Swisher Jr.

OPEN TALON PRESS

OTHER PUBLISHED NOVELS BY ROBERT K. SWISHER JR.

Historical Fiction: Trade and E-book
Published by Sunstone Press
The Land
Fatal Destiny

Contemporary Western Fiction: Trade and E-book
PUBLISHED BY SUNSTONE PRESS
How Far the Mountain
The Last Narrow Gauge Train Robbery
The Last Day in Paradise
Love Lies Bleeding
The Man From the Mountain

Literary: Out of Print
Published by Samisdat Press - Canada
American Love Story

Young Adult: Trade Only
Published by Echo Press California
The Weaver
Published by Sunstone Press
Only Magic

Humor: E-book only
Conversations With the Golf God

Mystery Series: E-book only:
Bob Roosevelt Mystery Series – 4 novels

Contemporary Fiction: E-book only
Hope
How Bridge McCoy Learned to Say I Love you
A Circle Around Forever

Satire: Trade and E-book
Published by Open Talon Press
Vent
Grammar Nazis Are Not Always Rite, Right, Write
Vent Revisited

Short stories and poetry in literary journals, articles in outdoor magazines.
Reviews by Publishers Weekly, Best Sellers, Library Journal, and many others.

PUBLISHED BY
OPEN TALON PRESS

EDITORS: Liz Gaidry

COVER DESIGNER: Samantha Fury

FORMATTER: Traci Wooden

Library of Congress - In Publication Date

Swisher, Robert K, 1947 - THE LONELY COWBOY:
A novel / by Robert K. Swisher Jr.
Summary: Historical fiction, a search for meaning before and after war.
ISBN: 978-0-9979096-3-0
LCN: 2020901535

DEDICATION

FOR THE MOUNTAIN HORSE KILLED IN A
MOMENT OF FREEDOM
I HOPE YOU FOUND A TRAIL IN THE SKY

THE LONELY COWBOY

CHAPTER ONE

Eighty-seven years old Ben Sharps woke up and felt like a brick - an old crumbling brick that wasn't even worth being used as a doorstop. The moonlight shining through the trailer window wasn't pretty or relaxing - it was oppressive.

Rolling his arthritic legs off the bed and grunting Ben forced himself up. He put his elbows on his knees and rested his head wearily in his hands - his face as expressionless as the shadowed room. "Besides feeling like a brick, I don't know a damn thing," Ben said, not forlornly or despondently, but matter-of-factly.

"Bullshit moon, what's your problem anyway?" Ben cursed. "Even you don't like old things. You should have better manners and let me sleep in."

The moonbeams only grew brighter - taunting him.

Ben picked up the half full bottle of Jim Beam from the bedside table. The windup clock with its radium hands glared 5:30. "Here's to you moon," he said wryly taking a long drink. He didn't drink as much as he used to but he had decided since today was going to be his last day on earth he would drink and smoke to his heart's content.

The whiskey burnt and was bitter but Ben did not grimace. He decided years earlier that sweet things only made a man soft and ended up festering and hurting far more than any physical wound.

Ben took another sip of whiskey and put the bottle back on the table. He then pulled open the drawer. There were four pouches of Bugler rolling tobacco and rolling papers, one of the pouches was open. He rolled himself a smoke and lit the cigarette with his friend's Zippo lighter he'd brought back from the war. The smoke drifted through the moonlight like restless spirits.

After only a few drags Ben stubbed out the smoke in an overflowing ashtray and stood. The off green linoleum floor was cold on his feet. His gray long-johns made him look like a ghost in the moonlight.

He picked up his black cowboy boots and socks and went down the narrow hallway of the trailer, flipped on the light, and sat at a red Formica table with two matching chairs - the seats were cracked and exposed the cotton bunting. There was a radio on the table but Ben rarely turned it on - all music was sad to Ben - he'd had enough breaking up in his life without listening to rich singers complaining how tough it was while driving around the country in their $250,000 motor homes. He put on his socks. A wind kicked up outside and he heard the agonizing creak of the windmill as the blades began to turn.

Ben turned on one burner to the two-burner stove and slid a dented and blackened aluminum coffeepot over the flame. He glanced around the trailer. There was a tattered blue sofa by the back window that had two worn saddle blankets tossed over it. In front of the sofa was a table made from two stumps with an old barn board between them. The table was piled high with True West Magazines, Modern Cowboy, National Geographic, Newsweek, Time, and Smithsonian. Stacked in every corner were books that ranged from history, to westerns, to fantasy, and even science fiction. When Ben journeyed to town he went to the used bookstore and always loaded up on books and magazines. If there had been one constant in his life it was reading.

There were no curtains on the windows. Being seven miles from the paved road Ben didn't need any curtains - he figured if someone wanted to look in the window and see his old scrawny naked ass they could. A double barrel shotgun was propped by the door. Ben use to enjoy shooting coyotes but he'd stopped years ago, deciding one day if they killed a calf they were only hungry - it wasn't their fault they were born into this hateful world as a coyote.

The coffee started to perk, filling the air with its rich aroma. The windmill outside sped up as the wind increased and Ben's old horse, Meathead, whinnied from her corral.

"I've never let you go hungry," Ben said, irritated for some reason by the horse's call.

"I should have turned you into glue a long time ago, or sold you to some Frenchman who likes horsemeat," he grumbled.

The horse whinnied again. The horse had never minded him. But Ben liked the old horse. An ugly old horse and an ugly old man - both ready to be put out of their misery. Besides, Meathead talked to him - not in audible words, but Ben heard her in his mind as clear as if he was talking to himself. He'd never told anyone she talked to him, no need to go into the particulars and get laughed at, but she did – in fact, most of the time Ben thought the horse was smarter than he was.

Ben turned the burner down and poured himself a cup of coffee so black and thick he could have cut it with a knife. He'd bought the cup at a gas station in Tucumcari twenty years ago. Painted on the cup was an old grizzled cowboy sitting at a bar drinking a beer and the phrase - "I spent all my money on beer and women - the rest I just wasted."

"I never had enough money to waste," Ben said, knowing it was a lie. But he liked the cup even if it had cost him four dollars. When he'd bought it he had six hundred dollars to his name, an old truck and a horse trailer, and Meathead was a young mare. Now he made three hundred a month and received a small social security check - half of which he put away each month to give to his daughter after his death. For part of his wages he also got all the beef he could eat, all the feed he needed for Meathead, and all the gas his gas guzzling 1974 ¾-ton four wheel drive pickup could waste. To top it off the trailer he lived in was free. Mr. Kutler even paid for the propane. "Never knew life could be this good," Ben said, sipping his coffee. "I've been luckier than most, can't say that I haven't been. But it won't change my mind about what I'm going to do, can't go back on my own word even if it's only to me."

Ben went back to the bedroom and got his tobacco and lighter. Back in the kitchen he rolled another smoke. "Wonder what my life would have been without vices?" he asked himself. But he didn't have an answer. "What is life anyway?" he added, but the answer that came to him he did not like and he drove it from his mind.

The horizon turned a pale red. The rolling rocky hills dotted with pinion and juniper trees became a dull dusty purple. The ghosts of the night scurried to their hiding places. Three coyotes yapped in the distance - their call not lonely but hungry. The windmill creaked and Meathead whinnied again. Ben stood, rubbed his left shoulder where he'd been shot during the war, tugged on the pants and put on a faded blue denim work shirt with snaps. The elbows were patched with pieces of worn out Levi's. He fastened his large silver buckle with a cowboy riding a bucking bronco engraved on it. It was the first buckle he had ever won. The only one of hundreds he'd kept. On the back of his brown leather belt was engraved BEN - so worn that only the letter B could be made out. "Famous saddle bronc rider my ass," he scowled.

He pulled on his boots - tucking the pant legs into the tops, and put a tattered hand-tooled billfold in his back pocket - the ribbing mostly worn out.

Ben went to the bathroom, turned on the light, and looked in the mirror. "Eighty-seven years old. My God how'd I live this long," he asked himself. His lean narrow face was worn saddle brown except for his forehead, which was white, always shaded by his cowboy hat. The deep creases in his face ran in no set direction, more like pieces to a puzzle - each the story of a year in the sun and rain and snow. His nose was big and round, creased with tiny red and blue veins from years of whiskey, and cocked off to one side - busted too many times from fistfights fought for no good reason he could remember. There was a large jagged scar on his left cheek - one too many tugs on a barb wire stretcher. His ears were large pieces of jerky, blistered pink and red, with large gobs of white hair growing out of them. His eyes were deep brown, half hidden by his droopy eyelids and bushy out-of-control eyebrows, but even hidden they were intense. Somewhere in the generations there had been an Indian, but neither his father nor mother had ever told him about any of his ancestors.

"At least I don't have to wear glasses," Ben said to his image. "Piss in a dribble, but I can see." Ben's white hair was cut in a crew cut. He'd always wanted longer hair, like those movie cowboys, but it got dirty - too hard to wash everyday. White splotchy stubble covered his face. He only shaved once a week now. Like everything else in life shaving had become a chore. For years he had worn a moustache but he'd cut it off last year - for some reason he woke up one morning and it had offended him. Ben turned on the cold water and splashed it on his face. His hands were darker than his face, almost mahogany, the knuckles twisted and swollen to the size of quarters, his fingers going off in different directions like they had a mind of their own - too many years of ropes and being tossed from horses. Where there wasn't a scar there were liver spots. Two Advil a day kept the pain in his hands, shoulders, and knees tolerable - Advil and whiskey and gritting his teeth. Ben took his teeth out of a glass on the sink. He'd gotten them fifteen years ago in Juarez, Mexico. The teeth, although too big, beat feeling his lips flop around on his gums and stopped spit from dripping down his chin.

Ben straightened his five feet nine inches the best he could. His tough sinewy muscles hugged his bones - there was no flab - no fat in his one hundred and fifty pounds - no gut hanging over his belt. Ben's cloths hung on him like his real purpose in life was to have been a scarecrow, but, even though he was 87 years old he moved like a man that was in his sixties.

Ben went back to the kitchen and poured himself another cup of coffee and swallowed two Advil. He didn't eat breakfast anymore. Every so often a can of beans or what was left over from dinner, but it was not a habit. For lunch he normally ate sardines, or tuna fish, or canned beef - not on bread or with crackers, but right out of the can, dipped out with his pocketknife, the only gift from his father he could remember. Ben knew now it was not his father's fault the way he had been - but he also knew he could never forgive him.

Most nights for dinner Ben ate fried steak with canned corn or beans. A doctor told him last year he should eat more roughage, but Ben was never a salad man - salad was for rabbits, and besides, if man was supposed to live off salad he wouldn't have been born with two canine teeth. But he did love fresh tomatoes when he could find them, bacon and tomato sandwiches drenched with mayonnaise, real mayonnaise, not the crap they called salad dressing and was low fat. "Lazy bastards work more and not sit on their butts all day they wouldn't have to worry about fat and cholesterol," Ben snorted stubbornly.

He sat down at the table with his coffee. The sun

was half way over the horizon - replacing the purple with a dull orange red that the cloudless sky would soon eat up. A flock of sparrows and a few doves landed in front of the trailer and pecked at the birdseed Ben tossed out every evening before he went to bed.

Ben had always liked birds. Birds didn't bother anything, they just went through their lives singing, and eating, and screwing, and building cute little nests, and trying to be left alone and do their little bird thing. Ben had always wished he'd been born a bird. "If I was," he chuckled, "I'd probably been born a dodo bird or one of those birds that's so ancient they don't fly anymore."

"If it was last year I'd put out the hummingbird feeders in a few weeks," Ben said, but added, "They won't need me anyway. They won't miss me. They'll go find feeders somewhere else."

Ben had twenty hummingbird feeders in the closet. He loved watching the little things buzzing and chattering at each other - fighting like mad but never hurting each other. "Play war," he muttered, "war with no malice, or hate, or greed."

The sun completely cleared the horizon and the wind stopped, which was unusual. The wind normally blew all-day, hot and scorching in the summer, cold and cutting in the winter. The windmill blades slowly ground to a halt like they really had no purpose, something foreign that should not have been allowed, a sin against all that was natural. Ben inhaled deeply the smoke and butted it. "It's taken me all these years to finally be satisfied with what I am going to do one day in my life," he said, not forlornly or sadly.

Meathead whinnied.

"I'm coming, I'm coming, you worthless hunk of dog meat," Ben swore.

He put on a fleece lined, weathered, Levi jacket that was more threads than cloth. His leather gloves with two of the fingertips worn out were stuffed in a pocket. He put his tobacco fixings in the other jacket pocket. He pulled his ten-year-old 4X cowboy hat on his head. The brim was ripped, there was a hole in the side, and it was covered with dirt and grease and sweat - making the once white hat an earthy gray. Pulling the brim tightly down on his head he stepped out on the unpainted wood porch to the trailer. The sparrows and doves did not fly away.

Going outside from the trailer was like walking out of jail. A thing he had done a few times, but with no regrets - sometimes a free man had to do a few nights in jail just to let the bastards know they didn't own everything and couldn't tell everybody what to do.

Ben loved the vista from the porch. There was no town for thirty miles. Only miles and miles of rolling hills that were covered with pinion trees, juniper trees, cedar trees, and cactus. In low areas gamma grass clung tenaciously to life. If there was a wet spring blue and yellow wildflowers dotted the landscape. The land around him was tough land, but good land - land that told a man where he stood - land that promised nothing but hardship and did not lie in its promise. Hidden in the crooks and crannies of the hills were pictographs left by ancient Indians, along with their arrowheads and beads and broken pottery - a testament to the futility of their lives no matter what spirits they believed in or worshiped. In the flats, next to old dried up riverbeds, were the crumbling rock walls of early Mexican and white settlers whose dreams lay scattered in the ruins - their desperate lives forgotten and swept away by the wind. On the sides of several of the hills were hand-dug mine shafts, years and years of toil looking for that one big gold nugget or that vein of silver, until one day the body could no longer keep up with the dream and the shaft was abandoned - a broken heart somewhere in its soulless walls.

Ben had been lucky when Mr. Kutler, the owner of the 90,000-acre Kutler Ranch in central New Mexico gave him a place to live. "Hell, I know I'm not worth my keep anymore," Ben had said, trying not to sound desperate the day Mr. Kutler hired him on.

Mr. Kutler didn't smile. "You've been a good hand all over the west Ben Sharps," Mr. Kutler said. "You watch my east fence, run in a few strays, keep the windmills going and I'll give you a place to die."

"It's more than a man can ask for," Ben replied, but he did not say thank you.

A man shouldn't have to say thank you to die. He should die on his own time. There had to be one true freedom in life. Ben knew he would die on his own time.

Off to the right of the run-down and sand-pitted trailer was a steel corral with three-sided plywood shed in the back for Meathead to get out of the weather. A two-inch pipe ran from the windmill tank to fill the water trough in the corral. A heavily cribbed and lopsided wooden feed trough in the corral kept the hay off the ground - which normally didn't work. Meathead took her hay and tossed it on the sandy ground. But she had never been prone to colic so Ben didn't worry about it. Besides, at her age, she might be better off dead. There was a weathered board shed next to the corral with a rusted tin roof. In front of the shed was a pipe hitching post set in concrete. Ben's dilapidated truck and beat up two-horse trailer were parked next to the shed. Numerous horseshoes were nailed to the shed - some pointed down, some pointed up - some luck ran downhill - some trapped luck wasn't what one needed. Six cattle skulls were also nailed to the shed, along with a goat skull and two coyote skulls. Ben had heard of artists who had made a fortune painting skulls but he couldn't understand it - bones were just bones, what was left of a futile and nothing life.

Meathead whinnied again, annoyed at being ignored. Ben rolled a smoke and enjoyed the view. It was peaceful. It was a late April day. Not too cool, not too hot, satisfying and nice - a good day to do what he was going to do.

High overhead in the cloudless sky six turkey buzzards rode the thermals – circling slowly, almost gently. Warm weather was not far away. Buzzards didn't come back from Mexico until warm weather was just around the corner. "Damn buzzards smarter than most people," Ben said. He'd always liked buzzards - people didn't mess with them. "You'll be picking my bones soon," Ben said to the buzzards. "And you won't even care if my meat is old and tough."

For a moment he wished he could fly, spread out his arms and step off the porch and sail up to the buzzards - tell them how lucky they were to be on top of the earth and looking down, and not standing on the earth and always looking up - like looking up would give a man solace or let him touch his dreams.

Ben thought about his sister and quickly drove the thought from his mind.

Ben stepped off the porch and mashed the smoke into the sandy brown hard as concrete dirt and put on his gloves. He walked over to the corral. Meathead whinnied, stuck her head over the corral and butted Ben playfully. Ben affectionately rubbed her neck. The bay was shedding her winter coat and hundreds of hairs floated into the air, many sticking on Ben's coat, but he did not bother to rub them off. "I'll feed you, you piece of junk," he said and went to the shed.

Meathead gave him a look that said, "Hurry up or I'll toss your ass next time you put a saddle on me."

The hand-forged iron strap hinges to the shed door creaked in protest as Ben opened the door. He'd been meaning to pour some used motor oil on them for months but never seemed to get around to it. The next man to stay in the trailer could oil the damn things. Inside the spider web filled shed, illuminated by the spaces between the boards and the fallen out knotholes, was a stack of hay, a sawhorse with several tattered saddle blankets and Ben's plain leather saddle on it. Ben had never liked saddles tooled with flowers and things - too sissified - something for some cowgirl riding in a parade or a big shot from Dallas. From various nails hung ropes and halters, bits and tie downs, a set of hobbles, a rifle scabbard, his polo spurs - he'd stopped wearing spurs with big rowels years ago - no need to hurt a horse, just prod it. There were also saddle bags, sections of chain, some horseshoe equipment, a metal curry comb, and a pair of chaps scratched and patched so many times the mice didn't even bother to chew on them. In one corner were an anvil and years and years of old horseshoes. They reminded Ben of unread books - each an untold story. In another corner were several shovels and a garden rake, the handles whittled from branches, and a roll of barbed wire and a fencing tool. "I'll never fix another strand of shitting wire," Ben said with satisfaction.

On a wooden bench were three sacks of sweet feed. Each morning and evening Meathead got an inch of hay and a tin can full of sweet feed. Sweet feed was her tobacco. "Everything has to have something enjoyable in life," Ben reasoned.

Ben took the hay and sweet feed and put it in the feed bin. Meathead pranced around like a young horse before eating. Ben smiled. "Happiness and joy should be that easy," he said to the horse. "I always seemed to make things too complicated."

Meathead looked at him, hay hanging from her mouth and seemed to say, "Leave me alone. Your services are no longer needed."

"You'll miss me. Nobody else will give a twenty-year-old ugly horse like you sweet feed," Ben said, turned, and headed back to the shed.

Ben remembered buying the mare as a yearling. It was probably the worst horse deal he had ever made. Six hundred dollars and the good looking bay yearling turned into a straight-backed, short-legged, small, slow, stubborn Meathead - thus her name. But she was gentle and for some reason Ben liked her and she talked to him better than any of his other horses ever had. Besides, he figured ugly things need friends more than others - hell - everybody could like something that was good looking, and even though she talked to him she never told him what to do. He hated to be told what to do.

Ben stood at the entrance to the shed. The light filtering through the boards illuminated the dust in the air. He wondered if man really came from dust. It seemed befitting to be only dirt. Most humans were dirt bags anyway and should have stayed dirt and not muddled up the damn world so much.

Ben put on his spurs, got the currycomb and a halter with a short rope, went back and stood by the corral and watched Meathead contentedly eating. She did not look up. Watching the old horse he suddenly felt lonely. It started in the bottom of his gut, circled his heart, and made him take a deep breath. "Go away," he muttered, "Too old to think about love now." But he saw Nancy's face in the back of his mind holding their newborn daughter, and even with the loneliness, he smiled inside - a sad defeated smile.

Ben wrote his daughter occasionally, but he never could say what he wanted to say and his letters only left him feeling sad and empty.

"I bet you don't get lonely," he said to Meathead. But then he thought maybe the old horse did. He wondered if she dreamed of being free or running with a herd. "If there is a God I suppose you have to be lonely," Ben said, and for a moment he felt sorry for Meathead. "At least I never lived in a box. Being alone was my own fault, not the fact someone wanted to break me and ride me."

The horse finished eating and took a long drink from the water trough. Ben went into the corral and slipped the halter easily over Meathead's head. She'd never been skittish or head shy. He looped the rope over the top pipe of the corral without bothering to tie it and started currying the horse. The hair came off in great globs. "My last day on this earth and you'll look the best you can," Ben said to the horse.

The old horse closed her eyes and sighed. Ben combed for an hour and then patted the horse on the rump and removed her halter. She nudged him appreciatively with her nose. Ben put the halter and curry comb back in the shed and went to the trailer, warmed up the coffee, and from the closet got a yellow note pad and pen. The words came easily and he felt no fear, only remorse, a remorse he knew he would die with. When he was done, he put the letter in his shirt pocket and poured himself a cup of coffee, rolled a smoke, and gazed out the window at no particular thing, thinking to himself, "It's been a hell of a ride, a little bumpy, but a hell of a ride."

Butting the smoke he put his gloves back on, picked up the shotgun, broke it open to make sure it was loaded and headed for the shed, not bothering to lock the door to the trailer.

Ben picked out a halter and tied Meathead to the hitching post. She stood, head down, looking like she wanted to be ridden about as bad as a rabbit wanted to be stew. "You only have to put up with me one more time," Ben said.

Meathead looked at Ben like he was a nuisance.

Ben went into the shed and got a saddle blanket and his saddle. Grunting, he half dragged the saddle outside. Meathead didn't flinch when he put the blanket on her, but she puffed out her gut in anticipation of the saddle. Ben slid the saddle on her back, ignoring the pain in his own back, and kneed her gently in the gut, making her inhale as he tightened the cinch strap. "You're not as smart as me, you old plug," he said. "You just think you are."

She swished her tail at him - hitting him in the arm.

Ben brought out the scabbard, attached it to the saddle, and slid the shotgun in.

He then got a brand new hemp rope he'd bought in town a few weeks earlier. The fibers were shiny like fresh straw. "It's a good rope. A rope fit for a hanging," Ben said, tying it to the saddle. "An old outlaw would be envious of this rope."

He picked out a hackamore and put it on the horse. He didn't need a bit. Old horse couldn't turn on a dime anyway. Hell, about all she was good for was plodding along and nipping at stuff she shouldn't eat.

Ben flipped the reins around the saddle horn, stood back for a moment, rubbed his chin and then went into the shed for the saddlebags. The bags attached, he went to the house and topped off the half full bottle of Jim Beam with water, got a can of peaches out of the cupboard and took all the packages of Bugler tobacco out of his dresser drawer.

He then tossed the remainder of the birdseed in front of the trailer causing the birds to jump up and down in surprise. "Last meal on me," he said with a grim smile.

He put the Jim Beam, peaches, and tobacco in the saddlebags.

He opened the gate to the corral, put a wedge of hay and a can of sweet feed in the feed bin and leaving the gate open he said to Meathead, "You'll know how to get back. All day long all you're going to be thinking about is that food that's waiting for you back here."

About to mount he stopped and went back to the house. "Old brain can't seem to keep things in order," he muttered to himself. He pulled a suitcase from underneath the bed that was full of newspaper clippings and photographs of him when he was one of the best saddle bronc riders in the country. There was also his purple heart and the title to his truck and horse trailer. He opened the suitcase and left the two titles on the table. "Mr. Kutler will make sure the truck and trailer goes to someone that needs," he said.

He closed the suitcase and went to the burn barrel. He did not look at any of the newspaper clippings or photographs as he poured them into the barrel. He lit the paper on fire, stood back, and watched the flames engulf everything. Greenish-blue smoke wisped into the air, carrying the words and pictures of his life for the sky to examine and then forget. When the fire died down Ben stirred the ashes with a stick, making sure no ember remained. The Purple Heart had melted into an unrecognizable blob. "None of us are more than a passing memory," Ben said.

He slipped Meathead's halter off, leaving it tied to the hitching post, and climbed into the saddle. The saddle creaked with his weight. He turned Meathead gently to the left, looked at the old trailer, and the corral, and the shed. "You were never a home," he said to the buildings. "But you were good to me."

He spurred Meathead lightly toward the western hills and did not look back.

CHAPTER TWO

Ben figured when he reached the right spot he would know. "If I'd let life take me where it wanted instead of trying to figure out a destination I would still have got somewhere," Ben said. "At least the destination would have been my own true course. Not something muddled up by all my wrong decisions. A person always knows when he's doing the right thing and knows when he's doing the wrong thing. I guess the wrong things are easier to do most of the time."

Meathead turned her head, rolled her left eye back, and looked at him. "Don't give me that look. You never had to make a decision," Ben ordered.

The horse snorted, but did not look away.

"What do you mean it's my own fault?" Ben demanded.

The horse snorted again.

"Life makes you do what you don't want to do most of the time," Ben said.

The horse looked away.

"Maybe life only makes you do what you would have done anyway," Ben said.

The horse shook her head as if bothered by a fly, but there was no fly.

"What the hell do you know anyway?" Ben snapped at Meathead.

Meathead shook her head. "You want sympathy you dumb old son-of-a-bitch. I got my own problems. One of them is called a saddle."

"Everything has a saddle of some kind," Ben blurted.

Meathead ignored him.

For awhile Ben's mind drifted off into a land of no thoughts. As they reached the top of a small hill, Ben came back to the world. He stopped Meathead and looked back. He could no longer see the trailer or the windmill, only the land. A breeze swept over the top of the hill and then was gone - a mere thought. Two crows sailed through the cloudless sky squawking back and forth to each other - whatever they were talking about seemingly important.

"Lucky bastards," Ben said, enjoying their freedom. "Wherever you two end up today won't make any difference to either one of you."

Ben nudged Meathead over the top of the hill. At the bottom were four huge cottonwood trees that were so twisted and gnarled it was though all their time had been spent in agony, but a force stronger than pain had made them reach for the sky. Many of their giant limbs were dead, but others had small green buds on them. "You boys are two stupid to give up the ghost," Ben said to the trees.

Meathead looked at him. "Maybe brave enough to see their life to its natural end."

"You don't know squat," Ben said.

At the trees, Ben dismounted and tied Meathead to a lower branch so she could nip at a few tuffs of last years' brittle gamma grass. A slight breeze rustled the new buds, sending many falling to the ground, their purpose destroyed before their true beginning. For some reason the falling buds reminded Ben of the desperate and pleading eyes of the children during the war - their bodies wrapped in rags, and their little hands and faces crusted with dirt as they begged for any crumb, but there never was enough to give. What was another meal anyway? Only a tease? A small respite before another hungry day - and another and another - until death in some ditch, or field, or behind a bombed out building - then to be picked up and tossed in a truck or cart and buried in an unmarked hole with other nameless ones - a gift only to worms and maggots. "No beginning," Ben murmured. "God, you son-of-a-bitch, you should be nicer to the young ones. Old bastards like me don't mean much, but harm to young ones is your sin."

The rat-a-tat-tat of a woodpecker cut through the air. Ben listened intently and saw a red headed woodpecker diligently pounding away for a grub. "I spent my whole life beating my head against walls," Ben said. "And you do it because you have to," he smiled ironically.

The woodpecker found his prize and flew off.

Ben loosened the saddle cinch one hole and then sat back against the trunk of a tree and took a deep breath. He looked up through the branches to the sky. "You're no god to me like you were to my sister," Ben said to the sky.

He rested the back of his head against the tree and closed his eyes.

******

"Ben Sharps, you get out of that apple tree and you go find your sister," his mother's voice cut like a punishing switch from the kitchen window. "And if you've been eating those green apples I'll tell your father and he'll blister your backside. I told you to watch after your sister, now you get."

"Yes ma'am," ten-year-old Ben called back, swallowing the last bite of apple quickly, and hollering fearfully. "Please don't tell Pa, please."

His mother did not answer and Ben scrambled down the tree faster than a squirrel. He raced barefoot toward the barn, his overly large overhauls flapping like wash on the line. The chickens scattered in his haste and he chunked the incriminating apple core into the hog lot where three skinny pigs chased after it. He pushed open the barn door slowly and heard his sister's quiet sobs from the hayloft. The light from the open door sliced through the dusty gloom. "It's ok, Lisa," Ben called quietly. "It's me, don't be afraid."

Ben climbed the ladder to the hayloft. His nine-year-old sister was sitting close to the open hay doors clutching a tattered homemade doll. One eye to the doll was gone and her calico dress was unraveling at the hem. Lisa's long blond hair was braided in two braids. Her bare feet were dark with dirt, almost alien to her white legs. She turned and looked at Ben, tears streaking her shallow face - masking the blueness of her eyes. Ben felt sad as he sat down beside her and he put his arm around her shoulder. "It's ok Lisa," he said. "One day you and I will be old enough we can run away from home and take care of each other and you won't have to cry anymore."

"Mama and Papa hate us Ben. I don't know if I can wait that long," Lisa sobbed.

"But we have each other," Ben said, holding her tighter. "It doesn't matter as long as we have each other."

Lisa put her head on his shoulder, looked out the hay door, and said in a far away, dreamy voice. "Isn't the sky something, Ben? Besides you, it's the only friend I have. I sit up here and look at the sky and it goes on and on forever and I wonder what it would be like to one day get up and just follow the sky. Stand here and spread out my arms and fly out the door into the sky. I can feel the air rushing on my face. I can see you waving at me and smiling and you wishing you could fly like me. The sky has to be God, Ben."

"God doesn't like us either," Ben said. "The sky isn't God. I don't even know if there is a God."

"No, Ben, God loves us. He just has more important things to do than worry about two poor kids from a Kansas farm."

"I'll be more," Ben swore. "I'm going to be the best saddle bronc rider the rodeos ever seen. I'm going to make us enough money to have nice things, and nice clothes, and food three times a day, and cookies and cake whenever we want them. You watch. And it isn't going to be because of God. It's going to be only because of me."

"Oh Ben, how are you going to learn how to ride a bucking horse?"

"I don't know, but I will and nothing will stop me," Ben replied, gritting his teeth.

"At least you have a dream, Ben. All I think about is the sky. I can't see my life being anything."

"It will be, Lisa. We just have to be strong."

"When I go to the sky, Ben, will you promise me that whenever you look at the sky, no matter how long you live, you will always think about me?"

"You can't go to the sky. The sky doesn't want anything but to be the sky."

"You must promise me, Ben. Will you always think about me?"

Ben looked out the hay door. There was nothing to stop the view, no hills, no trees, just the flat land and then the horizon - the land dwarfed by the sky. "It's pretty, but so big it's scary," Ben said.

"Promise me, Ben. You must. You will always

think about me."

Ben patted his sister's shoulder. "If you go to the sky I will always think about you. I promise."

Lisa sobbed, wiped her eyes and stood - tossing the doll onto a pile of hay. "We'd better get back to the house and help Mama and hope Pa doesn't come home mad."

"He's going to whip us one time too many. One time to many and when I'm bigger I might kill him," Ben said, hiding his fear and clinching his hands into tight fists.

"Don't you ever think about killing any man," Lisa ordered him. "Killing only brings you down to their level and makes you hate. Don't you ever hate, Ben, never, hate will only destroy you like it has Pa."

Ben did not answer. A corner of his heart already knew hate.

They went down the ladder, out of the barn, and walked toward the house, each hiding their fear and not talking.

******

Ben opened his eyes. His neck hurt and his legs had gone to sleep. Meathead was standing with her head down, her eyes closed - lost in a dream of a life with no saddle and green grass as high as her knees - not dry old gamma grass that only made her thirsty.

Ben looked up at the sky through the tree branches. It was not a Kansas sky. Here the hills invaded the sky, dared to invade its space - not afraid of the sky or overshadowed by it. "Ah Lisa," Ben said, "my poor, poor little sister. I hope you found God in the sky. I've never found Him here on the ground."

Ben got slowly to his feet and stomped them a few times to drive the tingling out of his legs. "I don't remember much of my life before I was ten," he said to Meathead. I guess all the whippings made me not want to remember."

Meathead looked at him. "Why don't you keep sitting and let me rest, you old fart," she said.

Ben tightened up the cinch, untied Meathead's reins and grunted up into the saddle. "If I had a dollar for every time I've got off and on a horse I'd be a rich man," Ben said.

Meathead swished her tail. "You'd have spent it."

Ben laughed.

Ben turned Meathead toward a trail that cut up the side of another hill. Near the top was a cluster of scrub oak, a few of falls red leaves still clinging to the budding branches like they would once again know life. Ben wondered how the scrub oak had taken root where it did. It was too low and too dry. "Guess some things just want to be alone, no matter how tough it makes their lives," he said.

"I don't think it had a choice," Meathead said.

"Nothing has a choice," Ben said.

"Most of you people do, but not all," Meathead said. "And you've had lots of choices."

"I can't say that you're wrong, you hunk of dog meat," Ben reluctantly replied.

Meathead shook her head. "Sometimes you think and talk too much."

Ben stopped by the scrub oak and inhaled deeply. He loved the dusty earthy smell of scrub.

Ben moved on to the top of the hill, which was taller than the previous hill. Stopping on the top he took off his hat and looked up at the sky for a few moments. His chin fell to his chest and his shoulders drooped and he shut his eyes - so tired, he thought, so weary.

Meathead also lowered her head and shut her eyes.

******

Ben lay on his bed, his fist stuck in his mouth, holding back his anger and anguish. "I'll kill you, I'll kill you," he swore.

Ben's father had whipped him good, whipped him for no reason, just came home drunk and grabbed Ben and started whipping him with his belt.

"You ain't worth the food I feed you," his father slurred.

Ben did not fight back, did not cry out - he would not give his father the satisfaction. He took the whipping and walked to his room and he held his tears. "I won't cry because of you, you bastard," he cursed.

His mother had watched, her arms crossed in front of her with a satisfied slice of a grin on her grim face, like whippings were all anybody every deserved. Even when her husband beat on her she said nothing. "We're not animals," Ben said getting out of bed and looking out the window.

It was an ugly place, dirty and run down, reeking of poverty and neglect. There were no flowers planted around the house. It took happy people to plant flowers and Ben could not remember ever seeing his mother smile. The wood fence was unpainted - the paint on the house long cracked and peeling - the porch leaning - the steps wobbly - the garden was weeds - the barn falling over. The one milk cow was pathetic looking - cursed like Ben and Lisa. The mule was skinny and dull eyed. The hog yard close to the house always stunk, stunk deep like sin, the smell creeping into sheets and curtains and clothes.

In school Ben was embarrassed for himself and Lisa – they smelled like hog shit. When a boy taunted them a terrible anger would come over Ben and even after he had beaten a boy down to the ground he would keep hitting until Lisa would tearfully pull him off.

Ben and Lisa would sit in the back of the room close to each other, both embarrassed, both in pain, wanting a friend - or a kind word, or somebody besides themselves telling them it would be ok - life wasn't all dirt and hog shit and mean people and being poor. But even the teacher ignored them. They were useless. Poor kids who would always be poor - poor made them stupid and ignorant - poor made them not people - but things - wretched things - things not worth her time.

But even with the embarrassment, Ben missed very few days of school and he studied hard and got good grades. He brought his books home at night and read and re-read them and tried his best to not talk like some poor hick. He also, whenever possible, went over to the neighbor and borrowed Mr. Riley's' rodeo magazines. He would spend hours looking at the pictures of rodeo cowboys and playing over and over in his mind how one day he would be the best saddle bronc rider in the world. It was a dream that never left his mind. He could feel the power of the horse under him and hear the crowd cheering when he rode as vividly as he could see the endless sky that his sister thought was God.

Ben watched the scrawny chickens scratching in the yard. He'd eaten so many chickens he hated chicken. "One day all I'll eat is steak," Ben said. "Big thick steaks with juicy fat and I'll let the fat run down my face."

Downstairs Ben heard his father screaming at his sister and then the sounds of another whipping. Lisa cried out, "No Papa, no Papa, please?"

"Whip her good, whip Satan out of her," his mother screeched, seemingly enjoying the pain on another.

Ben put his hands over his ears and closed his eyes, trying to block out all sound, all light, all sight. "I'll kill you, I'll kill you," he repeated over and over.

Lisa came into the room. Her legs red welts, her face flushed, tears streaming from her desperate and anguish-filled eyes. Ben held her. "We could run away, Lisa," he said. "I'm fourteen now. I can get a job. We could go to Wichita, or Kansas City, or maybe Denver. Go where nobody knows us."

Lisa stopped crying, slipped out of Ben's embrace, and stood by the window. Ben looked at her back. She seemed like a shadow, so skinny the light almost shone through her, exposing a tiny little sad heart that really did not want to beat anymore.

"Remember a few years ago when I asked you if you would always think about me if I went to the sky?" Lisa asked Ben.

"I promised," Ben said. "I'd never break my promise to you. But nobody can go to the sky, Lisa. The sky is just another dream. It's just there to keep us confused and baffled."

"No Ben, the sky is God and peace and calm. It's where birds live, and angels live, and all good things go to at the end."

"I don't think I'm good, Lisa. But I know you are, there are no wrongful thoughts in your mind. You don't hate Ma and Pa like I do."

"Ben, you're nothing but good, you just don't know it, or don't want to know it."

Ben stood beside Lisa. A wind kicked up, blowing dust from the dirt road toward Colorado. "Maybe the wind is God," Ben said. "A restless thing that keeps trying to do good, but all His good intentions got screwed up, so he keeps blowing, and moving, and looking for the right place, or the right person, or the right thing, so he can stop blowing and wandering and hoping."

Lisa smiled thinly at Ben and held his hand. "You and I are the sky and the wind," she said.

She released his hand and lay down on her bed with her back to him.

He turned back to the window. The sun dipped below the horizon and the stars appeared one by one. "Where do you go at night, sky?" Ben demanded. "You hide and ignore us. You could give a shit less about my sister - you bastard."

The dark filled the room and Ben went to bed. For a long time he gazed into the dark and listened to the soft, shallow, lonely breaths of his sister and he wanted to cry, if only to give his tears for hers, one time to be able to take her pain, just one time, but there were no tears, only an emptiness, an emptiness as deep as the dark and taunted with the knowledge he could never stop his sister's pain.

******

Ben opened his eyes. Meathead shook. "I wonder if my sister will smile at me when we meet again," Ben said.

Meathead started walking without being nudged. Ben reached back and took the bottle of Jim Beam out of the saddlebag and took a long pull and then put it back. "They say wine is the drink of the god's," Ben said. "Wonder what whiskey is?"

"Some gods have to drink whiskey," Meathead said. "Knowing they made a mess out of everything."

Ben rode parallel to the hill for a hundred yards and after rounding the bottom there was a small level clearing. In the clearing was the shell of an old rock house, no more than twelve feet square, that had been mortared with mud. There was a slot for a door but no windows. The roof and door were long ago rotted away and a pinion tree grew from within the crumbling walls - its branches extending over the walls. There were a few rusted tin cans, a lot of broken bottles, and an old pick head close to the door. "By the size of that tree, this place is well over a hundred years old," Ben said. "Hell, it's older than me."

"You're older than dirt," Meathead said.

"If there's a heaven I hope they don't let horses in," Ben said.

"Only if we get to ride people," Meathead said.

Ben grinned and dismounted, knotting the reins on the saddle horn, but slack enough Meathead could bend her head down. He took the bottle of whiskey out of the saddlebags and sat down on one of the fallen rocks from the house's wall. Removing his gloves he rolled a smoke and lit it, looking at the Zippo lighter closely before he put it back in his pocket. He stuffed the gloves in his back pocket.

"Whoever lived here was so shit poor I bet they never had any tobacco," Ben said. "Or whiskey. Bet they would have loved to sit a few times and smoke and drink."

Ben drank deeply then put the bottle back in the saddlebags. He kicked a few of the pieces of broken glass with the toe of his boot. "I wonder if your thoughts are growing with the trees," Ben said thinking about the people that had lived in the house. "I wonder where you came from to end up in such a lonely place."

Ben looked at the hills. "You weren't dumb though. Hills stop the wind, but you had to carry water from somewhere, sure as hell can't depend on rain in this country."

Ben sat back down on the rock and looked up at the sky. There were no clouds, no jet trails, not even a bird, just a deep blue. "Blue like your eyes Lisa," Ben said.

He rested his head in his hands. "Blue like your eyes," he said again.

******

It was late September and unusually cold when Ben woke up. The heat from the woodstove downstairs barely reached the upstairs bedroom. A sharp wind rattled the window. Ben looked over but his sister was gone. He figured she had probably gotten up early to gather the eggs.

Ben dressed quickly, hoping his father had already gone to work. His mother was sitting at the kitchen table drinking coffee and did not say good morning. Ben poured himself a cup, swigged it down, and put on his coat. "You'd better get all the wood your father told you to," his mother ordered, "Storms coming."

Ben did not answer and went outside. A terrible looking gray storm was brewing to the east and the wind grew in intensity. He went to the hen house but Lisa was not there. He looked under one hen and she still had her eggs. For some reason Ben grew worried and he ran to the barn. The cow was in the stall eating. The mule looked at him warily - like there was work to do. "Lisa, Lisa, are you in here?" Ben called nervously.

There was no answer. A gust of wind shook the barn. Ben scrambled up the ladder to the hayloft. The two hay doors banged back and forth from the wind. Ben went over to shut them. As he grabbed one he looked down. "No, oh no," he moaned.

Lisa was face down on the ground below the hay doors. Her arms were stretched out away from her body in a failed attempt to fly. Her head rested in a pool of blood. Ben raced down the ladder and ran around the barn. He frantically rolled Lisa over. Her blue eyes were open, unseeing into the gray sky, but bright and clear as if she had seen God. Blood, still bright red and warm, oozed from her nose and ears and was speckled with bits of dirt from the ground. Her face was peaceful. There was no pain, or anguish, or questions. "Oh Lisa, Lisa," Ben cried. "Nobody can fly."

He picked Lisa up and rocked her like a baby. His tears ran down his cheeks. When there were no more tears he looked up at the gray swirling sky. "You bastard, you bastard," he hollered. "You tempted her with dreams. I will never forgive you."

That night Ben waited until the house was quiet. He got out of bed, dressed, put on his coat, stuffed his few clothes in a pillowcase, picked up his boots, and as quietly as he could crept through the house. He opened the door slowly and once outside set the pillowcase down, put on his boots and went to the barn. The storm had passed. There was almost a full moon and the stars were bright and shimmering in the cold air. The cow moved nervously when Ben entered the barn. Lisa was wrapped in a sheet and placed on a pile of straw. Ben did not go over to her but picked up a short handled garden shovel that was in the corner. Walking back to the house his face was tight and masked. Inching the door open his breathing pounded in his ears louder than a train. He tiptoed to his parent's bed. "Pa," he whispered.

His father stirred but did not awaken. "Pa," he said louder.

Ben's father sat up, groggy from whiskey, rubbed his eyes, and then glared at Ben. "What do you want?" he growled.

Swinging the shovel with all his might Ben hit his father across the face. His father fell backward, knocked out, blood pouring from his nose. Ben swung the shovel again, hitting his father in the stomach. "You bastard, this is for Lisa," he swore and was about to hit his father again when Ben's mother bolted upright. "Ben, Ben, it ain't what it seems," she gasped.

Ben dashed from the house, grabbed his pillowcase of clothes, and ran, and ran, and ran, and ran.

******

Ben stood up from the rock and looked at the blue sky. Several small clouds drifted across the sun, turning the edges of the clouds gold and red. High up, only a dot, a red-tailed hawk scanned the ground for a rabbit or ground squirrel. "I promised you Lisa every time I looked at the sky I would remember you," Ben said. "But it hasn't been easy."

The sun came out from behind the two clouds. Ben smiled. "Fly Lisa, fly," Ben said, as a tiny tear dripped from his eye, slid slowly down the creases on his face and fell to the dry rocky ground.

Meathead looked away.

CHAPTER THREE

Ben rode for close to an hour. The day was becoming warm. Ben guessed low 70's. The wind was still not stirring. He had not been thinking about anything, more just looking - appreciating things like he really never had. The color of a rock - the way a branch grew out of a tree - a shadow falling on a hill - a chipmunk whose only problem was how to crack a pinion nut - a mountain jay that seemed to be pissed off at the world - scolding nothing in particular but anything that wanted to listen. "Maybe getting ready to die is the only time a person sees the world for what it is," Ben said. "There are some pretty nice things hidden in all the shit and struggle."

"A pretty thing is seeing a cowboy lying on the ground with a broken leg after he's fallen off a horse," Meathead said.

"How about a mountain meadow with a stream running through it with grass so tall and sweet you could never eat it all?" Ben asked.

"Never thought about it. I've always been stuck on some dried-up rock of a ranch with you," Meathead said. "You put me in a meadow with green grass I'd get the runs for a month."

Ben laughed and reached back and got his bottle of whiskey, took a pull and put it back. "I've tried to be good to you," he said.

"Could have been worse, could have been better, but I don't have any complaints," Meathead said.

Ben stopped the horse and rolled a smoke, lit it, and inhaled deeply. "I should have gone back to my father later on in life and told him I understood," he said forlornly.

"I couldn't forgive him for how he treated Lisa and me, but I should have gone back. He was just a poor man who never got a break and took out his hate and disgrace on those closest to him. Maybe instead of always looking for a little recognition I should have given him some instead of always giving him hate and loathing. Maybe it would have changed him.

Maybe if I would have said, 'Hey Pa, it's ok, I understand, we all need love,' it would have changed his life."

Ben took another drag on the smoke - watched the smoke disappear into the air like it had never really existed - it was only a dream.

"And poor Ma. What could she have done, taking her beatings from Pa like Lisa and me? In time she had to beat us every so often, she had to vent some of her rage on something weaker than her. She couldn't do anything against Pa. Hell, she never knew love. She never had flowers in the room, or a nice dress to just once promenade through town and walk down the street with her head held high and say, 'Look at me, I'm not always a poor farmer, eating potatoes and chicken, slopping hogs, and having kids, and getting beat by my husband because he's knocked down by life.' I should have once brought her some flowers. Some of those white daisies that grew in the ditch or those yellow buttercups that grew up on a wet year. Just brought them to her and said, 'Here Ma, something pretty for you, something for the table.' I bet she would have smiled, and maybe patted me on the head, and she might not been able to say anything, but she would have smiled. Poor Ma, never knew many smiles."

"Fuck me, selfish bastard," Ben said, taking a drag on the smoke and grinding it out between his fingers

- his fingers were so tough the ember did not really hurt, only a low burn, like a deep sadness or regret.

He tossed the butt on the ground. "We're all just a goddamn cigarette butt," he cursed and nudged Meathead, "something to be crushed."

Ben rode off a hill into a narrow valley about a mile long that was ringed in by hills. A sandy gully, over twenty feet deep and ten to fifteen yards wide snaked through the center of the valley - first going one way and then another - like it really couldn't make up its mind what it wanted to do. On the edge of the gully were a few cedar trees.

Ben followed the gully, saw a gentle slope to its bottom, and turned Meathead down the slope. She slid down easily and headed up the middle of the gully. It was cool with the sun cut off. There were jackrabbit and coyote tracks in the sand and then a pile of rabbit fur where the coyote had won.

"I ate a jackrabbit once," Ben said, "tough as leather and about as good as leather. But I was hungry so it was better than it should have been."

Ben followed the gully. It was a different world, a world beneath the real world, only a sliver of the sky above them, a small glimpse that if people had never been on the surface they would have thought the sky was only long and narrow and didn't amount to much.

When the gully ran into the base of the hill Ben rode out of the gully. Off to the side, over twenty yards up the hill, on an exposed limestone outcropping was a pictograph of a snake. The snake was not coiled but stretched out over fifty feet long and two feet wide - his fangs long and deadly - his tongue flicking out - his rattle upright in warning. Several portions of the snake had fallen off, the pieces of limestone shattered at the base - the etched fragments now indiscernible.

Ben dismounted, tied Meathead on the shady side of a pinion tree.

He looked at the snake and saw a trail that led to the snake that had been cut in the sandstone. There was a ledge that ran the length of the snake big enough for a man to walk along if he was careful.

Ben walked away from the snake until he could see the complete snake without moving his head. Looking down at the ground he saw chips of black obsidian where an Indian had sat making arrowheads or spear points. He looked back at the snake. "Whatever God you Indians invented here didn't do you a pissing bit of good," he said. "You got snuffed out."

Ben could see the half-naked Indians banging

away with their rock hammers forming the snake. When they were finished they would have killed a goat or maybe even a child to appease the image they had created, figuring all gods needed sacrifice. "God's sure as hell aren't friends," Ben said. "Masters have no friends."

A scorpion, for some reason caught out in the daylight, scurried a few feet from Ben, searching frantically for safety beneath a rock. Ben tried to step on him, but missed.

Ben didn't like scorpions, or flies, or mosquitoes, or black widow spiders, or centipedes. They all snuck up on people for no reason and bit or stung and then scurried away. He didn't mind rattlesnakes - they warned a person - they didn't bite people for the hell of it. They had a little pride in what they were - there was nothing sneaky or deceitful about them.

Ben felt like a drink of whiskey but didn't feel like walking back to Meathead.

He sat down on the ground and looked at the snake. "Maybe I should climb up there and chip out Ben Sharps was here and he doesn't believe in any god."

Ben thought a moment. "Hell, even if the snake god and all those invisible gods aren't real, maybe they do some good for the people that believed in them. Maybe it makes life tolerable and not so empty. Even if they are not real at least they served a purpose."

"It's a confusing mess," he added, taking off his hat and rubbing his head.

He then smiled a crooked wry grin. "Guess my god has been whiskey. It hasn't been a bad god though, just a little heavy on the money is all, but nothing I had to pray to."

Ben lay back on the sandy ground, not moving a small rock that was in the middle of his back. "Just a little rest," he muttered, shutting his eyes.

******

Ben ran as fast as he could after hitting his father, panting after awhile, panting so hard his lungs felt like they were on fire, but he still ran, ran until he no longer panted, and he'd become part of the run - part of the run like a bird was part of the sky. He felt like he could run forever and never get tired. He'd run until he was a young man, a middle aged man, and then an old man - run and run and run - never stopping to see anything or anybody and then he'd die running in some far off land he'd never dreamed of visiting.

The sun started to come up and Ben hid in a brush pile by a pond. He looked back the way he had come to make sure he was not being followed. As his heart started to slow down, and his breathing became normal, he was suddenly afraid. So afraid he started to shake. He held himself and shook like a frightened rabbit, or a beat down cowering dog - too afraid to bite its tormentor or even run. Then he started to throw up, chucked up fourteen years of pain and hate and anger, chucked up his sister who could not fly, chucked up hitting his father with a shovel. Threw up until there was nothing in his stomach and he gagged gasping for breath - gagged on fear and wondering where he would go? Gagged wondering what would he do?

When he was done, he felt weaker than he ever had in his life, and using his sack of clothes as a pillow, he curled up in a ball like a possum and slept so deeply his mind went blank. There was no father, no mother, no dead sister, no life, no future, no wants, no needs, and no dreams - only black. A black he would have wanted to go on forever if he would have known he was asleep, but he did not.

Ben woke up and for a moment did not know where he was. The sun was beginning to set. A pheasant called on the other side of the pond. Sparrows darted from the brush pile - startling him. Ben was cold. The cool of the earth had penetrated his overhauls and coat - sinking into his muscles and bones so deep he wondered if he would ever be warm again. He was also hungrier than he had never been - so hungry it hurt, and thirsty like his insides were a desert and he would never be able to drink enough water to quench his thirst. "Lisa, you up there in the sky, you watch over me," he whispered, trying to make his plea not sound like a prayer.

Ben thought about drinking from the pond, but pond water more often than not made a person sick and he did not want to get sick.

He waited until it was dark and he crawled out of the brush pile and started running. Like the night before he ran and ran until he became the run. He ignored his hunger and thirst. Several times he saw lights from farmhouses, but he veered away from them. When the sun started to rise he saw another large brush pile where a farmer was clearing out a ditch and he hid in it. He tried to sleep, but his tongue felt huge in his mouth from thirst, and his stomach felt like it would touch his backbone. Not caring whether or not he got caught, he crawled out of the brush pile and started running again. But his legs were tired, and his lungs hurt, and his hunger and thirst were mighty - mightier than he was and he stopped running and started walking. His scuffed, lace-up boots, dragged along the ground like an old drunk hobo who'd missed a train - not caring which way the train was going and knowing it did not really matter.

He walked for over an hour, his hunger and thirst like demons. He walked on, his eyes pointed at the ground - not the horizon - there was no hope and he started to cry. He didn't bawl or slobber but silent tears ran from his eyes, ran on their own accord like he had no control over them - they were their own world, but their world controlled his and would always control him. He would walk through life one to one with tears, not wanting them but never able to drive them away. "Damn sissy," Ben cursed.

"Hey son," a deep voice cut through the air.

Ben spun around, ready to race away quicker than a quail. His eyes were wide and full of fear.

"You don't have to be afraid of me boy," a man bigger than any man Ben had ever seen said.

The man had a long black beard and was wearing a heavy gray wool coat. He was riding bareback on a black plow horse that looked like it could have pulled ten plows. There was a rope looped around the horse's nose for a bridal.

Ben hurriedly wiped his eyes. The man looked away. There was no need to shame the boy - enough shame in the world anyway.

"You hungry?" the man asked, not sadly or like he really cared, but friendly.

"I'm not begging," Ben said, trying to be brave, trying to not show need.

"Didn't ask if you were begging, asked if you were hungry?" the man said.

Ben looked down at the ground for a moment, looked back up at the man, and trying to keep the quiver out of his voice answered. "Yes sir. I'm hungry and I'm thirsty."

The man inched the horse beside Ben and held out his hand. Ben took his large rough hand and the man pulled him up behind him on the horse like Ben was no more than a piece of kindling wood.

"I'll feed you son," the man said. "But you'll have to work for it. Nothing free in this world, if you don't buy it you have to labor for it. Money and labor the same thing in my mind - only difference is you can't steal labor."

The horse's back was so big Ben's legs stuck straight out and he put his arms around the big man's middle. His arms would not reach around the man. Ben's head was no taller than the man's shoulder blades. The heat from the man radiated through the wool coat - the warmth like forgiveness. A few more tears formed in Ben's eyes, but he rubbed them off on the man's coat and buried his face deep into the soothing wool. The man reached around, and without saying a word, patted Ben gently on the shoulder several times. "Move on now, Sam," the man said to the horse.

Ben shut his eyes. "Thanks, Lisa," he whispered.

Ben didn't know how long they had ridden. The warmth from the man and the warmth from the horse's back was the best warmth he'd ever felt. The steady slow walk of the horse was like a heartbeat - hypnotizing - peaceful. "Ho up, Sam," the man said.

Ben opened his eyes.

"You slide down now, son. Don't be afraid, old Sam's as gentle as they come."

Ben slid off the horse. They were in front of a large red barn. The paint was fresh like spring. Several milk cows were in a pen next to the barn. The cows were healthy, their udders' bursting with milk. In a field not far from the barn were ten black cattle - their ribs not showing from hunger. Next to the barn, beneath a tinned overhang, was a black as night car. The man got off the horse and led him into the barn. Ben hurried after them not wanting to be alone. The inside of the barn was clean. The hay neatly stacked and all the tools were in a row. Pigeons cooed from the rafters. Three calico cats rushed at Ben and rubbed on his legs. "Go get me an arm full of that hay," the man said, but not an order.

The man put the horse in a stall and Ben put the hay in the feed trough. "Now you get that bucket in the corner and on the side of the barn is a pump. Bring me back a bucket of water for Sam."

Ben ran to the bucket, ran to the pump, filled the bucket and hurried back, wanting to please the man more than he wanted to drink. "Hang that bucket from that hook inside the stall," the man said.

Ben did as he was told. When Ben was done the man smiled at him and held out his hand to shake. "I'm Reno Johnson. This is my farm."

Ben noticed Reno's eyes were as blue as his sister's had been - blue and big and kind.

"My name is Ben Sharps," Ben said, taking Reno's hand.

"Glad to meet you Ben, now let's get those cows in and milk them and then we'll get you something to eat."

Ben watched Reno milk the cows. Reno's chest was bigger than a barrel. The muscles in his arms were has hard and defined as oak tree branches. But Ben felt no fear of the man.

After milking they walked toward the house. The

house was a one-story frame, painted white, with a red brick chimney and a stovepipe sticking through the roof. They went through a side door into the clean kitchen - the wood stove was still warm. There was a hand pump by the sink and a towel. "You wash up," Reno said, building the fire back up in the stove. "And get a drink."

There was a tin cup hanging from a hook by the pump. Ben filled and refilled the cup. Trying not to slurp or spill water down his front. The water was better than fresh peaches. He then washed his face and hands with a bar of handmade lye soap.

Reno fried potatoes, heated up canned corn, and fried two steaks as big as plates. Ben sat nervously at the table overwhelmed with the smell of the food. Reno put a plate in front of Ben and sat down with his own. Ben only looked at the wonderful food, afraid to eat - afraid it was a mirage. Reno nodded and Ben started eating. "When you're done Ben, you can tell me what you're running from," Reno said.

"Yes sir," Ben replied, knowing it would not be right to lie to a man who had been kind to him.

******

Ben sat up from the ground. The spot where his back had rested on the rock was a little sore. "That was the best meal I ever ate in my life," he said and smiled, ignoring the pictograph snake.

He stood, rubbed his back, and went over to Meathead who was napping. She opened her eyes, "Hell, here we go again."

Ben rubbed her neck, got his bottle of whiskey, and took a small swallow.

A dust devil bounced along the ground a couple of hundred yards away - kicking up tumbleweeds. He took another swallow of whiskey, noticing there was a little over two thirds of a bottle left as he put it back in the saddlebags. He walked away from the horse and the pictograph snake and followed the edge of the gully. He'd heard that millions of years ago the whole area had been underwater and that fish as big as diesel trucks, with teeth as long as his arm had swam in the water. He couldn't imagine such a thing, or why such a beast had ever lived, but the limestone hills, layered from red to white to light brown showed how the water had slowly receded. "Millions and millions of years and I've had a hard time with eighty-seven years," he said.

Near the base of a creosote bush Ben saw several pieces of broken Indian pottery. Ben had heard Indians busted the pots on purpose during certain ceremonies, which sounded kind of stupid to him. Why bust a pot and have to make another one? It was like throwing away a good cast iron skillet so you could buy another one. "We people can sure come up with some piss poor ideas when it comes to gods and spirits," Ben said.

He didn't bother to pick up the shards. He'd seen thousands of them. They were little clay pieces of sadness to Ben - pieces of an unknown person's life and effort now scattered on the ground - so what was the purpose?

Ben had gone to a museum in Denver once and looked at exhibits of primitive man, how they had lived, and how man had developed to modern man. He'd listened to other people commenting on how happy they were to be alive now and not then. All Ben had thought was that we are all a walking museum - from the day we are born, just a piece of the past - a relic that future people will look at never realizing they too are relics. There never was or will be a modern man - present man - but not modern man.

"Shit," Ben said. "Someday they'll have stuffed cowboys in museums and on information cards it will say – 'Cowboy, not one of the smartest breed of people. They used to roam the western part of North America eating dust and roping cattle and working for little or nothing - often referred to as a saddle bum or hair brain.'"

Ben turned and headed back to Meathead. "Let's go get you a drink," he said, mounting and turning the horse toward a trail that led over the eastern hill. On the other side was a windmill Ben should have checked a few weeks earlier but hadn't. "Cattle are all over on the west side of the ranch anyway," he'd told himself, but he still felt guilty, not doing his job and all.

******

Reno pushed back from the table, watched Ben take his last bite of food, then went to the stove and brought back two cups of black coffee and a cup of sugar. He put two large tablespoons of sugar in his coffee, slurped the coffee loudly and smiled at Ben.

Ben had never had sugar in coffee. Sugar was for the occasional pie or cobbler, not coffee. Like Reno, he put two heaping tablespoons of sugar in the coffee and sipped it. The meal was so good, and the coffee so good, a tear tried to form in his eye, but he held it. The tear formed into a frog in his throat and he coughed on purpose trying to rid himself of the frog.

Reno took another drink of coffee, set the cup down loudly and looked Ben straight in the eyes. "Ok Ben, tell me what you're running from."

Ben could not look at Reno. He looked out the window at the flat western Kansas land and felt like he would always be searching for something that was always on the other side of the horizon - a place that was impossible to reach.

Ben started talking. His words were fast and quick, like they had to be told, even if there was nobody there to listen, they had to be told - told and gotten rid of like garbage - left to rot somewhere so far away there were not even coyotes to feed on it. He told Reno about his sister who could not fly, his father who whipped him all the time and who worked for a dollar a day on another man's farm and starved on his own. He told Reno about his mother. He told him of the feeling he always had in the back of his mind, even though he could not describe it the way it really was - it was a longing, a dream, an emptiness, maybe a sadness that he knew he would never rid himself of - it would always be there - something he did not understand, but he knew it would be there - something always setting him off from people or places - something to make him ponder what others would accept. Even at a young age Ben knew there was no justice, no real truth.

"After I hit my Pa I ran all night." He told Reno. "I slept most of the first day in a brush pile by a pond and when I woke up that evening I ran again. In the morning I hid in another brush pile, but I couldn't sleep. I tried to run but I was so tired and hungry I couldn't and then you found me," Ben said, looking away from the window, glancing at Reno without meeting his eyes, and then gazing at the empty plate with its shine of delicious beef fat. With both hands shaking he picked up the coffee that was so sweet it was like candy and sipped, set the coffee down carefully, and with all the might left in him finished by saying. "Mr. Johnson, sir, I never really meant no harm. I just really didn't know what to do."

Reno was silent for a few moments. His kind eyes gazed over Ben's head, gazed somewhere in his own past - somewhere it was nobody's business to know. "And so, Ben, what do you plan on doing with your life now?" he asked.

Ben did not hesitate in his reply. "I want to be a saddle bronc rider in the rodeo. I want to be the best saddle bronc rider there has ever been. I want to wear cowboy boots, and have a buckle shiny as the sun, and eat three meals a day, and have people look at me and say - that's Ben Sharps, he's the best bronc rider in the world. He could even ride a shooting star."

"How old are you, Ben?" Reno asked.

Ben wanted to tell him he was sixteen and almost did but he said, "Fourteen," adding quickly, "almost fifteen."

"How'd a farm boy like you ever dream about being a saddle bronc rider?" Reno asked.

"When I was a little boy I saw a picture in a magazine of a saddle bronc rider and from that day on it's been my dream to be in the rodeo. It's a dream so strong it's like it's not really a dream. It's more like something I've already done and now all I can do is remember it. But the remembering is so strong I can feel it all the way to my bones."

Reno finished his coffee, went and got himself another cup, but did not offer one to Ben.

"You ever been on a bronc?" Reno asked.

Ben reluctantly shook his head.

Reno smiled, but not a cutting or demeaning smile, more of an understanding smile.

Don't take me back home, Ben wanted to beg Reno. But he couldn't, and he knew if Reno said he had to go home he'd run. He'd get up from the table and run and run and run - even if he never ate, or drank again, and the running killed him.

Reno took a long drink of the coffee, set the cup down carefully, gazed once more over Ben's head, back into the past nobody needed to know about, back to the past that instead of making him mean and bitter had made him kind and gentle, but also made him alone - alone on a farm in western Kansas only talking to cows and horses and dry old land that most of the time didn't produce enough to pay any bill, just some of the credit - alone and only going from day to day knowing he would die here - here with the wind and the cows and the land.

"Most people never make their dreams," Reno said.

"I'll make mine," Ben said grimly.

"I know a man over in Colorado," Reno said. "He has a ranch by Buena Vista, mountain country, mountains so high you'd swear God couldn't reach their tops, colder than here in the winter, but pretty in the summer. More flowers than I have weeds. Meadows with so much grass cows and horses can be picky, and streams that are so full of trout you don't have to fish for them, they just jump out of the water and you catch them in mid air. About a week or so I'll take you over there. He'll teach you how to be a cowboy or you'll find out you're not tough enough and need another dream."

Ben did not know what to say. He did not know what to do. As if another being entered his body, he stood, walked around the table to Reno, and hugged him. He clung to Reno like Reno was hope and salvation and without warning Ben bawled unashamed.

Reno put his arm around the boy, did not speak

but thought to himself, son, one of these days you're going to have to shake those tears or this life will put a hole in you so big you'll never be able to dig yourself out.

CHAPTER FOUR

"Here's your drink," Ben said to Meathead, stopping by the stock tank.

Meathead slurped water for a few minutes with no thanks. Ben glanced at the still windmill blades. He then dismounted and checked the float that was supposed to make sure the tank didn't overflow, but most of the time didn't work. "Shit, if things worked the way they were suppose to work man wouldn't know what to do," Ben said. "More than half a life is spent fixing busted shit."

Ben angrily splashed water on his face and dried his hands on his pants.

Meathead looked at him like, what's your problem?

"What are you looking at?" Ben demanded still

mad about shit that broke down most of the time.

"Hell, you've been broke down most of the time during your life, too," Meathead said.

Ben gave her a dirty look and walked away. "Drink so much water you'll get a bellyache," he said over his shoulder.

The tank was in the middle of a section of rolling sparse land that was dotted with yuccas and clumps of bunch grass. It was fenced, but the cedar fence posts were past their prime and leaned in every direction like drunken soldiers. The wire was half falling down and rusty. Hills rose all around the flat, and behind them, over fifty miles away, were the dark outlines of real mountains - mountains so grand they did not want to be associated with mere hills. On the south side, the flat ended abruptly at a sheer drop off that fell at least five hundred yards. At the base of the drop off was the beginning of hundreds of miles of desolate land that jackrabbits didn't even like - the only things that survived on it were tumbleweeds and scratch grass. Dotting the desolation were white alkaline rimmed pools of stagnant water. On the alkaline shores swarms of black flies, mosquitoes, and gnats spent their lives. The gnats, and flies, and mosquitoes, are so thick that when they are disturbed they fly into the air in black clouds, biting and stinging with a meanness and vengeance that would bring any stray to its knees in minutes. "Indians used to take their prisoners out there and leave them naked with no food or water," Ben said.

"We should take our politicians with their empty promises and put them out there."

Ben stopped walking and lost his anger. "Here it is my last day. It doesn't matter anymore."

He took several deep breaths and looked back at Meathead. She was standing by the tank, head down, napping. "Horses are like dogs. When nothing is going on they sleep. What a good life," Ben said, shaking his head. "If man rested and slept most of the time they'd call him lazy."

Ben smiled a crooked little smile and sat down on a large flat rock that was covered with light gold and green lichen - the lichen older than the hills. A breeze swept through the flat, stopped as soon as it had started, not knowing why it had started and not caring why it had stopped.

******

Ben worked every day with Reno - Reno telling him what to do and never chastising him when he did wrong. They mucked out the stalls, brought in the last of the hay what with winter closing in. They milked, fed the cattle, painted a few cracked places on the house. Reno never mentioned about Ben running away - never treated him like a kid - treated him like a man - like he was a brother. Ben slept on a sofa by the fireplace in the living room at night. Reno slept in his own room. Ben would look at the fire and it was the first time he had ever felt calm. The fire would dance off the walls and Ben would dream of rodeos and cowboys. The walls were bare except a picture of Reno and a woman - both younger, both smiling. But Ben did not ask Reno about the woman. Ben would sleep warm and comfortable like a kitten full of his mother's milk. At times, waking in the morning, he wanted to tell Reno he didn't want to go to Colorado and learn how to be a cowboy. He didn't give a dang about being the best saddle bronc rider in the rodeo anymore. He wanted to spend the rest of his life working for Reno. But he didn't. Even though Reno was kind to him, there was something about Reno that Ben knew had to be alone - he could only give so much - and then he would have to be alone.

One fall afternoon Reno was going to town. "Best you don't go, Ben. Your father might have put out word to the police about you hitting him with a shovel and running off," he told Ben.

Ben watched the car for a long time. The dust from the road was like a brown snake at the bottom of the sky. He didn't have anything to do, and he didn't want to go sit in the house, so he walked out away from the house toward a skinny tree he had never gone to look at. The tree was about ten feet tall and had already dropped its leaves - the tree looked out of place and lonely. Beneath the tree were two graves – carved on simple wooden markers was - My Beloved Wife, and on the other - My Beloved Child. There were no names or dates. On each grave was planted a flower, now dead and wilted from the morning frost - the tree behind them not a guard, but a friend. Facing the graves was a green wooden bench. Ben sat on the bench. "I wonder where Ma and Pa buried you, Lisa," Ben said. "I wonder if you got a tree or a flower."

He looked up at the sky. There were no clouds, not even a sparrow to disturb the blue, only the sun, but now not giving much heat - ready to turn its back on the world and make man shiver - make man appreciate him more when he returned in the spring with his warmth, and then cuss him when the heat was oppressive and scorching. "You up there Lisa?" Ben asked quietly.

There was no answer - only the blue expanse and the sun.

"I'm sorry, Reno," Ben said to the graves. "I'm so

sorry."

Ben was filled with a sadness that was not his. The sun traveled the sky. The wind did not blow. Occasionally a mockingbird trilled in the distance, but nothing quelled the sadness.

Ben didn't hear Reno approaching - didn't see him until he sat down next to Ben.

Ben jumped up. "I'm sorry, Reno. I shouldn't have come out here. It isn't my place," Ben stammered, feeling guilty.

"Sit down, Ben. It's ok," Reno said.

Ben sat.

"My wife died giving birth to my daughter," Reno said with a sadness so deep it chilled the air around them. "My daughter clung to life for three days. We all have our grief and we do with it what we will. Don't ever forget in your life every living thing has its own grief. Now you go back to the house and get the stove and fire going."

******

Ben took off his hat and scratched his head. "Good people always seem to get more grief," he said. "Bad people seem to cause it and enjoy causing it."

"Even to this day I wonder what Reno's wife and baby were named," Ben said.

"We never talked about it."

Ben stood. His knees hurt and felt like rusty hinges. "If I was a rich man I could go get me some of those fake plastic knees," he said, heading back to Meathead. "But what good would it do, I'd still piss a dribble."

Ben got his whiskey. Meathead did not bother to open her eyes. He sipped the whiskey, put it back, and had enough tobacco left in the Bugler pouch to roll one more smoke. He lit the smoke and put the empty pouch in the saddlebag and took out a new pouch and opened it.

A raven landed on the top of the windmill - looked at Ben like he was the funniest thing he had ever seen in his life - squawked twice and flew off.

"You're a funny looking bastard, too," Ben said.

Ben leaned back against Meathead. She cocked her leg to hold his weight and did not open her eyes. Ben pulled deep on the smoke.

******

Reno had gone into town and bought Ben a suitcase and filled it with new clothes – four pair of cotton socks, two blue wool shirts, a pair of long underwear, lined leather gloves, and three pair of new Levi's. Ben had never had new clothes and could only manage to say, "Thanks," when he wanted to say more.

They left before the sun came up and as the sun was rising behind them, Ben, for the first time, saw the distant outline of the Rocky Mountains. The mountains erupted from the horizon like huge dark buffalo - shaking their heads and pawing the ground, daring anybody to challenge them or make them leave the world they controlled.

Reno drove but the mountains never seemed to get closer. "Will we ever get there?" Ben asked, so excited he could not sit still.

Reno smiled.

They ate lunch at a little town at the base of the mountains. The men eating were not farmers wearing work boots, but they all wore dirty cowboy hats, and cowboy boots, and had leather gloves tucked in their back pockets. They nodded at Reno but did not really acknowledge him. Ben devoured a hamburger and gulped a large glass of water - the water was the best he had ever tasted - mountain water.

Driving into the mountains Ben sat on the edge of the seat, his forehead against the window, and looked in wonderment at all the new things. There were tall pine trees and groves of aspen trees, the yellow leaves sparkling like contented butterflies. The scrub oak was turning blood red. Coming around a bend in the road the road suddenly ran parallel with a river - the river clear like diamonds - not muddy like Kansas farm ponds. It poured over boulders, churned the water white, and then slowed on the bends - the deeper water blue green and sparkling. There was tall brittle grass along the river - brown now from fall frosts - but Ben could visualize it in the summer - so green it would almost blind a person.

Reno did not talk.

In mid-afternoon they drove into Buena Vista. The river ran right through the middle of town. Reno pulled into a Skelly gas station, filled the tank himself, while a man washed the windows. Ben stood by the car in awe. The air was crisp, dryer than Kansas - invigorating.

"How's Dave Toole doing?" Reno asked the man washing the windows.

"Don't see him much, but heard it's been a good year, not much of a calf kill this spring and good grass."

"They haven't put him in jail yet?" Reno smiled.

"As long as people leave him alone," the attendant smiled back.

Reno paid for the gas and bought Ben an orange soda pop. He'd never had an orange pop - it was better than coffee - the sweet liquid was tingly and it made him smile.

Reno drove several miles north of town and turned left on a dirt road that headed directly into the mountains. To the left and right of the road were pastures filled with hundreds of cattle. In the middle of the fields huge haystacks were fenced off so the cattle could not get to them. "They run the cattle in the mountains during the summer and bring them down in the winter," Reno said.

Ben saw a cowboy riding his horse and he waved. The cowboy waved back.

They left the pasture land and started up a canyon - the walls of the canyon not much wider than the car - shutting off the sun - like the sun was forbidden to enter and if it did it could never escape.

They came out of the dark canyon into a sun filled meadow. The pine trees surrounding the meadow whispered to Ben, "We give you sanctuary."

The meadow was completely fenced with interlaced pine poles. The road went under a gate with a cattle guard. Burnt into a sign that stretched over the gate was, Toole Ranch - and the brand - a circle K. There were pine pole corrals and many log sheds, two log barns, two long cabins, and a large log cabin with the front side protected by a full-length porch. Nailed to the poles holding up the porch were numerous deer and elk antlers. There were also benches made from split trees and several chairs. There were tractors, hay rakes, and other machinery scattered in no set pattern and chickens were running everywhere. One of the corrals had at least twenty horses in it and three cowboys were looking at them. The cowboys had on drooping dirty hats, chaps, long-sleeved shirts, and lined leather vests. The cowboys waved at Reno nonchalantly as he drove by - paying no mind to Ben.

Reno parked in front of the large cabin. Three stovepipes belched smoke from the roof - the smoke rising straight into the sky and then drifting off into the trees - fitting into the trees like a welcomed fog. Getting out of the car Ben saw three giant stacks of cut firewood and off in the distance a graveyard with five crosses that were as shiny as piano keys. A lady about Ben's mother's age came out onto the porch. She was not much taller than Ben - thin and graceful like a willow tree branch. She had long dark hair like a raven's feathers, pulled back into a ponytail, and was wearing Levi's, black cowboy boots, and a bright red western shirt. Seeing Reno, her complete face smiled and she ran to him, throwing herself into his arms. "Reno, Reno," she cried happily. "It's been so long."

Reno held her, patting her back the way he had patted Ben.

After awhile they stopped hugging and Ben noticed when the lady stepped back there were tears in her eyes, which she wiped away quickly with the back of her hand.

Reno pointed at Ben. "Peggy," he said. "This is a good friend of mine, Ben Sharps. Ben, this is my sister, Peggy."

Peggy smiled and walked over to Ben. Ben held out his hand to shake but Peggy hugged him. Ben, without thinking, returned her hug. Ben was too nervous to say anything, but he noticed when Peggy let him go her eyes were a deep green and filled with caring. "Nice to meet you Ben, now you both come in. Dave will be back soon, he's out looking for a few strays."

They sat at a huge kitchen table drinking coffee and eating apple pie that Peggy had not let either one of them refuse. Ben listened to Reno and Peggy talk. There was nothing about the past, nothing about family, but they talked about the ranch and Reno's farm, and how things were going, and how tough it was to make it, but they always seemed to make it. Ben enjoyed watching them and felt happy and warm in their company.

It started to get dark and Peggy went around the house lighting kerosene lamps and stoking large ornate pot-bellied stoves. "We'll get electricity before long," she told them when she was done. "It will be such a relief."

A tall, thin man, with a black moustache that was over six inches long, with skin as brown as leather came into the kitchen. He had on high-topped cowboy boots and spurs. "Reno, you old bastard, good to see you," he said merrily.

Reno stood and shook hands with the man. "This is Ben Sharps. Ben, this is David Toole. This is his ranch, the Circle K," Reno said

Ben stood, feeling small and out of place. "Glad to meet you, sir," he managed to say nervously.

Dave chuckled and shook hands. "If you're a friend of Reno's, you're a friend of mine," he said, and they all sat down.

It was dark outside when they ate. The logs absorbed the kerosene light, making the cabin muted and soothing. Ben did not talk, nor was ever asked a question.

After dinner Reno told Ben to go sit on the porch. Ben knew they were going to discuss him and he left without comment. Ben did not sit but stood in front of the porch looking at the night sky. The stars were different than Kansas. Here he could stand on his tiptoes and almost touch them. In Kansas the stars were muted, like they existed in a haze - never able to show their true brilliance. From one of the cabins he had seen earlier he heard men laughing and then harmonica music - the song not sad but yearning - and the men stopped laughing. The notes from the harmonica set easy with the stars - seemed to fit in because the stars knew they would never really be happy - there would always be something missing no matter how bright they sparkled - but it was ok - it was just how it was, and no matter what, they would sparkle till they blinked out.

Looking at the stars Ben was suddenly afraid. What if Mr. Toole would not take him on? Now that he had been in the mountains, and seen the trees, and the river, and the cowboys. What if he had to go? He'd never be the best bronc buster in the rodeo. He'd never be a cowboy. "Dear God, please?" he prayed for the first time in his life. But his prayer made him feel like a traitor - hollow and begging.

Ben could hear Reno and Ben and Peggy talking, but he couldn't make out the words. The harmonica music stopped. The smoke from the fires went straight up for about twenty feet and then bent in a straight line over the cabins and corrals - trapped before it could rise to the night sky and be free.

Reno came out onto the porch and sat down by Ben. He did not talk for a long time, but seemed to ponder the stars, and the dark, and the ways of the world, but he did not question them. "Dave and Peg will take you on Ben," Reno said distantly like it grieved him deeply to let Ben go. "You must promise me you will do your best no matter what they have you do, never steal from them, or in anyway be deceitful. They are good people, Ben."

"Reno, I promise," Ben said, his heart pounding in his chest, and even though he was happy and relieved, his chin fell onto his chest and he said with more love than he had ever felt, even more than for his sister. "Reno, nobody ever treated me better and... and... and... well... oh Reno, I'll miss you terribly."

Reno patted Ben on the shoulder. "Shake on your word," he said.

They shook hands.

******

The cigarette had gone out in Ben's fingers. He field dressed the butt and let it flutter to the ground. He mounted Meathead. She shook her head in disapproval and snorted. Ben nudged the horse and pointed her west toward the top part of the flat. "And now I'm a cowboy thanks to Reno and Dave," he said.

"Isn't life some shit? Isn't it strange how some dreams get realized by accident?"

CHAPTER FIVE

"Always liked yuccas," Ben said, eyeing a group of yuccas about fifty yards away. "They just grow out here all lonely like. Then once a year they shoot out this huge nice smelling flower that few people ever see."

"Indians made soap from the roots, rope and mats and clothes from the leaves, and flutes from the stalk," Ben went on.

Ben had been to a few powwows in his time but he didn't like flute music - it was too sad and longing. There were never any happy tunes, or drinking tunes, or let's just go out and have a good time tunes. But Ben figured even before the reservations, true Indian life wasn't that damn good like the books said. "I'd rather been a cowboy, even if we did steal their land and wipe out most of them," Ben said. "Wasn't right, but too late for right. Besides, I could never believe rocks and mountains were gods."

"But I suppose the Indians would have taken better care of the land than any of us dumb cowboys. Maybe they respected it more."

Ben turned Meathead toward the group of yuccas, stopped by them and dismounted, took out his bottle of whiskey, took a sip, put the bottle back and sat down in front of a yucca. "Even if I like you, you don't give enough shade for an ant," Ben said to the yucca.

******

Ben and Peggy stood in front of the cabin the next morning and watched Reno drive away. Ben had slept on the sofa. Peggy waved, until with a honk, the car disappeared into the canyon where no light was allowed to enter. Ben stood with his hands in his pockets, one hand around the dollar Reno had given him. He felt like a part of his heart had been cut off and would never grow back. He wanted to cry, but held his tears, what with a woman by him and all. Peggy put her arm around his shoulder, pulled him into her side, and they stood for a long moment watching where the car had vanished. Peggy sighed deeply. "Well, Ben, let's get you situated," she said, adding with a smile. "I think you'll make a fine cowboy if you don't pick up any of the bad habits these men will want to teach you. But first, I have to ask you a question?"

"Yes Ma'am," Ben replied.

"Do you want to go to school?"

"I don't think school will do me much good," Ben replied truthfully.

"Being a cowboy is not a bad life," Peggy replied.

Peggy led Ben to the cabin where the harmonica music had come from. Half the porch was stacked with wood and there was a wooden bench. Inside were a potbelly stove and six bunks with a trunk at the foot of each bunk. Hanging by the beds from nails were coats and spurs and chaps. On the trunks were tobacco fixings, pouches of chewing tobacco, and a few framed photographs. The bunks all had different colored blankets on them, but they were all made. "I make them make their beds," Peggy said. "I can't stand a bum."

At the end of the bunkhouse was a scratched wooden table with a cribbage board, cards, and dominoes. "This bunk will be yours," Peggy said pointing. "And out back is a wash room with a wood stove to heat water and next to it is the outhouse. "You put your things away and then come over to the house and you can haul some wood for me."

"What's in the other cabin?" Ben asked.

"That's the chuck house where you men eat and where Maria the cook lives. Breakfast is at five, dinner whenever you get back in, but you won't be going out with the men for awhile. Dave wants me to show you around, teach you how to ride, and you're going to help Maria cook."

"I've never helped anyone cook," Ben said, trying to hide his disappointment.

"Everyone starts at the bottom, Ben," Peggy said soothingly. "You have to prove yourself and don't be in a rush to be more than you are. There's nothing in life to be ashamed about unless it was your doing." Then, looking at the table with the cards on it, she added sternly, "And don't let me find out these men are getting you in any card games now that you are going to be making a dollar a day."

"A dollar a day," Ben blurted.

Peggy smiled as she was leaving but Ben could see a touch of sadness in her smile.

"I don't want anybody feeling sorry for me," Ben said to the empty bunkhouse, but still amazed he would be making a dollar a day.

Ben put his things away and sat on his bunk. He suddenly felt alone and he remembered telling his sister, "I'll be the best saddle bronc rider in the rodeo and it will be only because of me and not any god."

But he'd already had help, even if it wasn't God. "Guess nobody makes it on their own," Ben said. "Everybody needs help."

******

"Peggy was my true mother," Ben said. "And even if I only spent a week with Reno he was my true father. I was real lucky, no telling how I would have ended up without them. I might have run all the way to the ocean and then turned around and run back. They taught me a lot."

He looked at the sky. "They never wanted to fly, Lisa, but then I suppose they never needed to know how."

"Maybe they wanted to fly but understood they never could."

"I do wish I would have learned more about Reno and Peggy. I know they were brother and sister but I don't know anymore than that."

Ben got his can of peaches out of the saddlebags and sat back down. He opened the can with his pocket knife and stabbed a peach. He'd always loved peaches. "Peaches are so good the government will make them illegal someday," Ben said.

Ben finished the peaches and poured the juice on

the ground and watched. Within minutes there were ants all around the juice and then a bee. "You'd better hole up soon," Ben said to the ants and bee. "Winter will catch you."

Ben groaned to his feet, stomped the peach can flat, and put the can in the saddlebags. Ben hated garbage tossed out on the land.

Ben took another shot of whiskey and got on Meathead and continued north.

******

Peggy didn't have any problem teaching Ben how to ride. Ben took to horses like they shared the same blood. Within a week he was riding like he'd been on a horse his entire fourteen years. He was never afraid and horses seemed to know him and appreciate him. Ben talked to the horses like they were people. At first Peggy thought it was strange, but then she noticed that the horses seemed to listen to Ben - even the skittish ones that most people found hard to ride rode easy with Ben. He'd pat them on the neck, whisper in their ear, and they would settle right down. Ben also had a gentle rein. He didn't yank on the bit or heel a horse hard.

Ben didn't show great joy in riding, but was always grim faced, like the riding was ok, but it was only something he had to do to be able to do what he wanted. He didn't tell Peggy his dream about being the best saddle bronc rider in the rodeo. He didn't tell anybody. At times looking at the sky as he was riding he'd say, "Lisa, you watching? I hope you're watching. I'm going to make my dream. And nobody is going to stop me."

Ben didn't like the kitchen work but he did not protest - always keeping in his mind what Peggy had told him. "Everyone has to start at the bottom."

Also keeping his promise to Reno he would do his best no matter what he had to do, but saying to himself, "Promises at times are hard to keep."

He liked Maria the cook. Maria was a Mexican woman no more than five feet tall and about the same around. She wore long colorful dresses that a parrot would be envious of. Her face was hundreds of folds of brown skin, and her eyes were black dots, and when she ordered a cowboy to eat all his food - all the cowboy said was, "Yes ma'am," and that was the end of it. She wore her black-as-night hair in a tight bun - so tight some of the folds on her forehead were pulled back. Her hands were large - manly hands - not brown like her face, but a light red from hot water and soap. Her only jewelry was a thin gold band, with a tiny cross on it that she wore on her wedding finger. She could carry two buckets of water - split wood for the cook stove quicker than any man, and if a man was late to eat when there was a set time and work did not get in the way they didn't eat. Any argument was met with a furious waving of arms and a stream of Spanish that nobody understood, but it was said so vehemently that the offender slinked out of the chuck cabin with his head down and stomach growling, never to be late again. Nobody knew her age, some said sixty, some eighty.

On one wall of the chuck house was a shelf overflowing with candles that were in glass containers. The containers had pictures on them of all the saints and saints nobody had ever heard of. In the middle of the shelf was a brightly painted wooden cross - the blood running out of Jesus' wounds was redder and brighter than any blood could ever be. In the windows were coffee cans planted with herbs. Little shiny rocks and multi-colored pieces of broken glass were placed carefully around the cans. When the sun hit the glass and rocks sparkles filled the room like daytime fireflies - fireflies that could never be caught and put in a glass jar to wonder on and kill their freedom. Maria had hung curtains that were red and blue and green and gold. They were almost brighter than the sunshine.

There was one small room off the chuck house

that was Maria's. Nobody had ever been in it or was invited. It was her room, her sanctuary, her place in the world.

She never spoke of her life in her clipped English, where she had come from or how she had gotten to Colorado. She never complained, out of bed before any cowboy, still not in bed after they were already sleeping. But Ben saw a deep veiled sadness in her eyes. At times she would stand by the window of the chuck house, look out past the canyon where the sunshine was not allowed to enter, and Ben knew she was looking back to another land, another time - back through the years and the circumstances that had brought her to a ranch with none of her own people. Ben would stand, silently, not wanting to invade her space, and in time she would turn, look softly at Ben for a mere second, and with a wave of her big arm, with its big red hand and the gold cross ring say sternly. "Get back to work, but eat a biscuit, you ezz too skinny, even for a gringo kid."

Ben stirred boiling kettles, chopped onions, greased pans, hauled wood, did dishes, set the table, brought in pitchers of water, and made sure a cowboy's coffee cup was never empty.

When the cowboys came in to eat they wiped their boots at the door, took off their hats, and had washed their hands and faces. Then they sat down at empty plates. Maria would stand at the end of the table, bow her head and pray in Spanish. The cowboys would look at each other, not quite sure what all this praying was about, but no one would say a word. Then Ben and Maria would serve the food - huge platters of eggs and bacon and biscuits for breakfast - occasionally a bowl of gravy. At night, fried pork chops or steaks, or chicken and potatoes, and corn or beans, and homemade bread that Ben would never forget the smell of. Sometimes Maria would make tacos or enchiladas. The men called the food 'Mex food' behind her back, but ate every bit, commenting later, while smoking on the porch of the bunk house, "That Mex shit is pretty damn good."

She made apple pies and cherry pies and rhubarb pies, leaving them on a bench on the porch to cool just to tease the men - who would never dream of stealing a piece - knowing stealing had no grace.

When the cowboys were done eating they always said as they left, "Thank you ma'am" or "thank you Maria," and Maria would wave them off like they were lower than the dust on their boots and then and only then would she and Ben eat.

Maria never spoke while she ate. She ate slowly and deliberately - chewing each bite carefully and savoring it. Neither Ben nor anyone knew the poverty she had been raised in and the many days there was no food. To Maria food was a blessing, never taken for granted and never to be abused - food had honor and grace and a satisfaction that nothing else in life could ever have.

When the kitchen was clean and ready for another day Maria would always send Ben back to the bunkhouse with a sack of cookies or some tasty Mexican pastry, telling Ben, "Take theez to those dirty cowboys and tell them someday Maria will die and no more cook for them and they will mezz her."

Her workday ended, Maria would go to her little room with its wood stove and pictures of Mary and Jesus on the walls, and she would sit in her chair and pick up her rosary. Sometimes she would cry softly, not because of what had been, but because she was full and warm and God had looked out for her, no matter her sins or transgressions He had blessed her, and she wished all people could be blessed.

******

"Ah hell, Meathead, I never took the time to really try and get to know Maria," Ben said. "I should have taken the time."

Meathead ignored him.

"It's a heavy transgression to not make an effort

to know somebody."

Meathead still ignored him.

"She was a good hard working woman," Ben said.

******

The cowboys on the ranch - Whitey, Mac, Crow, and Moose were good to Ben. Each in their own way was a loner and life had not been too kind to them, but they were not mean men although they had lived tough mean lives. Ben never knew, but Dave Toole had told them one afternoon when he'd first let Ben on, "Any of you boys ever do harm to that boy I'll whip you two inches from hell and send your ass out of here with no pay."

Whitey had replied, "Hell boss, we'd never hurt that boy."

"Didn't say you would," Dave had replied, "just saying if you ever did, besides, if you did, Peggy would be all over me like stink on shit and I'd just as soon lose a few teeth from one of you guys than have to tangle with someone I could never beat."

The men smiled, understanding completely.

For some reason all four of the hands could take cold, heat, dust, mud, rain, hail, snow, blizzards, getting kicked by cattle, stomped, run over, bucked off, but when it came to women they were more ignorant than a grouse and more afraid of than a bear.

The four cowhands were not young men, but never told their real age, and didn't really give a hoot about birthdays, but they were all in their forties or early fifties. They'd been raised with horses and mules and seen the first tractors and trucks. They'd all fought in World War I, but didn't talk about it - although they all agreed they hated Germans and couldn't really find much fondness for the English - figuring the English wouldn't have come over here to help save our ass especially after we whipped them to get our own freedom, and not one of them liked tea - tea was for sissies.

They all helped Ben each in their own way, not really out of kindness or sorrow, but it was the right thing to do. Whitey was a great roper and taught Ben all he knew. He made Ben toss a rope at a hay bale with an old bull skull on it so many times Ben was about to bust with frustration until one day the loop landed around the horns. Whitey only said, "It's about time." But Ben knew he was proud of him and Ben was proud of himself because he'd stuck it out and he'd made another man proud.

Mac could braid leather, and made halters, and tie downs, and bridals, and spliced rope so clean one couldn't see the splice, and he was the best farrier around. He taught Ben all he knew, and although Ben was never a great braider he did become a good farrier - although he hated it.

Moose didn't do anything too well, but also not too bad. But to Moose everything in life was funny. "Hell," he'd say, "Everything in life is so screwed up might as well laugh, might as well figure you're going to get shafted in the long run anyway."

Moose was about the only man that could make Ben laugh, but even then it was not a jovial laugh, but guarded.

When tempers were running short it was always Moose who calmed everyone down, either telling a joke they'd all heard or making up one on the spot. Moose taught Ben how to shoot. Something Ben didn't really like. He had no desire to shoot a deer or an elk - although he did so many times. There was something about killing animals that was sad to Ben. They lived in the mountains, minded their own business, and people shot them. It didn't make much sense when most hunters weren't hungry.

Crow played harmonica - yearning songs, telling of his life in music, but never telling of his life in words. He tried to teach Ben how to play but Ben had no knack for music. "If music was a shovel," Crow told him, "You couldn't shovel up a pile of shit."

All four of them taught Ben how to roll a smoke

and keep a match lit in the wind and more to please them Ben would smoke occasionally. They also wanted him to chew tobacco but Ben thought it was disgusting and would not even try it. And, cheating on his word just a bit, they taught him how to play rummy, and five-card stud, and seven card stud and cribbage, but they'd never let him play for money. "When you're eighteen I'll take every dime your skinny ass ever made," Crow told him, "But not till then. I don't steal from no boy."

Peggy had a lot of books and she let Ben borrow one at a time. Most nights Ben read. He didn't read nonfiction. The real world had no interest to him and he didn't see where history made much of a difference anyway. But he liked all kinds of novels. He especially liked Zane Grey, and he read Robinson Crusoe, and Moby Dick, and Alice In Wonderland several times. He also borrowed Dave's rodeo magazines. He studied the photographs of the saddle bronc riders – how they spurred the horse – how they held their arm up in the air.

Some days when there was nothing to do Dave would let the men take the truck and go to town. The men would be getting ready and Ben would be standing around wanting badly to go, almost willing to beg to go, but not being able to lower himself, and the men would ignore him like he was invisible, and then the truck would be running with three men in the front and one in the back bed and one of them would holler at Ben, "What the hell you doing standing there looking like some kitten without a mother. Get your ass in here."

The men would go to the bar, forgetting they needed toothpaste or razor blades, or socks, or there was a hole in the sole of their boot. Ben would sit with them while they drank beer and whiskey, talked about other ranches, and cattle, and cowboys they had known - the stories went into Ben's mind in colored pictures.

The bar was dark and there was a shuffleboard table along one wall - men played for dimes - cussing and arguing like the game was the most important thing in the world. There was a pool table - the velvet ripped and torn and stained from spilt drinks - the cues crooked as an elm branch. Spittoons were scattered around and the air was stale and filled with smoke - but to Ben it was blessed air - air breathed by men and it took a special boy to be allowed to sit with the men - blessed as long as he kept his mouth shut, didn't ever butt in when a man was talking and drank soda pop. "You keep drinking that soda pop all your life and you won't have half the problems life tosses at a person," Crow told him one day when he was so drunk he thought he was a philosopher. "And you'll end up an old man with more money in your pocket than any old broke-dick cowboy you'll ever meet." But then he thought for a moment, "That is the working cowboy, not the lucky bastard that owns the ranch."

At times they would slip Ben a half shot of whiskey, or a small glass of warm beer, and Ben would drink and be so happy he would almost cry.

At times fights would break out in the bar, one man would hit another, and then everybody would hit everybody just for the hell of it, and Ben would be picked up and tossed behind the bar like he was a sack of potatoes. Ben would hide behind the bar until the chairs stopped crashing and the bartender would hold out his hand for money to pay for the damages and everything went back to normal. "Don't hold no grudges. If the argument is not important enough to kill a bastard, don't hold no grudges," Whitey told him one day, blood running out of his nose, and ordering another beer. "Grudges only eat at your guts and makes a man meaner than he has to be."

At night in the bunkhouse Ben never fell asleep before the others. He would listen to the men snore, and fart, and moan, and even though his dream of being the best saddle bronc rider in the rodeo ate at him, he felt safe. He was a part of something bigger and grander than he would ever be, even though he couldn't put into words what the feeling was, he had friends, friends who would protect him and help him.

Occasionally in his bunk he'd think about Reno, and he'd miss him terribly, but he knew Reno was ok and he hoped Reno thought about him. He could see Reno, sitting alone on the bench in front of the graves of his wife and child, and he knew Reno carried a great hurt - a hurt no god should ever let a man carry unless he was testing him. But why would a god test any man - there were enough burdens without another test.

On some nights Ben felt like he was being watched. That there was something more than his sister in the night sky and that something only wanted the best for him. On those nights he felt like getting out of bed and getting down on his knees and thanking whatever was watching over him and protecting him, but he couldn't, and even though he couldn't, he felt guilty like he was shorting something that cared for him, and even though he tried to ignore the feeling he knew it was wrong to short any kindness or caring. The world needed more caring - more kindness.

******

"I don't feel sorry for myself," Ben said. "I'm just old and tired."

"You've been old since you were born," Meathead said. "No fault of your own, just how it is. You just won't face up to what you are."

"I'm nothing," Ben said. "I've never helped anybody. I've only caused pain in my life."

"You love those excuses," Meathead said, adding, "but even though you've been on my back for close to twenty years you aren't a bad man Ben, you've never been a bad man."

Ben pulled gently back on the reins and stopped the horse. He looked up at the sky. He looked down at the hard dry brown earth and said, "I never helped my Ma though she needed help. I never helped my Pa in his shame. I killed people for no reason that I knew except I was told it was right, but even doing it I knew it wasn't right. I never gave Maria a present though she fed me and took care of me and prayed for me. I never thanked Mac or Whitey or Crow or Moose for making me what I wanted. I never really thanked Peggy for hugging me or Dave for taking me on. I could have done more for my wife and daughter."

"You feel your sadness in your heart?" Meathead

asked.

"Never leaves me for a day. Like my sister not being able to fly. It isn't right. Some people just once should be able to fly."

"Ben, you're about as messed up as they come in your head," Meathead said and shook her head.

Ben nudged her, not hard, and they walked on.

CHAPTER SIX

Ben was almost seventeen when Dave bought six wild horses that had been caught in Wyoming. Dave didn't know why he'd bought them, he just did. One of those things in life a person does and doesn't know why. It had been a bad year, dry in the mountains with little forage for the cattle, and freezing cold in the spring. The money was scarce but he bought the horses. There was something about six wild horses that intrigued him.

When Dave told the men he was waiting for a delivery of wild horses Ben could hardly hide his excitement.

Ben no longer worked for Maria. Peggy helped her. Ben worked and ate with the men. While Ben worked for Maria he knew even if she did not show it, she needed the men as much as they needed her. The day Ben told Maria he didn't have to do any more chuck work Maria told him sternly, "You waz always in the way anyway, now get and go be one of those dumb cowboys who always get cow poop on their boots and dirty up my floor."

But as Ben started to walk away Maria grabbed him and hugged him goodbye in her big warm arms. Ben, after the hug, wanted to say, "You and I know sadness. I understand." But he was not able to. Ben could only bow his head and say, "Thank you, Maria," in a most humble way, feeling inadequate and not really worth her grace, or her strength, or her saint candles, or her Jesus on the cross whose blood ran brighter than any blood should be.

******

After three years Ben could rope and ride better than the older cowboys. It was like he and the horse were one and when he roped it was like he knew what the cow was going to do before it knew itself. The men laughed at him the way he talked to horses, but Ben just waved them off. "I talk to them. And they talk to me. Most of them are smarter than any of you guys," he'd say.

The men would walk off shaking their heads.

"Ben is a little crazy in the head, but he isn't a bad boy," they'd agree.

Ben was now making two bucks a day and he'd bought cowboy boots, a wide-brimmed white cowboy hat, spurs, a sheep-lined winter coat and a good heavy duty rain slicker. Whitey had made Ben a fringed set of chaps from a cowhide. The men told Ben he should buy a rifle, but he didn't want to. There was something about a gun that bothered him. But he did take a 30/30 of Dave's when he went deep into the mountains looking for strays for protection from bears and mountain lions. At the time Ben did not know there was a rifle in his future.

The day the truck brought in the wild horses Ben was sitting on the porch mending a rip in his chaps. Seeing them being unloaded Ben ran to the corral. They were the most beautiful creatures he had ever seen. Mac and Whitey were already there. "Those some mean ones," Mac said in admiration.

"I don't want to get on any of them," Whitey said.

"I'll ride them all for eight seconds and never get bucked off," Ben said, entranced by the horses - his dream vivid in his mind. "I'll never touch horse or saddle with my free hand and I'll spur them till I jump off."

The two men laughed. "The only thing you'll do

is break your leg or back," Mac said. "You've never been on a bronc."

"Bet you a buck each," Ben said, not looking at the men but at the horses.

"I always like beer somebody else buys," Mac said.

"I hate to take your money but I'll take that bet," Whitey said.

That evening Mac and Whitey were talking to Dave in front of Dave's house and they told him about the wager. "He's old enough," Dave said. "Might as well get busted up young and get it over with."

Peggy overheard the conversation and stormed out of the house. "Dave Toole," she scolded, turning beet red and pointing her finger at him, "You don't dare put that boy on any wild horse, not alone six."

Mac and Whitey started to leave. "You two stay put," Peggy ordered.

Both men stopped in their tracks and removed their hats and looked sheepishly at the ground.

"You two should be ashamed of yourselves, taking money from a boy," Peggy tore into the men.

"Peggy, it wasn't my idea," Mac said.

"Don't you make excuses to me," Peggy chastised.

"Now Peggy," Dave said calmly. "Ben is seventeen. He's no boy. If he wants to be a true cowboy he has to learn. All of us take chances on getting hurt."

Peggy's glare scorched each of the men. "If that boy gets hurt none of you will ever hear the end of this," she vowed and stomped back inside the house.

"I hope I lose my dollar," Mac said.

Whitey agreed.

"For some reason I think you already have," Dave said and went into the house.

Mac and Whitey headed quickly for the bunkhouse. "Dave might want to eat some of Maria's vittles for a few days," Mac said and then they both smiled - wishing they had a wife but also wishing they didn't.

That evening Ben stood by the corral with the six wild horses and looked closely at each of them. They went from dun to paint and all of them were wiry and strong - their eyes were fierce - saying keep away - no one will break me - their ears were laid back in warning. They raced around the corral watching and smelling Ben, at times kicking out when another horse crowded in too much. Ben talked to the horses in a calm voice. "It isn't all that bad being broke. It's just how it's got to be. When it's all over you'll get food and water all the time. People will doctor you when you are sick. You must realize I don't mean you any harm."

After awhile the horses stopped racing around the corral and bunched up as far from Ben as they could, but they looked warily at him and sniffed the air - still Ben talked. He told them about his dream of being the best saddle bronc rider in the rodeo. He told them about his sister who wanted to fly, and Reno who had treated him better than if he was his own. He told them about the ranch and Dave and Whitey and Mac and Moose and Crow, and he told them about his first ride up into the mountains - how there was no where in the world like the mountains. "The trees are so tall it's like they grow down from the sky and not up from the ground, and there's a smell of freshness that is no where else. It's a free smell - a smell of the sky and the trees and the wind. The streams are so cold the water numbs your teeth when you drink and the stars are so bright you don't need a lantern at night."

Ben talked to the horses until when the final light of dusk vanished the horses were listening to him - their nostrils not flared - their ears not laid back but upright, and their eyes not as full of fire.

******

"I rode every one of those broncs," Ben laughed. "Whitey and Mac and Crow and Moose didn't know I was scared so bad my stomach was tighter than a good fence and I felt like I was going to piss my pants."

He stopped Meathead at the northern fence to the

three sections. All five strands of the old rusty wire were down. He could picture some young cowboy in a few years stringing wire for months, cussing the bugs, cussing the sun, cussing the cuts on his arms, and cussing the wire.

"I remember Whitey, Crow, Mac, Dave, and Peggy watching me just before Moose let go of that first wild horse. The men were already counting their money and Peggy was trying not to show how afraid she was. Dave was keeping time. I'd never ridden a bronc before, although I dreamed about it thousands of times and studied it more than a man studies a picture of a good looking woman. The horse was like riding a storm, my teeth were rattling, my bones went in directions they had never been in. But it was natural to me - like I'd always been on a bronc. I never grabbed the horn and I never stopped spurring until Dave waved at me and I jump off. I knew my sister was watching me, and smiling, and she knew I'd make my dream. There was nothing going to stop me."

"Whoopee shit! What a day!"

"I rode five of them and when I was getting on the last one Maria came out from the chuck house. Standing by the corral she called out. 'You ride heem Ben, you ride heem,' and she crossed herself and said a prayer for me."

"I felt like a wash rag, all the strength rung out of me, but I rode that sixth horse like I was riding in a dream. When I jumped off everybody was silent for the longest time and then they all started to clap - not loud at first but then feverish. Dave and Peggy hugged each other. Maria hugged each of the men, huffing at them, 'See, it takes a cook to know theez horses.'"

"Then all the men banged each other on the back and whooped and hollered and tossed their hats in the air. I walked out of the corral feeling like my guts were a milkshake and my legs were so wobbly I thought I'd fall on my face. All the men shook my hand so hard in respect they jarred me as bad as the horses had. Maria was crying as she hugged me. Peggy took me by my shoulders, stood back, and with pride in her eyes said, 'Ben Sharps, you will be famous.'"

"Shit, famous. What is famous, but what's in your mind? But I didn't know that then."

"That night Maria barbequed steaks and boiled corn on the cob and Dave and Peggy joined us. Crow played happy tunes on his harmonica and all the men danced with Maria and Peggy. Dave brought out a bottle of whiskey and I got to take the first pull, but only one. Even if I could ride six broncs without eating dust I was still a boy."

"The next morning Mac and Whitey paid me."

******

Ben took out his tattered billfold. Inside one small compartment made for a photograph he pulled out two worn and faded one-dollar bills. He ripped the bills into tiny shreds and tossed them into the air. They fluttered to the ground like injured green moths. Ben watched until the last shred hit the ground. "Money only did most men harm anyway," Ben said.

He nudged Meathead and she stepped over the downed wire and followed a trail that led up the hill.

"Man should never gamble with his friends, even if it's for fun."

******

Ben didn't know it but word spread quickly in the cowboy world about him riding six broncs in a row without a spill. In another month the story had covered the entire state of Colorado and even reached Cheyenne, Wyoming. Soon the story went he had ridden seven broncs in a row and then eight. Then at least a thousand people had seen him do it and swore on their dead aunt's, or mother's, or father's grave, they'd seen it and it was the most wonderful sight they'd ever seen - except of course a naked woman they'd been with that was so pretty she could have been an actress.

One evening, a month after Ben's ride, Dave came over to the bunkhouse. "Got a letter for you Ben," he said.

Ben held the letter and looked at it like he didn't know what it was.

"Open it," Mac said, as all the men crowded around, more excited than Ben. Somebody getting a letter was about as wonderful as finding a treasure.

"I never got a letter before," Ben said. "I don't know anybody who would want to write to me. All my people are dead," he lied.

"The letter is from the Rodeo Association in Pueblo, Colorado," Dave said. "Jesus Christ, open it and read it," Crow said.

Ben opened the letter. All the men including Dave inched closer to him.

Ben read the letter out loud. "Dear Ben Sharps. We have heard about your great feat of riding eight broncs in one spell without being bucked off. It would be to our great satisfaction if you would return the enclosed envelope with five dollars and enter our saddle bronc competition on August 8th, 9th, and 10th. It is possible for you to win up to one hundred and fifty dollars."

"Son-of-a-bitch," Mac said. "That's almost two months pay."

"Can you believe that shit?" Crow said.

"Flip me like a pancake," Moose said. "Eight broncs. Those lying bastards."

Whitey was so in awe he couldn't speak for a moment. Then he said, "We could all go up, side bet Ben, and make us more money than we ever made in our lives."

Dave thought for a few moments. "Let me talk to Peggy, but one of you boys would have to stay behind and watch the stock."

Dread went through the men like wildfire. "We'll draw straws," Mac said.

"I'll send them the five bucks," Dave said. "This is an opportunity you cannot pass up, Ben."

Ben sat on his bunk not talking until it was dark. He'd never told the men about his dream. He'd never told the men about his sister, who couldn't fly, or his parents, or Reno. All they knew was that he was a sodbuster from Kansas, which was a sad thing to them anyway. Ben grew afraid. He had a responsibility to other people now and it was a mighty weight. He went outside. The light was still on in the chuck house. There was a half-moon just coming over the top of the mountains. "Lisa, you ever ride the moon?"

he asked.

A hoot owl hooted, trying to scare up a mouse.

"Hoot owl at night supposed to be good luck," Ben whispered. "See one during the day somebody is going to die."

Ben walked away from the bunkhouse toward the trees. The trees shimmered in the moonlight - tall and shiny - not afraid of the night - embracing it. In the moonlight Ben cast a gray shadow. His shadow talked to him. "Now you have a chance to reach for your dream and you're afraid."

"I might fail," Ben replied. "I might fall off and all my friends will lose money and not like me anymore."

"Then they are not your friends," the shadow said. "Everybody falls one time or another."

The hoot owl hooted again and for a mere second Ben saw him sail on silent wings between two trees. He was big and magnificent - one with the night - unafraid of even the blackest darkness.

"Thanks Lisa," Ben said and although he was still afraid he went back to the bunkhouse.

******

Meathead picked her way up the hill. For some reason Ben wanted to go faster, but Meathead was never one to go faster than she wanted to. Ben heeled her sharper than normal to speed up. Meathead stopped in her tracks. "Ok, ok, have it your way. I apologize," Ben said.

The horse moved on - no faster though.

"It's my dying day," Ben swore. "Show some respect."

Meathead did not bother to answer but flicked her tail sharply twice.

Ben got his bottle of whiskey and drank deeply - put the bottle back.

******

Crow drew the short straw and had to stay and watch the stock. His only comment being, "You bastards make sure my money gets laid down on Ben and not some bar top."

The day they headed to Pueblo, Dave and Peggy were in the front of the truck. Mac, Moose, Whitey, and Ben were in the back with all the camping gear. Dave was pulling a horse trailer with his best horse and had brought his best saddle and bridle, having told Ben, "You want a prideful horse for the rodeo parade."

Mac and Moose were talking but Ben didn't gather in on the conversation. He tried to lose his thoughts in the wind on his face, and tried to stop the thousands of butterflies that were swarming in his stomach and trying to fly out of his mouth. "I can't fail the men," he kept saying to himself over and over, but it wasn't doing much good, there just seemed to be more and more butterflies.

They pitched two tents at the rodeo grounds, one for Peggy and Dave, and one for the men. The rodeo grounds were busy with other people who were setting up camp. Maria had made enough fried chicken for ten people on a six-day trip and enough biscuits they could have set up a biscuit booth. Ben wasn't much help making camp. He had never seen so many people and never seen a true rodeo arena. He'd also never seen so many pretty young girls his age. They smiled at him and he looked away, uncomfortable, only looking at them again when they did not see him. "Shit," Moose said. "You win some money Ben and you'll have more pretty girls chasing you than there's water on a fish."

Peggy smiled.

That evening Dave took Ben to the entry table and signed him up. "You the boy rode the eight horses in a row," the man said, giving Ben the number fourteen to pin on his back.

"It was only six," Ben said.

"Six or eight, don't mean nothing, proud to have you here son. Parade through town tomorrow at noon. We line up here. You saddle bronc boys go off at seven tomorrow evening. Draw for stock at five. Mind you there are some rank horses in this bunch."

Walking away Ben said to Dave, "I've never been in a chute."

"Don't worry about it," Dave said. "Just keep your butt on the leather, your arm high and your spurs above the horse's shoulders. You're a natural."

That night they stayed in camp, ate chicken and biscuits, and Dave and the men talked about rodeos they'd seen and horses that were so tough no cowboy had ever ridden them. The horses had names like Busted, Killer Joe, Wild One, Comanche, and Thorn Bush. All the names were fearsome to Ben. Ben did not join in the conversation and he started to feel lacking in himself. Peggy, looking over at him, saw the look on Ben's face. "Ben," she said. "Why don't you and I go for a walk?"

Over the past two years Ben and Peggy had not talked much, although he had read most of her books, and he did not know that Peggy kept up with all that he did. He also did not know that Reno had told Dave and Peggy about Ben hitting his father and running away and about his sister. Peggy wrote Reno once a month, informing Reno on what Ben had been doing, and how he was turning into a good cowboy. Reno wrote to Peggy but told her it was best if Ben get on with his life and not look back, so not to say hello for him. But please keep him informed as he thought Ben was a good boy with a good heart but a little lost and confused.

Peggy and Ben wandered through the rodeo grounds. Groups of cowboys talked and laughed while others curried horses. The men would look sideways at Ben and Peggy, whispering after they passed, "That's the boy rode those eight horses." Many saying, "He don't look like much, wouldn't put no wages on him."

Women flirted with bachelor cowboys and young groups of girls giggled and laughed. Whiskey and beer made the rounds freely.

On the edges of the camp, vendors were selling hamburgers and hotdogs and barbecued beef. The smells mingled with those of horses and tobacco smoke and manure. The sights and smells were hypnotic to Ben, almost unbelievable, more a dream than a reality.

"You look sheepish," Peggy said to Ben in a caring mother's voice.

"I'm tighter than a knot in a rope that's been rained on," Ben said.

Peggy laughed. Her laughter relaxed Ben a little.

"Everybody here that's in the rodeo is nervous," Peggy said.

Ben didn't know what to say.

They walked, not speaking for awhile and for a reason he did not know Ben wanted to talk about his life. "My sister died trying to fly," Ben said quietly. "She thought God was the sky and that angels lived in the sky ready to help those in need. But I knew she was wrong and she died jumping out of the barn hay doors. God didn't give her any wings. He killed her with her dreams."

"She flew for a little while, Ben," Peggy said. "And maybe in that little while God was the sky. Maybe a little while is all any of us need to find peace or God?"

"My dream has always been to be the best saddle bronc rider in the rodeo," Ben said. "My sister knew my dream. I suppose it's a selfish dream. It doesn't help anybody. It only helps me, and now, well now, it's strange, all people got a dream and most people never even have a chance to get close to their dreams and here I am living my dream. It doesn't seem right my sister couldn't fly and I get to touch my dream. It just doesn't seem right that I've got a chance to have wings."

"Your sister is riding your dream, Ben," Peggy said. "She's up there in the sky and even if you get tossed off tomorrow she will be happy."

"I miss my sister," Ben said with a catch in his throat.

Peggy touched him lightly on the shoulder. "Life isn't right, Ben. But it doesn't mean that you quit or try not to be the best you can be. The thing in life is to try to be good and maybe one day a lot of what is not right in life will be so ashamed it has to be good."

"Whitey and Moose and Mac and Crow are all putting money on me." Ben said. "They shouldn't trust in me so."

"Ben, if they lose they won't care. They would have just spent it on something without much worth anyway. They're gambling on you just to show you in their own way that they care for you. If one of them were riding, you would bet on him even if you knew he was going to lose."

"I've never had a home like I've had on the ranch," Ben said. "It's a good feeling, a feeling that at times I don't know what to do with. At times I feel it would be better to run off and be alone and then nobody would expect anything from me."

Peggy stopped walking and hugged Ben. "Ben, you ride for your sister and when you catch that dream you tell your sister thanks. Don't muddle things by thinking too much."

Ben did not return her hug but stood with his arms at his sides.

CHAPTER SEVEN

"Meathead you should have experienced that first rodeo parade," Ben said.

"I've been in hundreds but the first one was the best. There were pretty girls wearing blouses that were covered with sequins of all colors. When the sun hit them they sparkled like thousands of tiny rainbows. There were rodeo clowns smiling and waving at everybody. The town band was playing. All the local clubs were marching and the fire department had their sirens blaring. All the rodeo cowboys were in the back of the parade. We were wearing our best clothes and best hats and were not talking much to each other, sizing up the competition, everybody hoping to count some money, but nobody mean or riley toward one another. We rode through town and people waved and shouted. I was on Dave's black gelding with his best saddle and saddle blanket. The horse glistened like a full moon at midnight. I was scared and proud and happy and so nervous I could barely stop my hands from shaking. I waved to the crowd, taking it all in like a sponge takes water. For a reason I didn't understand I wanted Ma and Pa to see me. Even if I hated them I wanted them to see me."

"The first night of the rodeo I drew a bronc called Summer Breeze and was first to go, but let me tell you that horse was no breeze. She was a tornado with more scars on her than barbed wire has cuts and eyes that were wilder than hornets. Cowboys manning the chutes told me she'd roll me off quicker than soap eats up dirt."

"Dave and Peggy and Mac and Moose and Whitey were high up in the bleachers, couldn't afford one of those fancy box seats. I saw them, but was too scared to wave. The crowd was cheering and the announcer blared. 'Ladies and Gentlemen, Ben Sharps from Buena Vista, Colorado. Word is he rode six broncs in one day without once hitting the ground. Let's give him a big hand.' The crowd cheered louder and I nodded my head - the chute opened and out we blew like a tornado. Everything was a spinning blur, faces went by like the wind and the noise from the crowd was like a thousand shotgun blasts. I rode and waved my arm and spurred that horse like a mad man and before I really knew it I was sliding off into a clown's arms. My ears were ringing so hard I couldn't hear a thing, but when I got back behind the chutes all the cowboys looked at me different, all of them saying, 'good ride,' but I could tell it was better than a good ride. When the broncs were all over I'd scored highest and got day money. Twenty dollars."

"Whoopee shit!"

"Mac and Whitey and Moose met me at camp counting up their winnings. Dave shook my hand and Peggy gave me a hug. All of us went to a cafe in town and we ordered steaks and baked potatoes. We were waited on by a young girl that kept smiling at me. 'You're Ben Sharps,' she said. 'I watched you ride today. It was something to behold.'"

"My steak was bigger than the rest and my potato had more butter on it," Ben laughed.

"That night lying in the tent I didn't think about the ride or the steak. All I could think about was the pretty waitress. I'd made somebody smile and it was a good feeling."

Ben reached back and got his whiskey and took another pull. "You were smiling that day too, Lisa. I know you were. You might not smile on me today, but you were smiling that day."

"The next day I didn't ride as well, but I didn't get bucked off, and going into the last night I was three points out of first place. A cowboy out of Texas named Bill Hanks was in first. He was in his late twenties and he wished me good luck."

Peggy had written Reno informing him Ben would be in the rodeo in Pueblo. Reno left early in the morning to get there for the last day and that night he was high up in the bleachers not wanting Ben to see him. Ben, being in second place, was scheduled to ride next to last. Bill Hanks, the leader, would ride last. As each cowboy rode, Reno grew more nervous.

"I tell you Meathead, getting in the chute for the last ride I wished I'd had butterflies in my stomach," Ben said. "I had worms, and centipedes, and rattlesnakes, and hornets buzzing around inside of me. The men had taken all the money they'd won and then some and put it on me, and even though they'd been encouraging all day, I could see in their eyes they figured they might have messed up and there were going to be a few lean months in the future."

"But as I settled on the horse I felt a hand on my shoulder. I turned but nobody was there. The touch was soft, gentle like a whisper, and I knew it was my sister. I also felt eyes on me, not hundreds, but one set and I quickly looked around the crowd. I felt Reno's eyes, but I did not see him. But to this day I know he was in the crowd. I nodded my head and the chute opened but there was no thrashing of my body, no twists and no jerks. It was like I was riding a smooth sailing cloud - all tranquil and content. I never wanted it too stop. I wanted to ride that cloud forever - ride that cloud to where my sister was and look at the sky all stretched out before us like we used to from the hay doors. Then the buzzer went off and I was standing on the ground and the two clowns were pounding me on the back in congratulations. The crowd was going crazy and I didn't care if I'd won or not. I just stood there and looked up at the sky and tears poured out of my eyes - tears that there were no words for or any way to describe them. They were not prideful tears or sad tears and I was not ashamed. But tears for my sister, and tears for my Ma and Pa, and tears for Reno, and Whitey and Crow and Moose and Mac, and tears for Maria, and tears for Dave and Peggy."

"I'd scored a perfect ten."

"I walked out of the arena and when the gate shut behind me I was no longer a boy. I knew I would never be the same. There would never be a ride like the one I'd just made, never be the same feeling, never the tears that couldn't be described - all tears would be shameful after that."

"Bill Hanks rode a good ride but I beat him by one point."

"Afterwards Bill Hanks came up to me and shook my hand. 'Hell of a ride,' he said. 'Hell of a ride. One day you'll be the best that ever was.' He walked away shaking his head."

"I made one hundred and fifty dollars, two days show money, and got a silver buckle bigger than a pie plate with my name on it. I'm wearing it now. It's the only buckle that ever meant a damn to me. That night there was a dance. I danced with more pretty girls than I'd ever seen in my life. I didn't know it at the time but they were dancing more for my shiny buckle than me, but even if I would have known it wouldn't have mattered. Dave let me drink beer and I drank and danced and drank and danced and the next thing I knew I was woke up by the sound of tires on pavement. I was in the back of the truck. Whitey and Mac and Moose looked as bad as I felt. I looked at my big fancy buckle and even though I wanted to puke, I smiled."

"If I'd have kept all the damn buckles I won through the years they wouldn't fit in the back of my truck."

"Most young people now don't even know who Ben Sharps is."

Meathead snorted.

"Guess it really doesn't matter in life if anybody really knows who a person is or what they did. Guess what's more important is to know yourself and get on with what you got."

Meathead farted.

"We're all a bunch of gas," Ben laughed.

The trail curled to the top of the hill. From the top the vista was immense, almost more than the eyes could take in. Hills rolled one after the other like swells on the ocean. Behind the swells were mountains as high as twelve thousand feet. "The mountains aren't the same as when I was a kid," Ben said. "Something about getting old takes the magic out of life."

"Maybe the magic is still there and you just lost sight of the magic," Meathead said.

Ben took off his hat and rubbed his head. Put his hat back on, reached back, got his whiskey and took a drink - put the bottle back. Flashes of bomb craters and bloated bodies stabbed through his mind. He pushed them away - back to shadows - always shadows.

"Close to Platoro, Colorado, there's a mountain that the top's nothing but black shale and rock, not even arctic spruce grows there," Ben said. The wind never stops, always howling like demons - warning people to stay away. A rancher hired me to find some strays and after looking for days I decided there might be a chance they'd wandered off in the wrong direction. I picked my way through the rocks. Through time, people had placed piles of marker rocks where a man could thread his way to the top. It took me over an hour to get to the top. There were no cattle but there was a three-foot tall tin cross propped up by rocks. Placed around the cross were rosaries, little crosses, and medals with saints on them. Looking at the cross you could almost see the curve of the earth behind it. The mountains went on forever and then just faded in the distance. The demon wind howled but the cross didn't flutter in the wind, it sang - the tin vibrated and sang a high pitched mournful song. A song nothing heard but the wind and the rocks and the demons. I looked at the cross and all I could think was God doesn't do any good on top of a mountain, and the people who climbed to the top of the mountain had to be powerfully sad - people who the green valleys and the trees and the rivers had abandoned."

******

After the rodeo life went back to normal at the

ranch. But when Ben and the men went into town the town people treated Ben differently. He'd brought the town some pride, and although Ben tried not to be taken up with it, he did swagger a little and told anybody who wanted to hear about the rodeo - and yes he did ride six horses in a row.

But times were getting tougher. The weather had turned on man. Farms were dust and more people than not were destitute – headed to places they had never been hoping for jobs. The cattle industry was at best a breakeven deal and the men working for Dave voluntarily took a pay cut. None of them had family or a place to go and didn't own anything but their clothes and a saddle and bridle. But at least on the ranch they ate. Crow stated, "Food is more important than money. All I do with money is gamble and drink."

Maria put in a huge garden. The men had to build a wire fence around it to keep the coons, rabbits, skunks, deer, and chickens out. When the men weren't in the hills chasing cattle, they hoed and pulled weeds, cussing all the time, "Damn farmer work." But when the radishes, and lettuce, and spinach, and green beans, and corn, and squash, and beets came in the men ate them with pride. When the tomatoes were coming in the men would look at them like they really didn't care if they grew or not. But when they were big and red and juicy some of them would disappear before Maria got to them. The same thing mysteriously happened to watermelons. Maria would storm to the bunkhouse, hurling Spanish accusations like bricks while the men looked at her as innocent as children.

Maria would stomp back to the chuck house and smile, "Dumb cowboys ezz no smarter than chickens."

The men were confused over the chili peppers Maria grew - long green ones and short little squat green ones - but when she put them in stew they all said it was about the best stew they'd ever eaten and it put regular stew to shame.

Over the next year Ben didn't go to any rodeos except local gatherings where the cowboys from all the ranches in the area drank and gambled. He did receive several invitations and answered them with a thank you but he could not make it - times were tough and he did not have the money. He did go to a few local ranches and break a few horses, saying he would charge nothing, but always getting a little money, mainly out of pride by the owner. The cowboys would watch him ride the broncs, all amazed and bewildered how easy Ben made it look. But Ben did take a few falls. The first one surprised him but he got up and brushed himself off - the cowboys laughing, "Hell, it's about time."

One hot August day Ben rode by the ranch cemetery that for some reason he'd never really paid any attention to. The five crosses drew him and he dismounted. One of the crosses was for Frank Toole. One was for Mary Toole - Frank dying in 1912 and Mary in 1924. Ben figured they were Dave's parents. The other three crosses were smaller and only had first names on them and a year: Mary - 1916, Gloria - 1919 and Suzi - 1920. On each of the graves was a tiny baby rattle, the colors faded and cracked.

Ben went to the chuck house. Maria was canning vegetables - the room hot from the stove and boiling water. Perspiration poured down her face. "Who are the three graves for?" Ben asked, seeing if there was a cookie or piece of pie he could eat.

Maria wiped her face with a dishtowel and sat down. "Sometimes it ezz good in life when God takes the little ones," she said. "He takes them to heaven to make Him smile after what this world has become. He needs goodness and lambs."

"Dave and Peggy lost three children," Ben whispered, deeply shocked and saddened.

Maria nodded her head.

"Dave nor Peggy ever say anything about it," Ben

said.

"Some hurts ezz too deep to talk," Maria said.

"Oh, Maria, why are so many things in life sad?" Ben asked.

"Me thinks it is so we can appreciate when good things happen to us," Maria said.

******

Ben got off Meathead next to an especially tall pinion tree that had to be at least two hundred years old. Two scruffy gray squirrels were scolding a blue jay that seemed amused by them and scolded back. Ben rolled a smoke. He didn't want a shot of whiskey. He gazed at a big branch on the tree that was parallel to the ground and then looked at the lariat for a long time, but he wasn't ready yet and he lit his smoke. "Those three dead babies saddened me about as much as Lisa dying," he said. "But I couldn't believe what Maria said about God needing good things around him. If he needed good things why'd he make bad things? Hell, you'd think He'd be stronger than the devil."

Ben took a deep drag on the smoke.

"If there is a God maybe He isn't stronger than the devil."

"Maybe they are of equal power."

CHAPTR EIGHT

It was a bitter cold January day, so cold ice crystals formed in the air, making shiny ribbons that marauded through the bleak sky. The wind could not make up its mind - blowing one way and then another and then flipping another way - cutting into the exposed flesh like tiny daggers - each breath a sharp pain in the lungs and freezing the hair in a man's nose. The cattle huddled up in the corners of the pastures - the ones left on the outside of the mass were sure to freeze if the cold kept up - the ones closest to the fence might get suffocated. The men tossed out extra hay and hoped the quickly approaching black clouds off to the west didn't turn into a blizzard and bury the huddled cattle. The ranch couldn't take any more losses. The cattle business had about gone bust on the backs of the migrating farmers, while mine owners, and car manufacturers, and railroad men, and oil men made fortunes - finding grace in erecting mansions, funding museums and libraries, and paying slave wages to any poor bastard who had to work for them. Dave complained one day, "What are all those rich fuckers eating, rabbit?"

The men gave the horses extra feed and put them in the barn and covered each with a blanket. The barn was so cold ice formed on the hair on the horses' chins. The men shut all the barn doors and helped Dave carry a lot of wood into the house - making a big pile in the kitchen. Peggy looked worried and did not talk. They then brought in a lot of wood for Maria. Maria looked tired and Ben asked her, "Are you ok Maria? If you're tired I'll help you cook."

Maria waved him off. "I eez always tired. Tired eez most of life."

Back at the bunkhouse the men huddled around the wood stove, slowly making fingers work that had forgotten how to bend, and bringing life back to toes that hurt as they warmed up. "I've lived in these mountains my whole wasted life and never seen anything this cold," Crow said. "Might as well be an Eskimo."

"No horses up there," Mac said. "You'd have to walk or ride one of those dog sleds."

"No horses for once in my life might be a blessing," Crow said.

"Hope Maria made some of that Mex food," Moose said. "Something so hot it would melt lead."

The men made a pile of wood close to the stove. "We take turns keeping the fire going tonight," Whitey said. "And we make sure, if it's all right with Maria, to keep her stove going also."

The wind swirled faster, screaming like a frightened woman, whistled off the mountain like a runaway train, bending trees almost to the breaking point, and then it started to snow. The snowflakes were huge, some the size of quarters. Caught in the wind they crashed into the windows like lost birds - rattled the panes like death demanding to get in. Snow built up on the porch in only a few minutes and then abruptly the wind stopped - followed by a silence so deep that within a few moments Ben, looking out the window, swore he could hear the snowflakes as they settled to the ground. As the snow fell the black sky turned a pale gray, barely keeping the sun at bay and they all knew the cattle wouldn't get smothered. The storm had blown itself out. Dave wouldn't go bust yet. "Son-of-a-bitch," Crow said in thanks.

******

"Those snowflakes falling out of the sky were something. In all my days I've never seen bigger," Ben said to Meathead. "I went outside and caught a few on my hat. They reminded me of babies, all filled with hope and dreams. Some of the flakes were stars with spikes going out every which way, some were beautiful spiders that didn't bite, and others had so many crooks and crannies in them it was like catching a frozen piece of light. But even now when it snows I think about Maria. Me out catching snowflakes, happy the wind stopped, and happy the sun was about to bust through, and Maria dying, needing me - maybe not to stop the dying, but to hold her hand and say thanks for all those fine meals she'd made me, and thanks for teaching me how to cook, and maybe to find out where she'd like her bones to lay. It had to be back home - a home she never told us about. It was like she told me when I found out about Peggy's babies - there's some pains too hurtful to talk about - she missed her home so badly she couldn't talk about it, but I knew she could not forget it."

"Ah Maria, you could have told me. I would never have betrayed your sadness."

Ben mounted Meathead and followed a trail that went down the hill. "There's a spring down there. Get your old bones a drink," Ben said.

Two buzzards rode a thermal. You're going to have to wait a spell. I'm not ready to die yet," Ben said.

A coyote stepped from behind a creosote bush not far from Ben, but didn't run. He was an old skinny coyote, some of his winter hair still hanging on, making him look disheveled like he was wearing a shaggy coat that was too big for him. He looked casually at Ben without a trace of fear.

Ben stopped the horse, returned the coyote's gaze. "You're like me," Ben said. "Too damn old to be afraid and not caring anymore if you live or die. Too many missed rabbits - too many hungry nights. Well, I'm not going be the one to put you out of your misery. You've got to figure out your own plan."

The coyote walked off, his nose to the ground.

"Good luck," Ben called. "Maybe you'll find your God. Maybe heaven's a place where you'll get fried rabbit every night sprinkled with lots of salt."

Ben nudged Meathead. She moved off quicker, smelling the water at the bottom of the hill.

******

"After it stopped snowing, the sun came out. The sun reflecting off the snow was so bright it hurt my eyes," Ben said. "I noticed there wasn't much smoke coming out of the chuck house, but it didn't really worry me. I bundled up and went over just to see if Maria wanted some help. When I opened the door it was quiet. There was no sound of food cooking or pots and pans being moved. 'Maria,' I called, thinking she was in her room. But there was no answer. I went around the big table and found her lying on the floor like a sleeping little girl. Her legs were pulled up to her stomach and her hands were clasped in prayer. I knew without bending over she was dead. There was a deep grief in her open eyes. I kneeled down and touched her forehead. It was warm, but not live warm, the cold already creeping in - finding its own life and needs in decay and loss. I didn't cry. But I was sad - a deep hurtful sad because I knew I had never been able to touch her sadness. I looked at her gold ring with the cross and wondered if her husband had died young, or if he'd been killed, or maybe he'd run off with another woman - any of which wasn't good. The sun shined brightly into the chuck house. The pieces of colored cut glass and shiny rocks sent little fairies all over the room and they seemed to congregate in a cluster above Maria. The blood pouring out of Jesus became redder, almost alive. For a brief instant I believed in Jesus and God and I lit all her candles in their glasses with all the saints. But my feeling for God went away and there were only the reflecting fairies."

"We built a huge fire in the cemetery, kept it going for two days to unthaw the ground so we could dig a hole. Peggy dressed Maria in her brightest dress and put her rosary around her neck and made sure her hair was pulled back and neat. Peggy went through her few things, but there were no old photographs, or letters, or anything from the past to notify any living kin or loved one. We kept her in the barn while Whitey and Crow made a nice white pine coffin and lined it with Maria's red and gold and yellow and blue curtains. After we put Maria in the coffin we put in the pieces of colored cut glass, and shiny rocks, and her bible, and her dresses, and all her candles, and her Jesus. The day we put her in the ground was cold but beautiful. They sky was as blue as a robin's egg. There was no wind. Peggy cried and said a few words. We stood hats off, heads bowed, wishing we had all done better for her, but knowing it was too late. After we filled in the hole with the frozen ground, Crow played his harmonica. It was a song he'd never played before - more a marching song - a strong song. That night nobody talked, we passed a bottle of whiskey, and nobody said a word - we drank and thought our own thoughts. When everyone was in bed and the light out, Crow said, 'God be getting one hell of a cook, lucky bastard.'"

******

Ben dismounted by the spring. A large willow grew by the spring, the seed carried from some far away riverbank years ago - a loner seed - needing its own distance to think. There were a few stands of red-stemmed alder, the smell of it earthy. Indians used to make baskets from the alder and Mexicans made crosses and chairs and benches. The pool the spring made was about twenty feet around and only a few feet deep, the bottom a slab of limestone. Grass grew around the spring, only spreading a few feet from its edge before there was not enough moisture for it to survive. There were tracks from all the creatures in the area in the sand - deer, bobcat, mountain lion, coyotes, dove, rabbits, lizards, quail, and other types of birds. The willow tree protected a few birds' nests. Getting off the horse, Ben wrapped the reins around the horn, got his bottle of whiskey and sat down under the willow, resting his back on the trunk. The shade was nice and he took off his hat and rolled a smoke and lit it. The smoke drifted up through the willow branches and then disappeared.

Meathead drank and then stood on the shady side of the willow, ignoring Ben.

"Dave hired an old grizzled cowboy who called himself Duke to take Maria's place. He was all bent up with every pain imaginable and had long white hair that he didn't bother to comb - it was like the wind was always hitting him in the face. Dave didn't pay Duke much wage but he got a place to stay and food. Duke didn't talk much, nothing about ranches he'd worked on or what he'd done in his life, but he read all the time. Duke had the newspaper delivered to the gate and he read fancy books - mostly history of everything imaginable. When he did talk he talked about the world and what was going on, which we cowhands never really thought much of. Hell, our world was the ranch, not much else mattered at the time. I never saw him laugh, but never saw him angry either. He didn't drink or smoke and only occasionally came over and sat with us on the porch. When he was done in the evening he'd sit on his own porch and look at things. Nothing in particular - the sky - birds - us working - the wind kicking through the trees. I figured there was a deep sadness in him – a sadness that forced him to be alone with his thoughts and grief. He wasn't the best cook, but of someone complained he'd say, 'You don't have enough money to be picky about what you eat and if you don't like it don't eat it - won't hurt my feelings.'"

"Meals were always on time, but unlike Maria, if a man was late you got whatever was left. We gave Duke the distance he wanted or needed, but we all missed Maria."

"And life went on, that's how it is, life goes on, a few changes, but it still goes on."

Ben took a pull of the whiskey and butted his smoke. Meathead swished her tail at a fly. A crow landed by the spring, got a drink, saw Ben, squawked at him and flew off.

Ben took another pull of whiskey.

"I don't remember what month it was or year, but it was spring. The winter had been mild and the spring rains had been good. The grass was knee high and flowers were blooming that were every color I'd ever seen. Things were doing better in the country - not good but better. There were work gangs all over the country making roads, and digging ditches, and working in towns building sidewalks. It didn't pay much but it put men to work, and they could send money back to their wives and kids, and maybe the wife could get a dress and the kids a pair of shoes, or an ice cream cone every so often. Plus it gave the men some pride and took some of the desperation away. Cattle prices were up, Dave saying, 'Those rich bastards finally eating beef and not rabbit, fuckers anyway.'"

"Duke, in a rare moment of talking, told me it wasn't because of the rich that cattle prices were up. It was because Europe was about to go to war and all the armies were buying beef. He also said the rich were only going to get richer when we were pulled into the war because they owned the gas, and the ships, and all those necessary things it takes to kill a lot of people and make more money. 'War is always good for the economy,' he said, and spit, making a sour face like he'd swallowed vinegar. 'No government gives a rat about its poor people, it's you poor dumb bastards that do the killing and get killed, not them rich politicians sitting on their fat asses filling you with slogans and dreams of pride and honor and why you are better than any other people in the world.'"

"At the time I thought Duke was just one of those book readers that didn't know squat. I had stopped reading by then. I don't know why but I just stopped."

"Crow and Whitey had both been in the First World War and when I told them what Duke said, Crow said real quiet like, 'He's got to be a vet like us.

He knows.'"

"Whitey said. 'Let them Europeans kill themselves and let our boys stay home. I don't like any of them anyway.'"

"At the time I figured if the country was ever in a war I'd go. If nothing else, it was my duty and there was something romantic and honor-bound that in some ways made me wish there would be a war. But I wasn't in love then."

"Glory my ass."

"I didn't get any honor or glory in the war. I lost it."

Ben took another sip of whiskey and shut his eyes.

******

One afternoon in late summer Ben drove to town to get barbed wire and staples. Dave wanted to split up two of the lower pastures. The men were wondering which two of them would be the unfortunate ones to have to build the fence. "We could all chip in and hire two boys from town," Moose said.

"We don't have enough money to pay ourselves," Whitey said.

"We could all come down with some mysterious aliment," Crow said.

"The only time any of us is sick is with a hangover," Mac said.

Building fence was a dreadful thought.

Ben didn't get to town often and he was enjoying the drive. Besides picking up wire, he had a list from each of the men for incidentals - mainly tobacco and booze. It was good to be alone. He rested his arm out the window. The air blowing in the truck was comforting in the summer heat. He didn't drive fast, enjoying the green pastures and the happy trill of redwing blackbirds singing from the bar ditches. The sky was full of powder puff clouds, reminding Ben of smiling old men telling lies to each other about all the pretty women they'd known in their lifetimes. The pine trees were covered with green pinecones and the spruces were so silver they shone. Two boys were fishing in the river and waved happily at Ben - proudly holding up a stringer of trout.

Ben parked in front of the feed store. A couple of cowboys from another ranch nodded at him and went about their business. The inside of the store was cool from the swish of the overhead fans. The odors of hay, sweet feed, salt licks, mineral licks, ointments, leather, and rope mixed into an aroma Ben found pleasing. He explored the store casually, going from row to row just looking, not needing anything, but enjoying the newness of everything. He tried on a pair of calfskin gloves. They felt so good he pondered buying them for over a minute, even though he didn't need them. "You should buy them," a girl's voice said from a few feet away.

Ben, slightly startled, looked over and seeing the girl he felt like somebody had hit him in the chest with a hammer. She was so pretty he couldn't talk. She was wearing Levi's with a belt that had a silver buckle almost as big as Bens. She had on brown boots and a man's white work shirt. Her long blond hair was pulled back into a ponytail. Her topaz eyes were so sparkling and happy he wanted to dance but he didn't think he could move. The girl laughed but not mockingly and said, "Ben Sharps, who can ride six broncs in a row struck dumbfounded."

Ben could not take his eyes off the girl who stared right back at him with no shyness or fear. Ben felt weak. He felt hot. He felt cold. Her eyes bore right through him. He felt like he was naked. Finally, taking a deep breath, Ben blurted, "You're the prettiest girl I've ever seen."

"Well thank you," she replied with a smile that would have made heaven blush. "My name is Barbara Mason and now you can take me to lunch. That is, if you have any money."

******

Ben opened his eyes. Meathead had moved

further around the willow, following the shade. "Lucky for me I had spending money in my pocket. I forgot all about barbed wire and staples, and Barbara and I headed for the cafe. Walking down the street my feet didn't touch the ground. Barbara was wearing perfume that was sweeter than any flower I'd ever smelled and almost made me dizzy. As we walked, she told me she had seen me ride in Pueblo and that it was the grandest ride she'd ever witnessed and she took my arm in hers which surprised me but made me feel happy and fuzzy inside.

Ben looked at the pool of spring water. "She was refreshing like you," he said to the water. "She made me forget about my Ma and Pa, and Lisa not being able to fly, and Reno, and Peggy's dead babies, and Maria dying alone. She also rekindled my dream about being the best saddle bronc rider in the rodeo."

"That first time we ate at the cafe was the first time I ever really felt alive. After my shyness we talked and laughed about everything. Her father was a forest ranger and her mother taught school. She had just graduated from high school. They lived in town in a government house behind the forest station. I told her about the ranch but nothing about my life. She seemed to eat up my words, like they were the best words she'd ever heard. Every time she smiled, I smiled until my mouth hurt. The time flew and before I knew it, it was close to closing time for the feed store. 'Can I see you again,' I stammered and she told me she'd come out to the ranch on Sunday if it was ok with me. She could have told me she was going to hit me in the head with a fence post and it would have been ok with me. Leaving the cafe, dreadful thoughts flew through my mind that I'd never see her again."

"I hurriedly got the wire and staples and dashed to the store for tobacco and booze for the men. Driving back to the ranch I felt wonderful but also terrible - wonderful for meeting Barbara, but dreadful that she would not come out on Sunday. It was not until halfway back to the ranch I was suddenly embarrassed. What would the men say when they saw Barbara? I was in for some kind of ribbing."

"That night sitting on my bunk Crow looked at me and grinned like he knew the biggest secret in the world."

"'You little son-of-a-bitch,' he said. 'You ran into some little filly in town today and got struck.'"

"The men all laughed as I shook my head."

"But in bed that night all I could see was Barbara's smile and her topaz eyes and a terrible ache came over me, an ache I'd never felt. I visualized Barbara naked and me naked and I wanted to be naked with her for all time. I wanted to be with her forever."

Ben stood, took a swig of whiskey, and put the bottle back in the saddlebags.

"There isn't anything for all time."

Ben mounted Meathead and pointed her toward two hills that were separated by a draw and led to another hill in the distance.

CHAPTER NINE

For the rest of the week Ben tried to hide his anxiety about Barbara visiting on Sunday. But no matter what he was doing he seemed to mess it up, not being able to keep his mind on anything but Barbara. He put a saddle on backwards. He tripped going up steps. He put his boots on the wrong feet one morning. He had not found the courage to tell the men or Dave that a girl was coming out to see him on Sunday, but he knew he was going to have to tell Dave. He didn't want Dave sending him off into the mountains. But he was still worried Barbara might not show up.

The men knew Ben had been smitten but they did not push the issue. They did talk to each other when

Ben wasn't around about their first loves, and seconds, and thirds, and although they laughed remembering the wonder and pain of it all, they, each in their own way, missed that wonderment and that sweet pain of love.

"I hope whoever this filly is don't break Ben's heart," Moose said.

"I think every heart gets broke once," Crow said.

"Well, I hope it don't make him bitter and sour on the world," Moose said.

"It's got a way of doing that," Crow said.

"That's why I like whores," Mac said.

"Them whores need love too," Whitey said.

"Must be a sad life being a whore," Crow said.

"All life is sad, just different degrees," Moose said.

On Saturday morning Ben got up the nerve to talk to Dave. He got up early and sat on Dave's porch waiting for him to come out. But instead of Dave coming out alone, Peggy came out with him. Ben stood, removed his hat, forgot what he was going to say and just stood there like a stump. "What is it Ben?" Dave finally asked.

"Well, ah, well, well," Ben stammered. "I've got to ask a favor."

Peggy started to laugh.

Dave started to laugh.

Ben didn't see anything funny about his predicament.

"We know Barbara Mason is coming out to see you on Sunday. Dave saw her father in town and asked if it was ok," Peggy smiled, secretly enjoying Ben's state.

"You can use two of the horses if you want to go for a ride," Dave said. "But you be a gentleman. I told her dad you were an upright man and trustworthy."

"You didn't tell the men, did you?" Ben asked nervously.

"No," Peggy said. "And I'll pack you two a picnic lunch, no need to ask Duke."

All Ben could do was say, "Thanks," and half fell down the steps as he hurried off with his heart all a flutter and his stomach more full of butterflies than when he was in the rodeo in Pueblo.

"Do you think he is trustworthy?" Peggy asked Dave, giving Dave a wink.

"I think so," Dave said.

"You weren't," Peggy said, and punched him playfully on the arm.

"Takes two," Dave said, and kissed her on the forehead.

******

"I tell you, Meathead, I didn't sleep a wink Saturday night and before the sun came up I took a bath, shaved, and put on clean pants and a clean shirt. When the others woke up I was shining my boots."

"'You going to church?' Mac asked with a sly grin."

"Nope, I answered, and wouldn't answer any of their questions although I knew they were terribly anxious to know what I was up to."

"I didn't go eat. I was so nervous I figured I'd just toss it back up so I went and picked out the two gentlest horses. I curried them and cleaned their feet and then I picked out the best two saddles and saddle blankets. But all the time I was thinking, what if she doesn't come? What if she doesn't come? Every time I thought it, it got worse until by mid-morning I'd convinced myself she wasn't coming. Hell, Meathead, it was almost a relief. I was in the barn when Peggy came in and brought a sack lunch telling me, 'now you go pick her some flowers by the house.'"

"But Peggy, I started to argue."

"'You like this girl. You let the men laugh. They'll only be jealous anyway.'"

"I picked six white daisies under the watchful eye of the men sitting on the porch, but since Peggy was outside they didn't poke fun at me."

"On the way back to the barn I heard a car approaching. Barbara was driving a big gray Oldsmobile and when she got close to me she waved at me with a smile so big on her face I thought the sun was coming up again."

"When she got out of the car by the barn she was wearing red pants, a sleeveless white shirt, black boots and had on the brightest red lipstick I'd ever seen. Her lipstick reminded me of strawberries and I wanted to lick it off right there on the spot."

"Whoopee shit!"

"'Bet you thought I wasn't going to come were the first words she said."

"I'm glad you're here, I said, and handed her the flowers, feeling like I was about six years old."

"'My favorite,' she said, smiled, and kissed me on the cheek."

"Mac and Moose and Crow and Whitey walked over acting all nonchalant like. They introduced themselves and told her what a nice young man I was and that I was the best saddle bronc rider in the country and that they were proud to know me. They were as captivated by her smile as I was."

"Duke didn't come over, but I could see him looking at us through the window of the chuck house. There was something in his look that was sad and forlorn, almost foreboding, like he knew what was going to happen."

"Book readers have a way of knowing things before

most people."

Ben fell into silence. Meathead meandered up the draw, picking her own way around the rocks and bushes and cactus. The sun was about noon high and Ben took off his over-shirt and tied it to the back of the saddle. A mule deer doe and fawn darted out of the draw in front of them and was halfway up the hill within a few seconds. "Teach that child to run," Ben called to the doe. "Take that child to the farthest and tallest mountain where man hasn't mucked everything up yet."

The doe and fawn went over the top of the hill.

"It probably isn't far enough," Ben whispered.

******

For the next three months Barbara and Ben saw each other as often as possible. They went to the movies, went riding, went on hikes, or sat around and talked, although Ben never told her about his early life. He only talked about the ranch. They held hands and hugged and kissed, but Ben was a complete gentleman. Even though at times he was so full of desire he thought he'd bust, he never made any improper moves toward Barbara. He didn't know it but Barbara was going through the same aches and hoping Ben would come on to her - but also proud he didn't.

Each time they were together their love deepened

- when they were apart it was like their hearts had been torn out of their chests. Barbara was caught between love and what she was going to do now that she was out of high school. Her father wanted her to go to college when most fathers wanted their daughters to get married and have kids. At times she wanted to be a nurse and at other times a teacher like her mother - most of the time she only wanted to be with Ben - nothing else mattered. She didn't care if he was only a cowhand. She knew one day he would be a famous saddle bronc rider and would have money and she could work at any job until he was famous.

Ben was caught between love and fear. Barbara was a part of his every waking moment, and most of his dreams, but Ben was only a cowboy. How could he take care of Barbara? He barely made enough money to take care of himself and he didn't have the money to try the rodeo circuit - dreams and money were two different things. At times he thought it would be better to tell Barbara they should not see each other, but when they were together, and he was going to tell her, he couldn't bear the thought of not being with her. How could he handle the loneliness after knowing love?

The men didn't joke about Ben's feelings for Barbara - they all knew they were genuine and not deceitful and they all knew the turmoil he was going through.

"The first time I was in love I couldn't even spit," Crow said.

"Who ever invented love was a mean-spirited son-of-a-bitch," Mac said.

"It's the reason most of us are busted out," Moose said.

"Maybe we should be like them Arabs," Whitey said. "Everybody has ten or twelve wives."

"Lord help us," Crow said. "None of us could handle one."

"Maybe women should have ten or twelve husbands," Crow said. "They could take care of us and all we'd have to do is screw."

The men pondered the problem for a few minutes and all decided in their own way it was too taxing on the mind to try and figure out. Dealing with cows and horses made life more simplified.

Over the past few months Duke had become more somber. A lot of times he didn't even say hello to the men when they came in to eat. While he served the food he looked distracted. He read more - ordering a big fancy paper from Denver, one all the way from New York City, and he bought a radio. Dave had a radio in the house, mostly to listen to the stock reports and weather. Duke only listened to the radio at night and only to the news – stock reports and music and skits didn't interest him - they were only distractions from the truth that most people weren't interested in. Duke figured most people didn't want to know the truth - it would only confuse them and destroy the myths they invented to make their lives have meaning.

Duke's being unsociable didn't bother the men. They all figured a man was what he was and it was really none of their damn business. What they didn't know was that Duke was worried. He knew there was a war coming and it bothered him deeply. Even if the United States wanted to, it couldn't stay out of it.

******

"It was April of 1939," Ben said to Meathead. "Barbara and I were walking along the river holding hands and not talking. I'd been up in the mountains moving stock around for a week and missed her so badly the week had seemed like two years. It was a beautiful day. The sky was calm and peaceful and all kinds of birds were singing like they were challenging each other to who could sing the best. Barbara stopped walking and suddenly hugged me harder than she'd ever hugged me before and she started crying. I didn't know what to do. I held her, and stroked her hair, but couldn't think of anything to say. Finally she stepped back and said, 'Germany just invaded Poland, and England and France have declared war on Germany.'"

"That doesn't mean anything to us, I said."

"'My father says within a couple of years we will be pulled into the war, she sobbed. And if he's right, you will have to go. I want us to get married and you do what you're supposed to do, ride broncs in the rodeo.'"

"Barbara I only have about a hundred dollars saved up. That would barely get us out of town, I said."

"Barbara started to cry again."

"Nothing can ever break us apart, I said. Not war, not anything."

"I should have married her right then."

"Back away from the river was a big stand of cattails. Barbara took my hand and led me behind them. The ground was lush with grass and there were tiny little white flowers no bigger than dimes blooming all through the grass. They had a sweet smell that wasn't overpowering. Barbara let go of my hand and she stepped away from me. She took her hair out of the ponytail and shook her head. The sun shining through her blond hair was finer than gold thread. She took off her boots. 'What are you...?' I started to say but she put her finger on my mouth to not talk. She took her pants off and underpants and then removed her blouse and bra. She was so pretty I wanted to fall to my knees and pray at her feet. 'You make love to me Ben Sharps,' she said."

"But there were tears in her eyes."

"Barbara and I made love gentler than a warm summer breeze. The birds sang and the scent of the flowers covered us with their blessing. For a long time afterwards we sat naked holding hands and we didn't talk, just sat holding hands. For one time in my life there was true peace in my heart. I didn't need to be a saddle bronc rider. I didn't need anything. All I needed was the sweet-smelling flowers, and the birds singing, and the cattails, and Barbara prettier than any of it."

"Meathead, what a fuck up a few good things in life can be," Ben said.

******

Ben and Barbara did not make love every time they were together. When they did, it was not planned or schemed over. It was only on the spur of the moment and it was always gentle and exploring, not wanting or taking. But Ben felt a difference in Barbara. No matter how she laughed or they joked or what they talked about, Ben knew Barbara was hiding a sadness from him. At times her gaze would go right through him - somewhere into the future that he could not see or fathom, and her eyes would lose their shine. "Are you ok?" he would ask, deeply concerned.

Barbara would blink - her eyes focusing once more on Ben - and smile and say, "Only thinking."

Ben would not pursue the matter, but he would feel a deep emptiness inside himself like he had never felt, not even for his sister.

******

Ben reached the top of the draw and turned Meathead around and backtracked the way they had come. "You spend too much of your time going backwards," Meathead said.

"My age, there's only backwards," Ben said.

"Bullshit," Meathead said.

"Barbara got a job working at the grocery store and we started saving money. I'd never had a bank account but Barbara opened one in her name. The money was going to be entry fees for rodeos and to save enough money for us to get married. We'd decided I would do rodeos and she would go to college in Denver and become a nurse. She hoped to start the next year. All I wanted at the time was to get married, but now she said we should wait. I'd gotten over my fear of not being able to take care of Barbara.

She always told me it would all work out, love had a way of making things work out, but at times she still had those distant eyes."

"In May of '39 I entered a rodeo in Farmington, New Mexico. Dave let me borrow the truck. I won one hundred and twenty-five dollars and another buckle, after expenses close to eighty-five dollars."

"I was in ten rodeos that year and won all ten, almost clearing a thousand dollars and I had so many buckles I put them in a trunk. I'd been bucked off more than once, but nobody in the area could come close to me. Local newspapers started writing about me when they heard I was going to be in the town rodeo and I started cutting out the clippings and saving them. Pretty girls at the rodeos started following me around but I never went out with any of them, not even going to the rodeo dances, but leaving town as soon as I could to get back to the ranch and Barbara. Dave didn't pay me for the days I was gone but he never told me I couldn't go."

"Barbara had been accepted to the University of Denver Nursing program and would start in April of 1940. She figured after she graduated we could get married and not have to rely on anyone. It would be easy for her to find a job and we could afford a truck for me to get around, and someday in the future we could buy our own little place."

"Her father was happy about her decision and had never done anything to try and get between us. Although I don't think her mother liked me much, even if I was getting written up in the paper."

"That fall I was in the Colorado State Fair Rodeo. The best cowboys in the area were entered. I was third going into the last day and had a good ride going on a horse named Buck Shot - he twisted left when I figured he was going right and I got bucked off. I landed hard on my shoulder and then the horse kicked me in the ribs. They carried me out of the arena on a stretcher and I was in the hospital for two days with four busted ribs and a dislocated shoulder. Besides being in pain I felt lower than dirt, but it never entered my mind to not get back on the circuit the next year."

"I should have quit then."

"Busted bones should tell you something."

"Busted heart tells you more."

******

It took Ben longer to heal than he thought but he started working as soon as he could. The only thing on his mind was to save money so Barbara and he could get married. He even took on breaking horses for other ranches for five dollars a head. Barbara told him to slow down but he would not listen.

Throughout the winter he figured out what rodeos he would enter in 1940. Instead of ten, he would enter twenty. It would be a lot of driving, but he didn't plan on losing, so he could almost double the previous year's take. Dave told him he'd sell him his old truck on time with no interest. During the winter all the men helped Ben work on the truck. He didn't want to worry about the truck breaking down between rodeos.

Ben bought a set of chaps dyed so they looked like an American flag with long fringe that would flap around while the horse was bucking, and a set of shiny spurs with big spiked rowels.

Barbara came out to the ranch a lot. She and Peggy enjoyed each other's company. Peggy didn't get to town much and it was good for her to have somebody to talk to besides a cowboy. Peggy was impressed that Barbara was so mature for her age.

Besides being deeply in love, Ben and Barbara were becoming good friends. Ben wasn't afraid to tell Barbara what was on his mind and Barbara wasn't afraid to tell him what was on hers. They argued occasionally but the arguments didn't last long and weren't stored away to fester.

It was not an exceptionally cold winter but there was a lot of snow and it seemed to drag on forever.

The men had fixed all the tack and grew bored feeding cattle twice a day. Most days after feeding they went into town and sat in the bar all day. Ben would stay with them awhile. Barbara told him he couldn't sit around her house all day pacing back and forth and getting in the way. Barbara had already bought her first years nursing schoolbooks and was going through them and Ben was a distraction.

Most of the conversation at the bar revolved around the escalating war in Europe.

Many people said the United States would get involved soon and just as many said it was none of America's business what those dumb European bastards were up to anyway. There was no talk about the Japanese. Ben didn't pay it much mind, but, unlike before he met Barbara and was willing to go to war, now the thought of war frightened him.

In April Barbara went to Denver. The night before they had not been sad - Barbara was excited about her adventure and Ben was looking forward to the upcoming rodeo season - the first rodeo being in May. But when Barbara was about to leave, she hugged him, and started crying, and as her father drove her away Ben had a dreadful feeling in his heart that he would never see her again.

CHAPTER TEN

Ben and Meathead rode back to the spring and startled a covey of quail that made Meathead jump. Ben laughed, "You're getting skittish in your old age?"

"You talking all the time lulls me to sleep," Meathead said.

"You don't have to listen. Man talks to himself most of his life anyway, nobody really listens. Most people only listen to the prattle in their own heads, what other people try to tell them they ignore."

Meathead seemed to sigh.

Ben dismounted. Meathead drank and Ben had a shot of whiskey and then sat under a tree.

"1940 was one hell of a year. I started out winning in Farmington, like the year before. Worse thing was

I was spending close to a dollar a day on phone calls to Barbara until she told me to write letters. I then won in Cortez and Durango. I got second in Santa Fe and second in El Paso, followed up by wins in Tucumcari, Abilene, Lubbock and Odessa. When there was time I'd drive to Denver and Barbara and I would have an evening or two together. Every time I saw her she was prettier and the more I missed her when I left. But it was strange, when I was away from her the world took on a whole different shine. I missed her and was sad but I was also happy. The sky seemed to be bluer, the trees greener, and it was like I was a part of everything. There was a reason for me to be alive. It was like I was a part of a living rainbow that would never fade."

"There are no rainbows now."

"I think 1940 was such a good year because I wasn't riding for me. I was riding for Barbara. I didn't think about fame or all the articles that were being written about me. I didn't drink much but I started smoking regular. Barbara, besides going to school, was working part-time waiting tables."

Ben rolled a smoke, took several long drags, butted it and put the butt behind his ear.

"The last rodeo of the year was in Cheyenne. All the big cowboys were there. At the time it was the biggest rodeo in the country. The Super Bowl of rodeos. They had wagon races and cook offs. The bars had dances every night with big name performers. Dave and Peggy picked up Barbara in Denver and came up to watch me the last night. Peggy and Barbara stayed in one room while Dave and I stayed in another. It was a little taxing but that's how it was in those days."

Ben smiled. "When you can't have something it makes it that much more desirable."

"I won in Cheyenne and within a week most cowboys in the country knew about Ben Sharps. I did so many interviews for magazines and newspapers I was dizzy with answers. Ben Sharps, who had ridden six broncs in a row without a spill. Ben Sharps, who just might be the best saddle bronc rider of all time. Ben Sharps, the kid with a future. Barbara just stood in the background smiling at me while flash bulbs popped and people asked questions."

"Barbara and I finally got away and even ditched Dave and Peggy. We went to a cafe and we didn't talk about the rodeo or her school. We talked about how nice it would be to have a little place outside of Denver. I wanted to get married that night. I told Barbara I'd work during the winter in Denver and we could rent a little house and then I'd rodeo in the summer again.”

“‘It’s not time yet, Ben, she said, and her eyes went through me the way they did sometimes, looking into the future and seeing things I couldn’t or didn’t want to see.’”

“I drove Barbara back to Denver and that night we rented a room. When we made love, she held me like I was going to go away somewhere, somewhere that was terrible, and ugly, and cruel. When we were finished she cried, telling me they were happy tears and how much she loved me.”

Ben took the cigarette butt from behind his ear and lit it. “Strange how women seem to know more than men. Seem to know things that there aren’t any words for at the time. Seem to have premonitions that men ignore. She was right. I was going somewhere that was terrible, and ugly, and cruel, and even after all the years I’ve never really returned.”

******

Ben spent the winter at the ranch. Moose, Mac, Whitey, or Crow didn’t treat him any different even though he was, “One of them famous rodeo riders now,” as Crow said, adding with a twinkle in his eye, “Now you can lend me some money since it takes a truck to haul your winnings around.”

Ben had cleared close to four thousand dollars for

the season after paying off Dave for the truck. Barbara and he now had over five thousand in their account. About once every two weeks he would drive and see Barbara and he would always ask her to marry him now and not later. She would look through him with her distant gaze and tell him not yet. Ben couldn't really understand why. But there was no changing Barbara's mind and he knew it. He did decide life would be much easier if women had to ask men to marry them.

Just before Christmas Ben and Barbara went shopping and he bought her a small diamond engagement ring. They both stared at it on her finger and smiled. "Now you tell me the date when you want to get married," Ben said. "I won't ask anymore."

"I want to be married to you more than anything, but the way the world is I know it is not time," she answered.

They made love that night and Barbara's embraces seemed desperate, as if she was consumed by a deep fear.

Ben drove Barbara to her parent's house in Buena Vista for Christmas break. There was fresh snow on the ground and it was sunny. The world seemed clean and sparkling and at peace.

The holidays were fun. Barbara's parents had a

party for all the townspeople and officially announced the engagement of their daughter. Everybody was excited for her, excited she was going to be a nurse and excited about Ben's success with the rodeo, but all the men told him, "Ben you'd better learn a trade. You could get hurt bad anytime and your rodeo days would be over."

Ben didn't tell them he didn't want to be anything else but a rodeo cowboy.

Peggy and Dave had a party that Christmas. Ben was talking to Moose on one side of the room and Peggy and Barbara were standing by the Christmas tree. Peggy had candles all over the room. Duke was being uncommonly sociable and was talking to Dave. Ben looked over at Barbara. The complete room disappeared and all he could see was her. Barbara was wearing a long white skirt with an off-white sweater. There were only white lights and silver ornaments on the Christmas tree and the tree lights and candlelight haloed Barbara. Her blond hair radiated gold, her eyes twinkled, and it seemed like she was not standing but floating in the air like an angel. Ben was transfixed. Barbara saw him looking at her and smiled a smile that was overflowing with love and happiness and contentment. Then she waved at him and for an instant Barbara reminded Ben of his sister

- all tender and gentle inside - always a child.

Ben was suddenly filled with a deep sadness - a sadness that didn't come from his heart but from the inside of his bones and ran through every cell in his body. He felt like he wanted to cry but he held it and thought to himself, oh Barbara, I hope we can fly.

The sadness went away as quickly as it had come and he smiled and waved back at Barbara, but she did not see him wave, she was talking to Peggy.

******

"I'll never forget that image of Barbara," Ben said. "She was never more beautiful."

A single tear ran down his face. Ben did not bother to wipe it off.

"During the time I was with Barbara I never thought much about my Ma or Pa, or my sister who could not fly. I didn't think about when I was young and dreaming about being the best saddle bronc rider in the country. Occasionally I'd think about Reno and wonder what he was doing or if he was ok."

"New Year's Day we all went to the bar to celebrate. Barbara and I danced and drank beer and we hooted and hollered and laughed about nothing really - just thunderstruck by love. It was terrible taking her home that night and not being able to be with her. After Barbara went back to Denver I spent the winter drawing up my schedule for 1941. There was no rodeo in the country that would not take me. I decided I would enter a few rodeos in Oklahoma and more in Texas and one in Omaha. I mailed out all my applications and got my returns. I was going to do twenty-two rodeos. My ribs were healed up and my shoulder was fine, although at times it ached deep inside the joint."

"Now I ache in every joint. Even my whiskers hurt."

Ben butted the smoke and took a long glance at the rope tied to Meatheads' saddle. "I should stretch it," he muttered. "Don't want too much give."

He sat on the ground a few feet from the spring. "You're like most things in life," Ben said to the spring. "You offer all these parched creatures water and coolness and then one day you dry up without a thought for any of them. You make all your gifts of coolness just lies - just something that strings them along till you don't want to mess with them anymore and you go away."

"Piece of shit wet ray of hope anyway."

Ben stood, got the rope, tossed it in the spring and sat back down.

******

In March of 1941 there were wet snows and then

freezing temperatures. Tree limbs were breaking from the weight of the ice on them and then the wind came - came like it hated everything and wouldn't stop blowing until everything was dead. The men would come in tired and half frozen - worn out worse than five-year-old boots. One night Ben ate slowly and all the men had gone back to the bunkhouse. During the winter, Duke had become more somber and standoffish, but he sat down on the other side of the table from Ben with a cup of coffee and started to talk. "I have dread in my heart for you Ben," he said.

Ben didn't know how to answer him.

"I have dread in my heart for all young men," Duke continued.

"I'm doing fine, Duke, you don't have to worry about me," Ben answered.

"You and Barbara are very fortunate, but it seems when those who find a true love in life something always comes along to destroy it."

"As soon as Barbara is out of college we are going to get married," Ben replied, not taken back or frightened by Duke's concern.

"Ben," Duke said, almost in grief. "Soon you will be in a war. The whole world will be consumed and millions of innocent people will be killed. I want you to do as many happy things as you can so you will have great memories to get you through what you will experience."

All Ben remembered saying was thanks and then Duke stood and walked away, all hunched over and with his head down like all the bad things in the world were on his back and he knew there was nothing he could do about it.

******

Ben took the rope out of the spring, tied one end to a branch of the willow, and the other end on the saddle horn. He led Meathead a few steps, which stretched the rope at least a foot and wrung most of the water out of it. He pushed Meathead back and repeated the process several times, stretching the rope a little more each time. He then untied the rope and sat underneath the tree, coiling the rope, all except the last three feet and started to make a hangman's noose.

******

1941 was a great year for Ben. He was in love, and won about every rodeo he entered - never finishing worse than second. He had so many silver buckles, new chaps, spurs, fancy boots, cowboy hats, head stalls, saddle blankets, and hand-tooled saddles he could have opened up his own store. Barbara was doing well in school and they saw each other as often as possible. They were looking forward to Thanksgiving when they could spend more than a few days together. Barbara told Ben one evening, "I feel like I'm becoming a wham bam thank-you ma'am. And you had better not be wham bam thank-you ma'aming any of those little cowgirls that hang around those rodeos trying to catch a good looking cowboy."

"How about all those educated men you see every day," Ben said, not seriously, but at times it did worry him she would fall out of love with him and fall for a city guy.

"I like my men stupid," Barbara said. "They're easier to control."

Her answer perplexed Ben. He had never considered himself stupid - maybe a little dumb, but not stupid.

******

Ben finished the hangman's noose. It wasn't the best noose, but passable. "Hell, I've never hung anyone," Ben said looking at it with a critical eye.

"Had to be a strange man that went around the country hanging people back in the old days," he said.

"Wonder how a man gets called to a job like that?" he asked, but he didn't have an answer.

******

Barbara and Ben decided they would spend

Thanksgiving together and not at her home or back at the ranch. Barbara's parents were upset but Barbara told them a white lie that she had to study for an exam. Ben rented a cabin in the mountains west of Denver that had a fireplace, new appliances and cooking and eating utensils. Preparing for the drive they stopped at an A&P grocery store and bought a ham, sweet potatoes, and a pumpkin pie, and at a liquor store on the edge of town they splurged on four bottles of inexpensive champagne.

It was a glorious fall day driving to the cabin. The Aspen leaves were falling and blanketed the ground deeper than a shag carpet - filling the air with a wet earth smell. The scrub oaks were brighter than blood and looked like red rivers on the sides of the mountains. A few of the mountaintops that were above timberline were already covered with snow. The air was not cold, but crisp. Ben was ecstatic because it had been a great year. He was up for cowboy of the year, and being a young man, there was no end in sight.

The cabin was nestled in a grove of pine trees - wood for the fireplace was already chopped and split and stacked neatly on the covered front porch. There were two wicker chairs on the porch. There were large windows on three of the walls. A double bed covered with a multi-colored quilt took up most of the room, with a small table and kitchen along another wall. There was a radio on a bedside table. The room was lighted by a moose antler chandelier.

"Oh, Ben," Barbara said. "This would be all we would ever need."

After unloading, they sat on the porch and Ben popped the cork on a bottle of champagne. After two glasses they started laughing. The sun was going down when they finished the bottle, and feeling like there were no cares in the world Ben carried Barbara into the cabin.

******

Ben tied the rope to the saddle and mounted Meathead. "Something about champagne that gets rid of inhibitions in a woman," he said, shaking his head and smiling.

"I've ridden a lot of wild horses in my life, but that night with that pink champagne, Barbara gave me the ride of my life."

"Whoopee shit!"

Ben nudged the horse. "Go wherever you want to go," he said.

Meathead started up a trail that ran up the eastern hill. "Smart horse would go down hill," Ben said.

"Smart horse wouldn't listen to you," Meathead

said.

Ben glanced at the hangman's noose. "You won't have to wait long," he said to the rope.

"Barbara and I had three glorious days. We didn't see anybody else or even listen to the radio. I tried not to listen to the radio at all. All there was, was talk of the war in Europe and talk about the Japanese. I guess I was ignoring the war, like it would all go away. Barbara and I went for long walks and we really didn't talk much, but we looked at the same things. It was like I was seeing things through her eyes and she was seeing things through mine. On Thanksgiving we cooked the ham and sweet potatoes and drank two bottles of champagne. It was strange, but before we started to eat Barbara looked at me seriously and asked, 'You ever pray, Ben?'"

"I told her no. God is a mystery to me."

"'I would like you to start praying. I think it is important,' but why it was important she didn't say."

"That night before we went to bed we knelt down beside the bed and she prayed. She prayed for the people at war in Europe. She prayed for poor people, and then she unclasped her hands and laid them on mine and said, 'and please God, protect Ben. He is a good man and I love him.'"

"Strangely, for a brief moment I felt like God was

in the room with Barbara and me and He was sad. It was the sadness of an eternity of wasted time."

"Then Barbara said, 'Now Ben I want you to pray.'"

"I just knelt there and no words came to my mind. All I could think was what good would it do? Then I thought about my sister who could not fly and I mumbled to Barbara, I can't."

"She was not mad at me, she only bowed her head and prayed silently for a few moments and then said to me, 'One day Ben you will have to.'"

That night, after they made love, Ben told Barbara everything about his life. He had never really told her about his sister or his parents. She had never really asked how he got to the ranch. But he told her everything. How his sister could not fly, hitting his Pa with a shovel, and how Reno saved him. She lay in his arms and did not interrupt him and when he was done she kissed him gently and said, "Ben, you've been very fortunate in your life."

******

Meathead stopped on the top of the hill. A strong breeze blew from the west, kicking up dust in the valley between the hills. Ben took a shot of whiskey, was about to put the bottle back, took another shot and then put it back.

A red-tailed hawk circled, spied something in the

valley, set its wings and dove toward the ground faster than an artillery shell. It hit something hard behind a small bush and sailed back into the sky with a rabbit in its talons. The rabbit screamed - a scream that knew there is no pity.

"You kill because you have to," Ben said to the hawk.

"On December 7, 1941 the Japanese bombed Pearl Harbor," Ben said. "I should have prayed. Not for myself but for Barbara."

CHAPTER ELEVEN

When Duke ran out of the chuck house and told the men the news that the Japanese had bombed Pearl Harbor nobody believed him. But he was so adamant they all hurried to the chuck house and gravely listened to the news on the radio. When the reality of it all had sunk in, no one spoke. It was like the air had been sucked out of the room and no one would ever be able to breathe again. Then everybody looked sadly at Ben. Ben knew he had to join the military, but his earlier resolve was gone. How could he explain it to Barbara? Was duty stronger than the need for love?

Within a week the United States declared war on

Germany and her allies and on Japan.

"It's a big ball of shit now," Duke said. "War is nothing but a big ball of shit. Why couldn't the bastards just leave us alone?"

Barbara knew before she came home for Christmas that Ben was going to join the military. Although she didn't want him to, she knew her wants meant nothing to the world. She was not going to be the only young girl in love whose husband or boyfriend would be going overseas. Ben hadn't decided what branch he wanted to join. Crow told Ben to join the Navy - they were always clean and ate. But Ben didn't want to die from drowning. Mac told Ben to join the Marines saying, "If you're going to have to fight a war, fight with the fighters." Duke told Ben to not join anything. "One more dead body won't make a difference one way or the other." Moose told Ben to join the Army if he could take the piss ant officers screaming all the time and not really knowing what the hell they were screaming about.

After hearing the news, Peggy cried a while and then grimly went into town and bought large quantities of sugar, salt, flour, and canning jars.

Dave had the gas delivery truck come out and fill all the gas barrels and bought extra ammunition for all the rifles.

Ben finally decided he'd join the Army.

******

Ben started Meathead down the other side of the hill. "Indians who used to live here had to fight all the time," Ben said. "The poor bastards barely eked out an existence and some other tribe decides they want the land because it has more rabbits on it, or more deer, or a spring, or just for the hell of it, so they start a war."

"Fucking people have been fighting for time immemorial."

"Fucking cavemen even fought and those dumb bastards couldn't even talk."

"It's like Duke said, one more body won't make a difference."

"What's one body to thousands and thousands of bodies killed by one war or another?"

Ben looked up at the sky. "God, if you're up there you must have some powerful enemies, either that or they've already whipped your butt and you're off hiding somewhere in the universe licking your wounds and trying to figure out who you can get for an ally."

"Christmas was a sad day but everybody tried not to let on how sad they were. Most of the young men in town and on the surrounding ranches had joined one branch of the military or another. Mothers were full of tears. Fathers were trying to be stoic and brave and telling their sons how proud of them they were, but they were crying inside knowing that a lot of the boys would never come home."

"Barbara cried when I told her I was going to enlist, but saying she knew I had to go."

"But it was strange. The Christmas tree that year was the prettiest I'd ever seen. Barbara was radiant. At Dave and Peggy's party we all laughed and joked like the war would be over in a week, and everything would be back to normal before we knew it had really started."

"When Barbara and I could sneak off we made love. She had never been gentler and I had never been so caring. She didn't hold me desperately but tentatively, almost shyly. I'd told her when I bought her the engagement ring it was up to her when we got married but she never brought it up. I knew she was frightened like I was and I knew she was afraid to marry me knowing I might get killed - it would only double the burden, so I never brought it up either."

Ben rolled a smoke and exhaled slowly.

"Getting married wouldn't have made us more in love anyway or strengthened our bond."

"We cried a few times and then we would laugh

over stupid little things. We talked a lot, talked about our love and what we would do when I got out. We talked about our dreams mostly. We talked so we wouldn't fall into silence and let each other know how afraid we really were and how lonely we felt inside."

"Barbara went with me to Denver the day I enlisted. There was a line of men over a half mile long waiting in front of the recruiting office. Ladies were serving coffee and cookies. All of the ladies were smiling, but all of them were holding a sadness behind their eyes. Some of the boys were with their parents and others were alone, but all the boys were boasting how brave they were and how the Japanese and the Germans didn't have a chance. What they didn't know was that the Japanese and Germans were telling their boys the same things. When it was my turn, the officer looked at me for a second or two. 'You're in good shape cowboy,' he said. I signed my name to several papers and was told to report back on January 10th. The officer shook hands with me and the next boy in line stepped up."

"Sign your name and take a pledge and then you can kill with no shame."

Ben frowned and drew on the smoke.

"Sign your name and you can kill women and children, and old people, and you can bomb cities full of civilians, and make orphans, all under the name of country and God and right."

"Even when another country starts a war killing's no good, Meathead."

"Necessary, but no good."

"There are no winners in war."

"But who will ever stop it?"

Ben stopped the horse. "There's one race of people that never really fought a war," Ben said. "The Eskimos. Go figure. Maybe it's too damn cold or they are the smartest people in the world and they are not going to tell the rest of the world their secret. They figure in time the rest of the world will kill itself off and then they can move to a warmer climate without some bastard trying to kill them."

"They're smart."

Ben butted the smoke and took a shot of whiskey. "I know one thing," he said, putting the whiskey back in the saddlebag. "I know I really don't know a damn thing and I don't know if it would do any good if I did."

******

Barbara went back to school and Ben was going to go to Denver a few days before he was to report. Ben spent a lot of time alone. He'd walk around the ranch, recounting things that when he had done them didn't mean much, but now were important and worth remembering. The men talked to him somberly. The Christmas spirit was gone and the real world was back. Ben started reading Duke's newspapers and following the war.

Sitting on his bunk one evening Ben suddenly wanted to go see his parents. He wanted to tell them he had enlisted.

The next morning he got up early and drove toward Kansas. Every little town he went through had flags flying from all the stores. It was dark when Ben got to his parent's farm. He stopped the truck a quarter mile from the farm and got out, pulled on his coat, and started walking the rest of the way.

******

"It was cold and the wind was blowing," Ben said to Meathead. "I'd forgotten how flat the land was in Kansas and how the night sky went in half a circle around a person like you were standing in the middle of a glass dome. There was a half-moon giving everything a shadow. The stars were not bright like the mountains, but they were out by the millions - little sparkles that didn't give a damn about war, or love, or hate, or anything that is important to anybody on earth."

"The first thing I saw in the moonlight was the

barn. The hay doors were banging back and forth. My sister's ghost was standing in the doors. She looked at me and waved but she was crying, 'Don't go Ben,' she called to me. 'Don't go. I told you never to hate and all that is going to happen to you is you're going to learn how to hate.'"

"I went into the barn and I climbed up the ladder to the hay doors, but the ghost of my sister was gone. There was just the doors banging back and forth, and the stars filling in the opening like somebody had painted in the hole. I looked down at the ground and Lisa was standing there looking up at me but she was no longer crying. 'I will protect you,' she said and she melted into the night."

"I turned from the doors and propped up on a hay bale was Lisa's little doll. She had a new eye, and a new dress on, and she was placed facing the door. Ma must have done it. The doll seemed very lonely."

"I went back outside and started for the house. Even in the cold I could smell the hog lot and I remembered taking baths and trying my best to wash off the smell of hogs but it would never go away. I remembered the kids laughing at me and how angry I would get and start fighting the boys and Lisa pulling me away, begging me not to become like them."

"There was a light on in the living room of the house and smoke was coming out of the stovepipe. The wind caught the smoke and swirled it around, tossing it every which direction. The curtains were not closed and I could see my Pa sitting in a chair drinking whiskey and my Ma sitting on the sofa knitting. They were listening to the radio but I couldn't make out what they were listening to. They both looked ancient, like all life had finally been sucked out of them, but life would not let them die - it wanted to punish them."

"I stood there watching my parents and even though I felt sorry for them I had no good feelings for them and I no longer wanted to tell them I was in the army. All I felt was bitterness and sadness and remorse."

"I walked back to the truck, stopping one more time and looking at the barn. The wind had stopped and I could see the ghost of my sister standing in the opening of the hay doors again. She smiled at me and then she jumped but she did not fall to the ground. She spread out her arms and she flew out away from the barn toward the stars. Higher and higher and higher she went until she disappeared."

"My sister could fly and it made me feel good. Not happy, but good."

"I drove to Reno's. When I got there it was almost midnight, but Reno's bedroom light was on. When I got out of the truck I felt like I was back at my real home even though I'd only lived there a week. I knocked on the door. Reno came to the door fully dressed. When he opened the door he smiled and said, 'Welcome back cowboy.'"

"He hadn't aged much. His hair and beard were getting white but his eyes were still vivid blue and gentle – made gentle by sadness, which I didn't understand until later in life."

"We sat drinking coffee with two tablespoons of sugar in each cup and talked about the farm and Peggy and Dave. I told him about the rodeos and I told him about Barbara. It wasn't until dawn that I told him I had enlisted in the army."

"'Damn wars anyway was all he said.'"

"Damn wars anyway."

"When the sun was coming up it was time for me to go. We stood on the porch looking out at his farm and I could see the tree over his wife's and daughter's graves had grown taller. It stood like a crucifix in the dawn light but I didn't know if it radiated hope or despair."

"I want to thank you for everything, I told Reno and I was going to say more but Reno cut in. 'No need for more words,' he said and hugged me. And then he said, 'You take care but I don't want you writing me. I don't need another hurt. But you know I will think about you each day.'"

"When he let go of me there were tears in his eyes but I didn't cry until I was driving down the road. I cried for Reno and I cried for my parents, even though I had no feelings for them, and I cried for my sister even though she could now fly, and I cried for Barbara and me."

******

The night before Ben was about to leave the ranch he told Dave that if anything happened to him all the buckles and bridals and saddles he'd won should be divided up between the men. Dave gave his word it would be done and told Ben when he got out of the army if he ever needed a job he had one.

Dave also bought back his truck he had sold Ben and would drive Ben to the train station in town. Barbara would pick him up at the station in Denver.

It was hard for Ben to leave the ranch. Peggy sobbed and kissed him. Mac, Crow, Moose, Whitey, and Duke shook hands with him and each man gave him ten dollars, which Ben tried to refuse, but couldn't. Crow telling Ben, "You take Barbara out to a fancy restaurant on us."

Peggy told him to write or she would whip him good when he got out.

Peggy and the men were all standing outside and waved goodbye when Dave drove Ben to town. Dave and Ben didn't talk during the ride. At the train station Ben told Dave, "Just leave me and go on back. I'd rather it be that way."

They shook hands with no words between them.

******

"Most of the time life would be better with no words," Ben said to Meathead. "Seems words always get misunderstood, or what a person really wants to say never comes out right, or is never really enough."

Meathead looked at him sideways.

"There are goodbyes and then there are goodbyes," Ben said.

"Barbara and I had two nice days. We had two photographs taken of us smiling and holding each other. One she framed and the other one I had made billfold size so I could carry it with me. We went to a fancy restaurant with the men's money. There were candles on the table and I had lobster for the first time and Barbara had something I can't remember the name of. But as each hour passed until it was time for me to leave we grew quieter and quieter, until both of us wanted it to be over - me to be on the train and then me coming back on the train with the war over."

"The morning I was leaving the loading dock was crammed with people. Couples were hugging and kissing, women were crying, and men were trying not to cry. Most of the people had American flags. Barbara and I stood silently holding hands. Then a sergeant hollered and all goodbyes were cut short and everything became a blur. I felt Barbara press something cold into my hand. The next thing I knew I was on the train and looking out the window at Barbara and waving, and the train lurched, a whistle blew three times, and within a few seconds we were on our way to another world."

"I never felt so hollow or empty. No man on the train said a word. We all sat empty-eyed. A few sobbed."

"I opened my hand. Barbara had pressed a gold ring in my hand. I put it on my wedding finger and from then on every time I looked at it I could see her face, not when she was waving goodbye, but our first Christmas party at the ranch when she was bathed by the candle light and the white lights from the Christmas tree and she looked like she was floating in the air like an angel."

"Then a buck sergeant walked into the car carrying

a clipboard. 'All right you sissies,' he hollered. 'Get this straight. Somebody else is going to be fucking your wife or girlfriend now. It don't wear out so don't worry about it. What you don't know won't hurt you. When I call out your name you holler out loud and clear, 'here sergeant,' and remember one thing, I ain't your mother. Your mother is the 'mother fuckin' army now and the army really don't give a shit if you like it or not. So get over your sniveling-feel-sorry-for-me-bullshit. You're only born to die anyway. Now Sam Broom where the fuck are you?'"

"I tell you what Meathead. From that day on we all knew that we were in the 'mother fuckin' army. There was no question about it. And the sergeant hadn't lied to us, the 'mother fuckin' army doesn't give a shit. Its job is to win wars, not to make friends."

"It's too bad we need an army."

"But we need one."

"Fucking world anyway."

CHAPTER TWELVE

Meathead and Ben got to the bottom of the hill but another steep hill started up immediately to the front of them. The hills cut off the sun and Ben put his coat back on. About half a mile to the left were two other hills. Their bases were so close together the sky between them looked like a wedge of pie. Ben had never been to this portion of the ranch and he turned Meathead left.

Ben followed an old trail that was about ten feet wide. He took the letter he had written back at the trailer out of his pocket and reread it. Satisfied, he put it back in his pocket. "I wonder when they find me if they will bother to go through my pockets," he said.

"It would have been better to leave the letter on

the table," Meathead said.

"I can even screw up dying."

Ben drank a shot of whiskey.

"This is kind of a nice trail," Ben said to Meathead. "Quiet. It's so hidden I bet outlaws in the old days used this trail - maybe after they robbed the bank in town or held up a stagecoach. Unless you knew this was here you'd never find it."

They reached the pie in the sky that separated the two hills. It was the entrance to about a five-acre piece of flat sandy land that was completely circled by vertical rock walls that were over fifty yards tall. Ben couldn't see any trails crossing the faces of the walls. The trail he was on was the only way in and the only way out. There were a lot of pinion trees and an area that at one time had been a cultivated field but was now overgrown with juniper trees. There were also the crumbling remnants of three rock buildings that had a good vantage point of where the trail came into the bowl. "Had to be outlaws or somebody on the run," Ben said, "Or some old hermit who really didn't care much for people."

Meathead snorted, "Like you."

"I like some people. I just don't like life," Ben said and headed for the three rock buildings.

Propped up against one of the buildings was a rust

covered horse-drawn plow. "I did that when I was a boy," Ben said as he dismounted. "It would be hot as hell. The bugs would be biting and the mule would plod along knowing her life would be nothing but toil and hardship."

"I guess there has to be some pride or satisfaction in just plodding along."

Ben figured whenever someone had lived here hadn't been more than seventy or eighty years ago. The roofs to the structures were falling in but were not rotted completely away. The roofs were cedar posts set close together, covered with cedar shingles, and then covered with dirt. Brittle grasses grew out of the roofs. There were no openings for windows. One of the structures had two rooms. The rusted-out remains of a wood cook stove was in one room and a rusted out bed frame, no bigger than an army cot, was in the other. A few scraps of the canvas mattress cover remained - the cotton filling long ago carried off by birds and mice for nesting material.

One of the other structures was a three-sided shed that had had a double wooden door - a few remaining boards hung from rusted iron hinges like discarded clothes. There was nothing in the shed.

The last structure was smaller than the others and only one room. In one corner was an old metal trunk, its secrets held secure by a rusty lock. Ben dragged the trunk outside.

He picked up a rock and beat off the lock. The lid squeaked open. The trunk was filled with worn-out cowboy boots. The heels were worn off at an angle and the soles were split and full of holes - boots against the earth, but the earth had won.

Ben counted them. There was eighteen pair. Eighteen years of boots. There was nothing else in the trunk. "I guess this was your legacy," Ben said. "We all seem to want to make a shrine of some kind, even though we all know all shrines crumble in time. Your shrine was a trunk full of worn out boots that you knew somebody would find one day and wonder over. I hope you rest in peace now that your shrine has been seen."

Ben closed the trunk and dragged it back inside the structure.

He walked over to the edge of the once cultivated field that was overgrown with juniper trees. He could picture in his mind whoever had worn the boots walking behind the plow. "You couldn't have had any dreams," Ben said. "Out here by yourself. You were like I am now, merely moving through life, not really caring, but doing something just to be doing it. No dreams, no hope, only wishing for death. Or maybe you were running from the law and somewhere in this dry old sandy dirt you buried your money - money you couldn't spend anyway. Or maybe you just didn't give a shit about anything and you thought you would find peace all by yourself."

"All you found was worn-out boots."

Ben walked back to the two-room structure, sat and leaned back against the warm rock wall. Meathead looked at him but had nothing to say.

Ben looked up at the sky.

"The war was what war is supposed to be," he said to the sky, "ugly and frightening and insane, but at times more touching than anything in life."

"I did my basic in Ft. Polk, Louisiana. The training wasn't bad. I ignored the screaming drill sergeants. They were only doing their job. We ran and fired rifles, tossed grenades, patched up fake wounds, crawled through the mud, and learned to hate the Japanese and Germans, which didn't take much doing since the Japanese had attacked us first and the Germans started the war in Europe. We were the good guys. The country had glory and honor then. Now we do not practice what we preach."

"Every chance I had I wrote Barbara since we could not make phone calls. We were told to never say where we were or what we were doing. I just said over and over how I missed her and how big the hole was in my heart not being able to see her."

"I got a letter from her most nights. But it's strange, you can only tell somebody how much you miss them in so many ways and then with time even the hurt and loneliness start to go away - not completely - but it fades and at times you find yourself not thinking about who you are missing. The love is still there, but not the hurt. When life changes you have to follow the changes. It slowly sunk into my brain that the war was going to go on for a long time and there was no need to dwell on it. I was in the army and would be in the army until I was either killed or the war was over."

"I guess coming to a realization of life is becoming a man."

"I guess becoming a man isn't really what it's made up to be."

"The world would be better off if men kept some good parts of being a boy in them."

"There's no boy in me now."

"Being a cowboy, which became my nickname, I was made an infantry rifleman.

Even though I never like the idea of killing I found I had a knack for shooting like I had a knack for horses. Both trades won't get you far in life."

Ben mounted Meathead and headed back for the trail. Leaving the bowl, he looked back at the three structures. "Too bad," he said. "You also found out there is no place to hide."

Ben rode the way he had ridden in, back tracked to where he had crossed the broken down fence. Instead of heading toward the trailer he headed east. The land was not as hilly to the east and the pinion trees were larger. In scattered draws and gullies were large stands of cottonwood trees. When the cottonwoods released their seeds the pinion trees looked like they were covered with snow. There was a dirt road several miles away that ran to the ranch headquarters, which was another five miles away. Mr. Kutler, during bad years, let people come in and cut dead pinion for firewood - charging them so much a cord. They could not get off the ranch without going by the headquarters and there was no other way to enter the area so they had to pay. Ben had only been on the road once and that was to take a friend of Mr. Kutler deer hunting. For some reason the big bucks liked the cover of the larger trees in the fall. The man was a big shot from back east and only wanted to kill a deer with a big rack so he could have the head mounted in his office or den. He didn't care about the deer or the meat. It was all about the head and the killing. "Put the bastard in the infantry if he really wants to know about killing," Ben cursed.

Ben rode along the edge of the larger trees. Most of the trees were over thirty feet tall, which took several hundred years to reach. Most of the big pinion trees in the state have been cut down, years of firewood depleting them to a few remote stands. "Necessity is an evil thing," Ben said. "I can't count all the things man has destroyed because he had to."

"It's a curse to have to stay warm and eat."

"Man shouldn't have to destroy things now. Man is smart enough to not destroy all he touches."

"Maybe we destroy things because we like to."

"We must have a mean streak."

"Maybe just greed."

"Fuck, maybe...just greed."

"God, if you are up there? If there was only one good man in the world would you kill him out of mercy and not make him suffer so? Or would you just sit and watch him suffer and wonder how much he could take?"

"If there are saints, You are pretty taxing on them."

The pinion trees grew on an average about twenty yards apart - the tips of their branches touching each other like they needed each other's strength to survive. There were numerous birds flying from tree to tree - blue jays, sparrows, and a few yellow finches. Gray squirrels scampered on the ground scrounging for last year's pinion nuts and did not run from Ben as he rode by, but sat up and looked at him seemingly confused. High in the sky two hawks circled, one calling out in a high-pitched cry, hoping to scare a rabbit or squirrel into running and becoming a welcomed meal.

Ben rolled a smoke, lit it, and drank a shot of whiskey. Meathead meandered through the trees not really looking where she was going. Ben didn't really care.

"We were told that after our training we would get a two-week leave and were allowed one collect phone call. When we got back after leave we would get our assignment. Barbara was living at a dorm and when they finally got her to the phone my heart was beating so fast and loud I thought my feet would come off the ground and my eardrums would explode. I could hardly talk but managed to stammer out I love you and that when I got to Denver on the train I'd call. Barbara cried. After the phone call, all the emptiness I had covered up during training came back stronger than ever."

"I met people from all over the country during training - people from New Jersey and Maine and

Wisconsin - people from Texas and Oklahoma and Georgia - one guy all the way from California. At first it was strange hearing all the different accents, but we all discovered that being privates the majority of us were from poor families. The rich kids were officers."

"Meathead, don't ever let anybody tell you that being poor is a good thing. The poor are the poor and get the shit end of the stick. Simplicity in life is only a choice for those who can eat."

"Nobody in training became close friends. We were all headed in different directions after training so there was no need. We did drink a lot at the beer garden and talked about girlfriends, and wives, and home, and what we'd been doing before the war, but there were no friends. I made one friend later, the best friend I ever made in my life, but after he was gone I didn't want to make any more friends. It was like Reno said, 'I don't need another hurt.'"

"Riding the train to Denver I felt proud. I had on my uniform and my shoes were spit shined so bright you could see your face in them. Even with only private stripes I was as proud as a general. I felt like I could walk across the ocean and whip those Japanese or Germans all by myself. I would never get shot, only the other guys. I'd come back with so many ribbons and medals for bravery they'd write books about me."

"The train was filled with soldiers. We drank and sang and talked about when we got home the first thing any of us wanted to do was get the girl friend or wife naked and make love for ten or fifteen hours."

Ben smiled.

"I got into Denver and called Barbara. She borrowed a car to pick me up. I stood in front of the station pacing back and forth like a caged lion. I saw a car stop and Barbara got out. The first sight of her made me dizzy. She was wearing a knee length blue dress and bright red lipstick. The lipstick was brighter than strawberries. She ran to me and I picked her up and swung her around. She hugged me and kissed me, and we slobbered words back and forth, and then we were in the car and at a motel in fifteen minutes. Our clothes were off in a heartbeat and we thrashed around on the bed like wild animals - not giving to each other but taking - taking out the loneliness and the emptiness and the longing. But we didn't make love for ten to fifteen hours, maybe ten minutes."

Ben chuckled.

"Or maybe just five minutes."

"Then we just held each other and didn't talk and we slept. I slept so deep I don't remember sleeping.

When I woke up I felt more rested than I ever had

in my life. I lay in bed looking at Barbara while she slept. Her face was calm. Her strawberry lips smudged. Her eyelids twitched in dreams, dreams I would never see. Her skin was soft and milky and I never wanted her to wake up. I wanted her to live with her dreams forever. I wanted her never to get hurt or feel pain. As long as she slept she would never die, but go on forever in a land between living and death where all things were possible, and there were no wars."

"When she woke up she smiled at me. Not a happy smile but a contented smile and she whispered I love you."

"I told her not as much as I love you."

"We made love again."

"The ten days went by in a daze. We went to the zoo, we went to parks, and we walked around town looking at all the wonderful sights. We made love each night not as desperate as the first day - each time more caring and thoughtful as the day drew closer when we would once again feel the emptiness, and the longing, and the loneliness. Once again we never talked about marriage. A lot of military people were getting married but neither one of us wanted to feel pushed into marriage or desperate. It was not until the day before I had to go back that Barbara told me the army was starting a nursing corps and she was planning on joining. She felt it was her duty."

"I tried to talk her out of it but she insisted."

"I finally told her it was a noble thing to do but it worried me, she could get hurt."

"Not being a nurse she assured me."

"There are no assurances in life."

"When we waved goodbye as the train pulled away I imbedded her image in my mind from the ground up. Her feet, her legs, her stomach, her hands, her arms, her breasts, her neck, her smiling face, her golden hair, her eyes overflowing with love for me and that bright red lipstick."

"Her lipstick looked like blood."

"I should have known. Life is always full of signs that most of the time I miss."

"I should have known."

Ben stopped Meathead and drank another shot of whiskey.

"It was late at night on the train. I didn't have the shade down on the window. Occasionally the train would stop at a small town, a few people would get off, and sometimes a soldier would get on. Then the train would be back in the country and passing a few scattered farm lights. I thought about my folks, and Reno, and I thought about the ranch, and all three of them seemed like a place I had visited so long ago I didn't know if they were real or not. They were more like a dream that is only vaguely remembered."

"I kept looking at the ring Barbara had given me and I felt like it was my protection. Barbara's gift of love was stronger than any crucifix or prayer."

"I didn't feel it then but I know now, if there is a God he has forsaken us."

"I was still awake as the sun started to rise. It was a beautiful sunrise. The horizon was light red, then crimson red, and then the sun came out as gold as Barbara's hair. I looked at the ring and I realized it would have been better for both Barbara and me if we had never met. Love would only be a burden - a heartless distraction that could never fulfill its promise. You cannot love and kill."

"I knew that for a time I would have to learn to not feel, not out of choice but necessity."

CHAPTER THIRTEEN

Ben was assigned to the Seventh Army as a rifleman and was transferred to Ft. Campbell, Kentucky for more training. During his time at Ft. Campbell no one was given leave. In 1943, under the command of General Patton, he was on one of the 2,590 vessels headed to invade Sicily. None of the enlisted men knew where they were going nor were they allowed to write anyone before they departed. They only knew for sure that they were not on the ocean for the fishing.

Ben had told himself he must learn to not feel and had done his best, but after several days on the troop ship he was overcome with longing for Barbara. Ben tried to fight the feeling, but he could not get Barbara out of his mind and the thoughts of her tortured him. It had nothing to do with passion, but there was a hole in his heart that only grew bigger with each passing day. He even found it hard to eat. In defense, he started to read again. Most of the books circulating through the troops were westerns and mysteries. Ben read two to three a day, concentrating so hard to forget everything that was going on around him. To some degree it worked but when it came his time for night guard duty on deck, his longing was the worse. Walking the deck, when all the lights were out, he felt like he was the only person on board the ship. He was stranded forever to go around and around in circles on the ocean and he would never see land again. He would never see Barbara. He would only see the dark forms of the other ships that surrounded them - ships with no one manning them, only pieces of cold, uncaring steel. Ben would look at the stars, vastly different from the Kansas stars or the Colorado stars. They seemed to emerge from the ocean on either side of the ship and then fan out to fill the heavens. But they were not formed in the heavens they were born in the water. During the day the ocean would take the stars back and try with all its might to quench the fire in them, but it was not powerful enough and it would reluctantly have to release them again the next night.

******

Ben stopped Meathead by a large pinion tree and dismounted. He examined the tree. "You've lived through the Civil War, the Spanish American War, the War with Mexico, World War I, World War II, Korea, Vietnam, Panama, Afghanistan, Iraq, and will live through others," he said to the tree. "And none of them had any bearing on your life. While men have been killing each other for no reason except power you have just let it all go by and grown."

"I wonder how a person could go about being a tree?" Ben asked Meathead.

"Probably takes good connections," Meathead said. "Something you're lacking."

Ben walked around the tree, looking closely at all the branches. "You're too good for a hanging tree," he finally said and then lay on the ground, propping himself up on his elbows.

"I was never more afraid during the war than on that troop ship," he said.

"It was not only me, every soldier was morbidly afraid of the ship getting hit by a torpedo. I didn't want to drown in the ocean, or live and then get eaten by sharks, or die slowly from lack of water or food."

"But it's funny I was talking to a sailor one day and he told me it would scare him to death to have to fight on the ground."

"Takes all kinds I suppose."

"I tried everything I could think of to not miss Barbara, but nothing worked. I even tried to write and break up with her, but I threw the letter away when I was done. Being away from her was bad enough, but knowing she was not a part of my life would have been worse."

"I took off her ring, thinking it would help, but I only felt naked without it and put it back on."

"I did not write her for a few evenings, thinking if I didn't write her I wouldn't think about her but it didn't work either."

"For a few days I stopped looking at the photograph we had taken in Denver."

"What a strange thing love is. It takes every emotion to the very limit."

Ben sat up and rolled a smoke and lit it.

"What a strange thing hate is. It also takes every emotion to the limit."

"I think they are brother and sister."

"I got to know a lot of people on the ship but most of them I tried not to get close to. They were more like strangers I'd meet while traveling. But there was one fellow named Lazun. I don't know why we became such good friends. He was an Italian from New Jersey who was always smiling. He and I were good friends from the minute we first met and about as opposite as black and white. He was five feet six inches tall with black hair and black eyes. His black whiskers were so thick that even after he shaved it looked like he needed to shave again. He had big arms and a bull neck and muscular legs, which did him well in the infantry, and he had a wife and a baby girl back home. He was a devout Catholic and wore half a dozen religious medallions around his neck. He never tried to convert me but each night he knelt down and prayed."

"'Cowboy,' he'd say to me, 'one day you're going to have to learn how to pray.'"

"Wop, I'd say. It's never set right with me. I feel like I'm lying when I pray."

"'Then pray for the world, or pray for horses, or some other bullshit thing you dumb ass cowboys think are important.'"

"Lazun had never been on a horse nor wanted to be on one. He had never been to the mountains and couldn't have cared less. Roughing it to him was going to a city park and having a picnic. His father owned a meat market back home and when he got out he was going to work for his father until he inherited it."

"He never showed me the photograph of his wife and daughter he carried with him. He never talked about missing them or how much it hurt to be away from them. But he would go off by himself and look at the photograph. He carried his sadness within himself. It was more because of him that I learned how to control my longing for Barbara."

"I did show him the photograph of Barbara and me once. He smiled and asked me how an ugly guy like me got such a good-looking woman?"

"Lazun, are you flying with my sister?"

"In July, Lazun and I were on the same landing craft at Piano Lupo Beach. It was a nightmare, a day all the demons of the world rejoiced at our misery and relished our fear. I don't know how anyone survived. Lazun and I were together through the complete attack - sharing the nightmare - sharing the fear. After that we were always together - brothers of anguish. At night we would share a foxhole, or a shell hole, and Lazun would tell me about pizza, and sauces his wife made, and all types of food I'd never heard of like calzones and clams and different types of sausages."

"Biscuits and gravy, and steak, and baked potatoes,

and bacon, and lettuce and tomato sandwiches to him sounded like things a person had to eat in prison."

"'When we get out you'll have to come to Jersey and my wife will make you a meal so good you'll never eat that cowboy crap again he would tell me all the time.'"

"We talked about everything there was to talk about. We talked about dreams and hopes. I told Lazun more about me than I ever told even Barbara."

"After several months of advancing we were given a few days rest and everybody took a bath in a river, shaved, washed our hair, and got haircuts. They even brought us a hot meal from the rear. Somebody had stolen some wine from a shelled-out house, which we weren't supposed to do, but dead people don't drink wine. We were all sitting around drinking wine. The birds were singing and for a little while the war seemed far away although we could still hear artillery fire. Lazun handed me his Zippo lighter. By then I was smoking like a fiend, we all were, something about war makes a man nervous. 'Here,' he said, 'I want you to have this, I don't think I'm going to need it much longer and I think it will give you luck. You need more luck than I do since you don't pray.'"

"You going to stop smoking? I asked him."

"'No, cowboy, I think the war is about over for me.

I saw God the other night and he was calling for me to come home.'"

"He didn't elaborate on his vision. He almost sounded relieved."

"I wonder why I've kept the Zippo lighter?"

"I guess it was fitting he got killed in Italy. Him being Italian. I didn't cry when he got shot in the head. I was past crying by then and knew it wouldn't have done any good anyway."

"More tears on the ground won't grow flowers or melt crosses."

"I felt empty like my heart had been ripped out but there were no tears."

"Emptiness is beyond tears."

"I hope he knows I did pray over his body. Not much of a prayer. But I prayed." "Since I didn't pray for myself it didn't feel hollow and needy. But coming from me it probably didn't have much value."

"Lazun you piece of shit wop anyway."

"How can God take a man with a family?"

"Are God's needs more important than a family?"

"I wrote his wife telling her what a brave man he was and how it had been my pleasure to know him. I told her that he talked about her and his daughter all the time and I sent her the photograph he carried of them and the medallions he wore around his neck."

"I think the saints had run out of power with all the killing going on. They didn't have enough grace to go around and had to be picky."

"I gave Lazun's wife my address, but she never wrote back."

"It's funny. I've never had a close friend since Lazun and I've never eaten any of the Italian food he told me about. It never sounded good after he was gone."

Ben took a drag on the smoke and butted it and rolled another smoke and lit it with the Zippo. He looked at the Zippo, most of the finish was worn off - only shiny silver metal showing.

"The night after Lazun was killed I was in a foxhole by myself. There was no moon and the stars were brighter than Christmas tree lights. My sister appeared above the foxhole. I hadn't seen or really thought about her in months. There was my sister, with the stars shining through her, making her radiant, but she was sad. 'When you look up at the sky you don't think about me anymore,' she said."

"It's been hard to think nice thoughts, Lisa, I told her."

"'You just have to look deeper and harder, Ben. Remember I told you never to hate. You have had to do bad things but you can't hate. Promise me you won't hate.'"

"I don't think I can but I'm trying."

"'Please, Ben, promise me.'"

"Have you seen a friend of mine in the sky? I asked"

"'No.'"

"Why do some people get killed and others don't?"

"But she was gone."

"How can you kill and not hate?"

"Philosophers say the only way you can know love is to have experienced grief and hate."

"They're full of shit."

"Stupid bastards."

"Hate only destroys love."

"The only way to know love is to teach it."

Ben stood, butted the smoke, brushed the dirt off his pants and got a shot of whiskey. "Meathead, if you don't do good while you are alive what is the purpose of life?"

Meathead didn't answer.

Ben mounted Meathead and rode away from the tree. He noticed the sky was beginning to cloud up, not clouds that in a few hours would bring rain and lightning, but long wispy clouds that meant in a few days there might be a storm. He didn't know the name of the type of clouds, he just knew what they signaled for the future - more than once in his life he had ignored the clouds and paid the price.

"More than once in my life I've ignored what I knew was right and regretted it," Ben said.

"Regrets are part of life," Meathead said.

Ben took a deep breath and exhaled loudly.

"You're right I suppose, but sadness shouldn't be."

"It is a great transgression," Meathead said.

"New faces came in and out of the unit and after awhile nobody really looked at each other. The war went from day to day, wounded to wounded, killed to killed, and then another new face. The new faces were either overly brave or scared shitless. The old timers made side bets of coffee or cigarettes on which ones of the new faces would get hit first. The lucky ones got a million-dollar wound early and were sent to a hospital. The unlucky ones didn't have to worry or be brave anymore."

"Mail came sporadically, but it came. Sometimes not for a couple of weeks and then I'd get three or four letters from Barbara and every so often one from Peggy. Barbara was in nursing training at Fort Des Moines, Iowa, and when she was done she would get her assignment. She figured she would be sent to England. Her letters were always upbeat, telling me what she was doing, what was going on in the real world and how much she loved me, and that the war would be over soon and I could go back to becoming a famous saddle bronc rider in the rodeo and she would be a nurse."

"I looked forward to Barbara's letters, but as time went by sometimes the letters were a burden. The day-to-day grind left me tired but at least I knew what would happen from day to day. I would either get killed or kill somebody. Then a letter and all the hopes and longing would come back in a great rush. Hope and longing in a war are not good things. They might keep a man going, but it also hurts. It made me dream and I didn't want to dream. It made me look at Barbara's ring and her picture and see things I did not want to think about."

"Peggy would tell me about the ranch. At the time things were ok. There was gas rationing and food rationing, but they were making ends meet. Whitey, Crow, Mac, Moose, and Duke were fine and always said to say hello but they never wrote. Reno had been over to visit and looked well."

"I didn't write Peggy many times and I tried not to think about the ranch. Freedom is a terrible thing to lose and a terrible thing to think about when you really don't have any."

"We did have freedom to kill, though."

"What a freedom."

"Strange. War gives you freedom to kill and the rest of the time killing only gets you put in jail."

"Someday killing might be the only freedom we have left."

"Damn government's trying to make it that way."

"Not just ours but all of them."

'I learned one thing in the war though - all blood is red."

'Makes all people the same."

"We might all be messed up but we're the same."

******

After fighting through Italy, the Seventh Army was moved away from the front and made a part of the Sixth Army group. In August of 1944 they invaded southern France. It was Ben's second amphibious landing and he was promoted to Buck Sergeant. Barbara received orders for a hospital in England. The nurses were going to be transported on a troop ship and she was excited about going.

It worried Ben about Barbara going on a troop ship. Many ships were being sunk by German submarines.

******

A fly landed on Meathead's ear and Ben swatted it. Meathead did not show any thanks. Ben looked up at the sky. The clouds were speeding by overhead like they had an important appointment. They reminded him of people in big cities - going so fast through their lives they never really stopped to look around them, or wonder why in the hell they were in such a big hurry.

"Only in a hurry to die," Ben said.

"It had been over a week since I got a letter from Barbara. I knew she was on the troop ship and I was terrified. Then another week went by."

"And another week."

"I tried my best not to worry about her and started thinking about my sister. I had not seen her since Lazun got killed. I felt her at times looking down at me and I even thought that she might be the only reason I hadn't been wounded or killed."

"Sometimes at night I'd talk to her. Not out loud, but I'd tell her how I felt, and how I was trying not to hate, and how when I got out I was going to get married and try my best to be the number one saddle bronc rider in the rodeo."

"At the time she never answered or appeared to me."

"I felt like I must have let her down."

"I started to think about the men I'd killed. I started to wonder if most of them were like me. Common men caught up in duty and things they had no control over."

"I decided most of them were. They were just young privates and sergeants who thought about their home, and family, and really just wanted to go back home and make love to their wife when she would let him, and have a couple of kids, and maybe go fishing every so often, or go to the bar and have a few beers with the boys."

"By then I'd killed ten men that I knew of."

"I never went to look at them. But I knew when they hit the ground they were dead."

"I'd probably killed more but didn't know it."

"At the time I really didn't hate the men I killed or tried to tell myself I didn't. I just had to kill them."

"How do we dehumanize our enemies so? How do we make them animals so we have no feelings about killing them?"

"I finally got a letter from Barbara. She was in England somewhere out in the country, where exactly she couldn't say. She loved the people and between shifts at the hospital she worked at a USO Club. She told me all the men made passes at her but not to worry because none of them were a stupid cowboy. She sent me a photograph of her wearing her uniform and she was holding up her hand so I could see the ring I'd given her. She was older and more mature and prettier than the day is long."

"I was happy she was in England and not stationed in Africa or Italy."

"We fought our way through France and one day I got a letter from Barbara informing me she was being sent to Italy."

"I read and reread the letter and I remembered the last time I had seen her and I could picture her with her bright blood-red lipstick."

"For days all I could think about was her lipstick."

"Damn lipstick anyway."

Ben stopped Meathead but did not dismount. He rolled a cigarette slowly, lit it, and took several drags. A steady breeze picked up, strong enough to rattle the branches of the trees and make the clouds seem worried.

"During the winter of 1944 I was in the Battle of Alsace and I made E-6. In the spring of 1945, I crossed the Rhine River into Germany. We all knew the war in Europe would soon be over. I had walked half of Italy, most of France, and been on two beach landings, most of the time really not worrying about getting killed, or maybe worrying but not dwelling on it. But now I started to worry - the end was in sight and most of my thoughts were about marrying Barbara and getting back into the rodeos."

Ben butted the smoke and rolled another one and lit it.

"For the first time in close to two years I started to ache with thoughts of Barbara.

I'd done my best to push any desire for her out of my mind, but now I wanted her. I wanted to be in bed with her and feel her softness and hear her laugh. But the thought of it also scared me. How could I be soft? Would I be able to be caring once I got home?"

"Mail kept up with us fairly well but then for over three weeks there were no letters from Barbara."

"I was in the Black Forest when I got a letter from Peggy."

Ben took a deep drag on the smoke and his eyes started to tear.

He wiped them away roughly with the back of his hand.

He took another drag from the smoke.

"Barbara was killed at Anzio, along with five other nurses, when the German's bombed and strafed a tented hospital area. They knew it was a hospital. There were large red crosses painted on the top of the tents."

"She had been buried in Italy and received the Bronze Star and a Purple Heart."

"Damn blood-red lipstick."

CHAPTER FOURTEEN

"With Barbara's death I went crazy, Meathead. I hated the Germans. I didn't sleep or eat much. Nothing mattered to me. I took every dangerous assignment they wanted volunteers for. I even shot two German soldiers that were trying to surrender. I shot the first one between the eyes after he got down on his knees and begged me to not kill him, and then I shot the other one in the back as he tried to run away. I then shot each one of them twice more in the head and then I spit on them. They could surrender in hell. All I wanted to do was kill Germans. Every one of them."

"I really can't remember how long I was that way. Everything was a blur."

"I killed every German I saw."

"Then one afternoon I was out alone on a recon mission. I was sitting on a hill behind a bush when something snapped in me. A bright red flash exploded in my head that almost made me black out, but when it was gone my mind was clear. It was like I was sitting in a crystal clear bubble. I saw trees, and green grass, and I heard a bird singing. The trees and the grass were beautiful and the bird's song was the prettiest thing I had ever heard. I picked a few blades of grass and rubbed them between my fingers. It smelled fresh and full of life and promise. Tears started pouring out of my eyes. I didn't try and stop them. I just let them pour on and on. The bird kept singing. When the tears did stop I no longer felt anything. I did not feel happy, or sad, or lonely, or guilty, or remorseful, or filled with hate. I was only a shell. My skin only covered uncaring bones. My heart was gone."

"On the way back to the front lines I heard sobbing. Instinctively I dove behind a downed tree and inched to the end of it, peaked around the corner, and I saw a German soldier. He was sitting on the ground with his back against a tree and he was looking up like he was beseeching God. His rifle was lying beside him and his uniform was torn and tattered. His face was smeared with dirt. He was sobbing so hard his shoulders shook with each sob and his hands were clasped in front of him in prayer. I put the rifle sights on his heart."

"God hadn't listened to Lazun's prayers why should He listen to the German's?"

"God hadn't protected Barbara."

"God hadn't protected my sister."

"My finger squeezed the trigger slightly."

Ben rolled a cigarette and lit it. The Zippo lighter sounded like a distant bell when he closed it.

The clouds that had been building on the horizon separated into smaller clouds that seemed peaceful and content. The wind settled.

"Meathead, for some reason, all at once, all I could see was the German's face. His tear-stained face filled every inch of my vision and his sobs were like thunderclaps echoing down a mountain canyon."

"He was only a fourteen or fifteen-year-old kid - a kid who should have been in school, or thinking about feeling up his first girl, or taking out the garbage for his mother."

"I knew then that nobody has any control over where we are going to be born or what we will become. We are all born and live out our lives in the culture we are born in to and become whatever that culture expects us to become."

"We are all what we are by accident."

"We are all products of propaganda."

"Some of us are lucky and some of us draw the short straw."

"The sun hit the ring Barbara had given me."

"My sister's voice whispered in my ear. 'Don't hate. Please don't hate, Ben.'"

"Lisa, I said. I am nothing."

"'Look at the sky, Ben. Look at the sky. I can fly.'"

"I looked up at the sky and it was a deep turquoise blue like back on the ranch."

"'Don't hate, Ben. Please don't hate.'"

"I stood up but kept my rifle pointed at the boy. He suddenly saw me but he did not go for his rifle. He only looked at me and his eyes were lost. He did not beg me to not shoot him. He did not cover his face. He only kept crying and praying. I lowered the rifle and ran toward our lines."

"Two days later I was shot by a sniper in the left shoulder."

"I've always wondered if it was that kid that shot me."

"There are no answers, Meathead. There are only questions."

******

For Ben the war was over. He was flown to England, received his Purple Heart, and was in the hospital when Germany surrendered. Although his wound was almost healed and he could have gotten a pass to go into town to celebrate, he did not. He lay in his bed silently looking out the window. But all he could see was Barbara waving at him as he was leaving the train station.

Ben got out of bed and stood by the window. He took off the ring Barbara had given him and he threw it as far as he could. He tore up the photograph of her in his billfold and watched it flutter to the ground. "Love is only for dreamers," he said.

While Ben was in the hospital he spent all his time reading. He didn't play cards with the men, or dominoes, or talk about home. He didn't write any letters to Peggy telling her what had happened to him. He stayed by himself. He was not aloof or unfriendly, but people left him alone. There was a distance in his eyes that even the nurses knew they could not penetrate. For the first time Ben read history and religion. He devoured books like they were food. He tried his best to cover all his thoughts with words - to blanket reality with other people's thoughts and emotions and needs.

One afternoon it suddenly dawned on Ben that it

wasn't that he didn't feel anything in life - it was that he didn't care anymore and he decided that life was just like riding a bronc - everybody in time got bucked off, and when the time came, he would buck himself off.

******

The clouds that had dotted the sky were suddenly gone, like they had displeased some power and the power had wiped them away with one stroke of its uncaring hand.

"At the time I'd never made love to any girl except Barbara," Ben said.

"I had been tempted a few times during the war by whores but they always seemed sad and I never wanted to add to their sadness. There's enough sadness in the world without adding more."

"It was March and I was getting close to being released from the hospital. As soon as I was, I would be shipped back to the states and discharged a free man. The army didn't want me anymore so I wouldn't have to go to the Pacific. Although my shoulder was healed, it would never be one hundred percent again."

"I was sitting outside one afternoon reading. 'Sergeant Sharps,' a soft female voice said. 'I would like to talk to you.'"

"I looked up."

"Her name was Betsy Simmons and she was a nurse. I had seen her around the hospital, but although she was attractive I had never paid any attention to her. I noticed she had green eyes and a soft smile."

"Maybe it was pain from seeing all the wounded and maimed soldiers."

"I smiled at her. The first smile I could remember since Barbara's death."

"'I hate to bother you, Sergeant, Betsy said to me. But there is a dance tonight and I would really like to go. Would you take me?'"

"To this day I don't know why I said yes, but I did. Maybe it was her big green eyes, or her soft smile."

"Maybe it was her body."

"Maybe I just needed somebody to talk to."

"Maybe it was because she needed somebody to talk to."

"'Seven tonight, she beamed. I'll meet you in front of the hospital.'"

"I took a shower, shaved, put on a clean uniform, and even borrowed some cologne."

"I felt like a kid going out on his first date as I waited for her to show up."

"We walked to the dance. She was wearing a

yellow dress and she reminded me of a spring flower. Betsy did most of the talking and never asked me what I had done during the war. She was twenty-two years old, from Indiana, and had been raised on a farm. She was going back soon and in time she knew she would marry some farmer. When she told me, she laughed. I remember her laugh. It seemed foreign to me at first - something alien that I should not trust - something I had forgotten existed. But the more she laughed the more I enjoyed it. It was refreshing. A big band was playing and the dance hall was packed. People were laughing and the cigarette smoke was so heavy in the room it seemed like fog. I took her hand and led her to a table for two. The warmth of her hand scared me at first. I hadn't felt anything warm in years. But her hand held mine like she never wanted to let go. Before we knew it, we had drunk four or five beers and we were dancing to every song the band played. I'd never danced the jitterbug or any of those new fancy dances, but nobody cared. It was fun. Her eyes sparkled and we laughed and drank more beer. During a slow dance I pulled her close to me and kissed her. She returned my kiss feverishly. When we were finished kissing we looked in each other's eyes and we both smiled - not a long lost love smile - not a friend to friend smile - but a warm smile

- a smile only interested in the moment."

"We left before the dance was over and without her asking or me asking we rented a room. It was as if we knew before the last dance we were going to end up in bed together. Betsy turned off all the lights except one and undressed slowly. As she undressed I had never felt such raw passion. When she was down to her panties I undressed. We were like two beasts that had been caged for years, fierce and ferocious but not hurting - our groans and moans erasing part of what each of us had been through - finding for a few hours with a stranger what had been taken from us in war's name."

"In the morning we walked back to the hospital holding hands. We did not talk. We hugged each other lightly before we parted but I could still see a deep sadness in her eyes."

"I did not see her the next day even though I went around the hospital looking for her."

"The next morning I boarded a ship back to the states. Betsy and I had not exchanged addresses and I never saw her again. I bet she married her farmer and had six or seven kids. I hope every so often she thinks about me and wonders how I am."

"I have often thought about her and wished the best for her."

"I should have told her thank you."

******

Ben rode into the middle of a small clearing. The trees circled the clearing perfectly, like they had been groomed for a purpose they did not know, nor did they question or care why.

Ben took a small sip of whiskey.

"As the ship was pulling away from England the decks were lined with soldiers.

No one cheered. We all stood, lost in our own thoughts, and watched the shore disappear and then we were alone on the ocean. It was different not being in a convoy surrounded by destroyers and frigates and minesweepers. That evening I stood on the deck and watched the sun set inch by inch until it was gone - gone like the ocean had swallowed it. I was like the sun. Something had swallowed me."

"The ship was two days out from New York and I was standing by myself by the rail. A low cloudbank hung on the western horizon. The sun had just set making the clouds a bleached wispy red. I wanted to believe that the blood from all the soldiers killed was being cleansed away and now there would be no more wars."

"The urge to jump overboard overcame me. If I jumped, there would be no more emptiness."

"I put one foot up on the bottom rung of the rail."

"The ocean called to me. It would release me. It would give me peace."

"I put my other foot on the rail and was about to climb to the next rail when Lazun's face appeared in the clouds and he smiled at me."

"'Cowboy, you're going home', he said. 'I'm glad you're going home. Now don't be stupid.'"

"I was about to answer, but his face vanished."

"Then my sister flew through the clouds. 'Not feeling is better than hating, Ben,' she said. 'You will never forget what you have been through but in time it will not be a burden and you will feel again.'"

"Thanks Lisa, I said. But I don't think so."

"Then I felt the soft touch of Barbara's hand on my face and her lips on my cheek and a whisper. '"Find love, Ben. Only love will save you. For me, please find love, and become the most famous saddle bronc rider in the rodeo.'"

"Oh Barbara, I miss you so."

"'Every time you ride think about me.'"

"I don't want to be a saddle bronc rider anymore."

"'You must.'"

"Will you help me? I begged."

"There was no answer. She was gone."

"I stepped back onto the deck."

"I shut my eyes and the past months of my life ran through my mind like I was watching a movie - the landings on the beaches - the blood coloring the ocean red - the bodies floating in the water - the bombs and mortars and the various sounds of battle - and the resulting pieces of arms and legs and guts littering the ground - the destroyed cities and the vacant eyes of the children and women and old men who now had nothing - the beseeching eyes of whores. I saw all the men I had killed and the young German soldier sobbing and praying. I saw Betsy - Betsy with her smile and soft eyes and I felt her warm hand as we walked."

"Nothing is real, Meathead. All life is an illusion. We are all bit players in a movie we have no control over."

******

As the ship moored in New York a band was playing, flags were waving and the docks were packed with wives and girlfriends and children. Walking down the gangplank Ben did not feel proud or filled with glory. He felt alone. He was not a part of the festivities. There were no hugs or kisses waiting for him. All he loved was gone - all he had wanted and longed to be before the war seemed useless and without meaning.

He went to the army station, was discharged, and was told he could file for a small amount of disability for his wound. He never did file even when he was broke. He did not file out of pride. He would not take money with Lazun and Barbara dead - it did not seem right.

Ben went to a store and bought a set of civilian clothes, a light coat, and a small suitcase for his toiletries, leaving his military belongings behind. He took a cab to the train station and purchased a ticket for Denver. He thought about calling Dave and Peggy and telling them he was coming to the ranch but decided not to. Six hours later he was on the train.

Ben slept the sleep of the dead most of the time on the train. With each sleep the adrenaline that had flooded through his body during the war slowly receded.

As the train neared Denver Ben saw the Rocky Mountains - for the second time in his life they reminded him of huge buffalo daring anyone to invade their territory. A pang of relief shot through his heart. He remembered the first time he had seen the Rocky Mountains while riding with Reno on his way to Buena Vista, and how the pain of losing his sister and the hate he felt for his parents had vanished, and how he only looked forward to working on the ranch and becoming the best saddle bronc rider in the rodeo.

Ben took the train from Denver to Buena Vista - still not calling Dave or Peggy. There was a lot of snow on the mountain tops. The aspen had barely started to bud and the air was clear and fresh.

It was early afternoon when Ben got off the train in Buena Vista. Nothing had changed. Two boys were happily fishing the stream in the middle of town. A few people were sitting in front of the feed store and the jukebox was playing inside the bar. All the stores still had flags flying in front of them. Ben did not go see Barbara's parents. He knew he would have to in time, but now was not the time. He walked out of town quickly, headed toward the ranch. He did not want to be recognized by anybody and have to stop and have people feel sorry for him.

******

Ben rode out of the clearing. A dust devil skipped through the middle of it and was destroyed by the trees as it tried to escape. He rolled a smoke and lit it.

"I didn't make it to the ranch until about midnight," Ben said to Meathead.

"I didn't try and hitch a ride."

"I just walked."

"Home is a great place. Buena Vista was my home.

Still is in my heart. I've been all over the damn country but a person only has one home."

"When I walked through the gate to the headquarters, the lights were out in the chuck house, the bunk house and Dave and Peggy's. A thin haze subdued the stars. But there was a new pole light that illuminated everything like it was painted a dark gray. There were three horses in the corral. I went and stood by the corral. The horses snorted a few times and then came up to me like they had known me their entire lives. I patted each of their necks and breathed deep the odor of the horses."

"I stood there talking to the horses. I told them everything bad I had done in the war. I told them about Barbara and Betsy. I told them I was a big mess inside."

"They all told me they understood."

"I went into the corral and I mounted a bay. Holding onto her mane she walked around the corral. The other two followed us."

"The haze lifted and the stars came out like they only do in the mountains - bright and vivid and full of life."

"My sister appeared in the sky. She was smiling and she flew around in huge sweeping circles and then she floated in the sky. The stars were her eyes and nose and mouth."

"'Ben,' she said. 'Don't ever forget I am in the sky. Whenever you think life is too much for you, you look up. Promise me.'"

"I promise, Lisa."

"Then she was gone. I rode around the corral all night. I tried to count the stars. I wanted to pick one and put it in my pocket. For awhile there was no past, no future, only the stars, and the horse, and the freedom of it all."

"Everything in my life became a dream except for that moment."

"The sun was coming up when I heard my name being called. 'Ben, Ben,' and Peggy was running toward me. Tears were streaming down her face. Dave came out on the porch. Moose and Crow and Mac and Whitey came out of the bunkhouse. Duke came out of the chuck house."

"They all were running toward me."

"Home. I was home."

******

Ben butted his smoke.

"But Lisa, I never lived up to my promise to you. I looked down at the ground more in my life than I looked up at the sky."

"Some promises are just too hard to keep."

CHAPTER FIFTEEN

Ben went back to work on the ranch but he only stayed in the bunkhouse for a few weeks. Although he felt like he was home he did not feel a part of the ranch and found it difficult to make conversation with the men. He lived day-to-day, but his mind was in the past. He asked Dave if he could build a cabin up in the mountains. He needed to be alone. In a week, Dave and the men and Ben built a twenty-foot by twenty foot one-room log cabin in a small clearing a mile from the main headquarters. The cabin had a tin roof and a porch that faced west. Each wall of the cabin had two windows. They also built a small corral with a shed. They put a sheepherder's stove in the cabin and several kerosene lamps and candles. There was a spring close to the cabin and Ben had a wash tub for a sink. Ben made a bed frame from logs and hauled in a mattress, a wooden table and four chairs - two chairs for inside and two for the porch. He did not put any pictures on the walls and no curtains on the windows. He bought a lot of books - all fiction. History no longer interested him - it seemed history just went around and around and man never learned from his mistakes. He also subscribed to countless magazines.

Everybody at the ranch saw the differences in Ben. At times he would be surly and sharp and he was easy to anger. He drank and smoked a lot and he looked through people when he talked to them. It was like he really didn't see other people, but was looking at something far off on the horizon, so far he couldn't even see it, but he searched for it thinking if he would see it, it would fill in the emptiness that he had become.

The men gave Ben his space and did not try to help him - all of them figuring a man had to work things out by himself. They knew time would heal Ben if he let it - if not, he would crush himself in his own misery and regrets.

Ben worked harder on the ranch than he ever had. It was like work was his vengeance on what life had done to him, or what he had done to life. He got up early and worked until dark. Then he would ride back to his cabin, cook a simple meal, drink, and be alone with his thoughts and his books.

In August the United States dropped two atomic bombs on Japan and the war was officially over.

Ben was glad the war was over but the thought of all the women and children who had been killed from the atomic bombs bothered him and did not seem right. If a country was supposed to be righteous killing women and children was not righteous. He got drunk that night, but it was not in celebration.

******

"I spent one year in the cabin without thinking about getting back on the rodeo circuit," Ben said to Meathead.

"I spent a year dreaming bad dreams and getting drunk and trying to sort things out in my mind. But the more sorting I did, the more I felt I was not a part of the world. I felt like I was two steps out of touch and that nothing in life made any sense. It was like the world went on around me but I was not a part of any of it."

"Looking back, it was a good year in many ways.

Everybody should be alone for a spell during their life. I'd sit on the porch, look at the trees, and the birds, and the sky, and marvel on them. I knew they were not gods and could not save me but they also did not taunt me or want anything from me. They were just something to look at, and occasionally smile over."

"Early in the year my sister appeared to me several times but she would not talk. She'd float in the air, looking at me, like she understood, but she did not question me or ridicule me. She would not smile or frown and then she would be gone."

"Each time she left I felt a small portion of my hurt go with her."

"At times at night I would sit in the cabin and talk to Barbara, although I never saw her. I would tell her how badly I missed her and how I felt guilty about being alive when so many others were dead. I wished she was still alive and we could get married and have that little house close to Denver."

"I think she didn't appear to me because she knew if she did it would only have burdened me more."

"A person can't walk through life depending on ghosts."

"A person should never walk through life always looking back."

"I did learn to look forward once again."

"But it didn't last."

"There were times I'd fly into a rage. I'd scream and holler at the trees. I'd beat on the walls with my fists. Then the rage would leave and I'd feel like a lump of clay that wanted to be molded into something useful but didn't know what."

******

The first year after the war Ben only went into town one time and that was to see Barbara's parents. Ben did not stay long. There was nothing for them to say. The grief of Barbara's death was etched into their faces. They talked small talk and then all three of them cried. Ben hugged Barbara's mother and shook hands with her father and he left. Going back to the ranch, he wished he had not gone to town - it had only made his wounds fester.

That night, drunk from whiskey, he realized for the first time he would never see Barbara's grave, or be able to put flowers on it, but he supposed graves were only for the living anyway - a reminder that life is only dirt.

******

"At the time I thought life would be better without love," Ben said.

"A person can come to grips with loneliness. But

when love is taken away it's the deepest pain there is. It makes loneliness seem almost like a blessing."

"Towards the end of the year I started eating occasionally at the chuck house and I found myself enjoying the small talk of the men."

"One day I noticed how Moose and Crow and Mac and Whitey were getting old and it made me sad, not so much for them, but the fact that I would miss them."

"There's a whole lot of missing in this life."

"During that year I had not been on a bronc and didn't even think about it. The only world there was, was going on in my own head."

"Man can be a selfish bastard."

"It was late October. Before the war I'd always loved the spring the best. But I like fall now. Fall comes in short and sweet and brings with it all the colors there are. It knows it's going to die, and taunts death with its color, and when the winter finally kills it fall doesn't cry. It goes out with a chuckle like it really doesn't give a shit and had a great time making everything so pretty."

"Even in the dead of winter a tree or a bush will have a fall-covered leaf hanging from it, the leaf telling the winter to 'fuck off, you only think you're the strongest.'"

"I was sitting on the porch watching two squirrels burying acorns and there was a mountain jay that would fly down and mess with them. The squirrels would get agitated and scold him and the jay would squawk at them like he had never had so much fun in his life."

"For some reason I thought about Betsy and I knew she was fine and by now she'd married some farmer and was probably pregnant."

"I remembered the deep warmth I felt with her."

"Warmth is a great gift in life. Maybe it's what men and women are really about. Not need, not desire, but warmth."

"Peggy walked up the trail."

"Peggy and I had talked very little during the year and she had never been up to the cabin since it had been built. But as she walked toward me she had a smile on her face. I suddenly felt all her sadness at losing three babies and I wondered how she could bare it."

"Some people are stronger than others."

"But even the strong grow old and tired."

"Peggy sat on the porch with me. For awhile she did not speak and I didn't know what to say. She made me feel nervous. She just looked out from the porch at the trees. There was a cool breeze and it carried the crisp scent of fall - a scent of decay that is also filled with life."

"Finally, she said without looking at me. 'It's beautiful up here. I suppose the world is what we make of it.'"

"At times it's peaceful, I told her."

"'Do you think there will ever be peace in this world?' she asked me.'"

"I don't think so. I told her the truth."

"'I don't either, Ben. So you'd better get off your ass and get back to living.'"

"And she stood and walked back down the trail."

"I watched Peggy until she was about to disappear into the trees. She stopped, turned around, and waved at me but she did not smile. She waved like she would never see me again."

"I waved back feeling ashamed."

"It grew dark and I was still sitting on the porch and Peggy's words kept coming back to me - so you'd better get off your ass and get back to living."

"Get back to living."

"Get back to living."

"Then Lisa flew in from the stars and stopped in front of the cabin. 'Ben, you can fly,' she said. 'You go ride those broncs and you fly. You make people smile and say, 'That's Ben Sharps. He's the best saddle bronc rider the rodeos ever seen.'"

"But Lisa."

"'I'll be with you.'"

"But Lisa."

"'You ride.'"

"Then Lazun appeared to me. He was smiling. 'Cowboy, let me see you ride a bronc and get your ass bucked off and get back on again.'"

"I fell asleep - a sleep as deep as when I had run away from home and slept in the brush pile - a sleep that only earth knows - a sleep put a small amount of fire in my heart."

"I got up while it was still dark and I rode to the chuck house. When I got there Duke was making biscuit batter and the coffee had just perked. Without asking, Duke poured me a cup of coffee."

"I'm going to get back on the rodeo circuit next year, I told Duke."

'It's about time, he said. You want more coffee, get it yourself.'"

******

During the winter of 1946 Ben set up his rodeo schedule for 1947. He was going to do twenty rodeos. Ben still had the money he and Barbara had saved and a small amount of savings from his wages and army pay. He bought a Ford pickup truck and a 14-

foot Trailette camper. It would be his home while going from rodeo to rodeo. Ben put all his old rodeo gear Peggy had saved in his cabin. The word spread to town that Ben Sharps would once again be riding in the rodeo. A writer from the newspaper in Denver came to the ranch and interviewed Ben. The writer wanted to put things in the article about Ben's military service. Ben told him, "Wars aren't anything to be proud of. They are the sin of man and his greed and selfishness. If you write about me in the war, I'll kick your ass all the way across Colorado."

The writer did not mention in the article anything about what Ben had done during the war. He only mentioned he was a veteran and proud of it.

January was bitter cold. There had been little snow but the wind blew constantly and several times it dropped to ten below zero. The men could handle feeding the cattle so Ben decided he wanted to go see his parents and Reno. He didn't hate his parents anymore even he would never understand their treatment of his sister and him.

Ben left the ranch as the sun was coming up. A stiff wind blew from the west and the air was so cold ice crystals hung in the air. The sunlight through the crystals sent tiny rainbows bouncing across the windshield.

As Ben drove he didn't think about his parents. He

thought about when Reno had pulled him up from the ground onto the horse and how warm Reno's wooly coat had been. "Who keeps you warm, Reno?" Ben questioned.

Ben stopped in Tribune, Kansas, for the night. He ate at a small cafe and then went to the bar. Three men about Ben's age were in the bar and eyed Ben suspiciously in the normal small-town manner. Ben nodded at them. They nodded back and then one of them looked at him closely. "I know you from somewhere," the man said.

"I've never been in these parts," Ben replied, and ordered a shot of whiskey and a beer from the bartender.

"I know where I've seen you. I saw you ride in Cheyenne before the war. You're Ben Sharps the saddle bronc rider from Colorado."

The man walked over and held out his hand. "Glad to meet you," he said. "You ride better than any man I've ever seen."

Ben returned the shake and mumbled, "Thanks."

"You going to ride again now that the war's over?"

"Start in May," Ben said.

"Damn, Mr. Sharps, I'm proud to have met you," the man said and went back to his friends.

Ben drank his shot and beer and went to his room.

Lying on the bed he was suddenly afraid. What if he could no longer stay on a bronc?

At four in the morning he headed for his parents' house.

It was close to eight in the morning when he drove into the homestead. The sun was shining and a stiff cold wind was blowing. There was no snow on the ground. There was nothing left of the homestead. All that remained of the barn and house were charred marks on the ground from a fire and a few boards that were burnt up so badly they had not been worth salvaging. The apple tree he used to climb had survived. He heard his mother's scolding voice, "Ben Sharps, you get down from there and go find your sister."

Ben got out of the truck without putting on his coat. The cold wind cut into him and made him shiver. He looked up at the sky. "Why didn't you tell me, Lisa?" he asked.

His sister did not appear.

******

Ben stopped Meathead by a pinion tree that had been hit by lightning years earlier. A scorched trunk barely three feet tall was all that remained. Its branches had been blown into oblivion - all their years of growth not worth the struggle.

"It was strange, Meathead, standing where the house and barn used to be. I didn't feel anything. There were no good memories to recount. I went to where the barn used to be and looked at a point in the sky where the hay doors would have been. I thought of my sister and me sitting there and looking out over the flat land to the edge of the earth, and I wondered what my life would have been if I would not have hit my father with a shovel and run away. I wondered if one day my father would have come home from work and suddenly loved me and we would have made the farm work."

"But going back to the truck, I doubted it."

"My father would have always been a mean drunk. He would have only beaten on me until one day I would have stomped him in the ground and maybe killed him in my rage."

"I started the truck and turned on the heater. The warmth slowly took away my chill as I drove to a neighbor's house."

"Mr. Riley told me my parents had been killed in the fire and were buried in town next to my sister in the pauper's corner of the cemetery. There was no will and nobody had known where I was so the bank sold the land."

"I wouldn't have wanted the place anyway."

"I drove to town and went to the cemetery and found where my sister and parents were buried. I felt bad that my sister was next to my parents. I knew her bones couldn't rest next to bones that had only shattered her dreams and made her try to fly."

"Looking at my parents' graves I didn't say I forgive you, rest in peace. I said nothing. What was there to say?"

"I told my sister I loved her."

"Then I drove to Reno's, strangely glad that all history of my childhood had been erased."

Ben dismounted and rolled a smoke and looked at the charred tree stump. "Nature is as mean spirited as man," he said.

Ben got back on Meathead.

******

When Ben drove into Reno's farm, he noticed it had run down some. There were a few spots on the house that needed painting and some of the fence needed repair. The barn had settled some and listed off to one side like an overloaded ship. The tree where his wife and daughter were buried had grown four or five feet. Even stripped of its leaves by the winter it was still a proud and honorable guard.

There was smoke coming out of the chimney and

Ben noticed Reno had a propane tank now. Ben knocked on the kitchen door but there was no answer.

Ben found Reno in the barn. Reno was restacking some hay bales. Reno's hair was almost all gray and his beard was white, making his blue eyes bluer. He smiled when Ben walked in and limped over to him. "Arthritis is the curse of living too long," Reno said as they shook hands warmly. "Let's go get some coffee."

Reno walked slower and his back was bent forward. His fingers had about doubled in size and Ben knew his hands hurt. Ben felt a pang of pity for Reno but knew he didn't want pity, so he drove the pity away.

Sitting at the table drinking coffee with two tablespoons of sugar in it the men did not talk for awhile. Ben looked around the kitchen and remembered telling Reno about hitting his father with a shovel and running away from home.

******

Ben butted his cigarette. "Sitting in Reno's kitchen I truly felt like I was home," Ben said to Meathead.

"The ranch was home but not Home. Mac and Moose and Crow and Whitey and Duke were friends, but they were not Reno. Reno to me was my father. Dave and Peggy had made me a cowboy but Reno had given me the opportunity to pursue my life."

"Maybe I should have told Reno I was looking for a job and would gladly work for him."

"It was a turning point in my life and I knew it."

"But I never asked and Reno never asked me."

"I wouldn't have been a famous saddle bronc rider."

"I might not be here now on the Kutler Ranch."

"Who knows?"

******

"Well Ben, I guess you're a cowboy now," Reno finally said, like he had been weighing his words and had finally decided on a way to start a conversation without delving into the things he thought Ben might not want to talk about.

"I guess I am," Ben said.

"Most people in life never get to be what they want," Reno said. "You're a lucky man."

"I suppose I am," Ben had to agree. "But sometimes a dream isn't really what you thought it would be."

"I heard about your misfortune and I'm sorry," Reno said.

"I guess we share a pain," Ben said.

Reno looked out the window toward the tree. "I guess we do," he replied, but with no sadness or remorse in his voice.

"I think about you a lot," Ben said.

"I kept track of your rodeo days," Reno said. "I hope you are going to go back."

"I'm going to do twenty rodeos this year. I wish you would come to one and see me ride."

Reno did not comment on the remark. "Peggy wrote me and said you're living in a cabin by yourself."

"It's been nice in a lot of ways and bad in a lot of ways."

"Does the good outweigh the bad?" Reno asked.

"I suppose it does."

Reno smiled and sipped his coffee.

"Are you ever going to sell this place and move to a place you won't have to work so hard?" Ben asked.

"No Ben, I'll drop dead out here one day and hopefully somebody will find me before the coyotes or the buzzards have picked my bones clean. When I was a young man I wanted to go to Alaska and buy a fishing boat. I dreamed about the ocean. I could see the nets overflowing with salmon and almost touch the seagulls as they flew around the boat. I dreamed so hard I could smell the seawater and the fish. I would have never milked a cow, or plowed dirt, or watched a crop fail. But the worse thing is, if I would have followed my dream, maybe my wife and daughter would not be out there by that tree. I've never even seen the ocean and dreams don't really matter much to me now. I've learned you have to play the hand you're dealt although most of them are only worth folding."

******

"It was different talking to Reno after not seeing him for several years," Ben said to Meathead.

"I wanted to tell him thank you for everything he had done for me. But I never did."

"We sat for a few hours talking about small things, things that don't really matter in life, and then I left."

"Riding back to the ranch I realized time changes us all, pulls us deeper into our own minds, so deep we stop looking out at the world and we only see the fleeting images that dart through our minds. We take those images and make them what we are. We take our own thoughts and think they are better than other people's thoughts, but everything we think is true might not be true to another person. Funny - there is truth but there is no real truth."

CHAPTER SIXTEEN

It was a dry early spring and the first week of April Dave bought ten wild horses. Peggy had asked him to buy them so Ben could practice before he got back on the rodeo circuit. Dave figured he could at least break even on the deal and hoped it would help Ben. He told Mac, Moose, Crow, and Whitey not to tell Ben.

One morning, when Ben rode into the headquarters, Dave and all the men were standing by the corral looking at the just delivered wild horses.

After tying his horse Ben was so excited he ran to the corral. "Some of these might test you," Whitey said with a wry grin.

"Your old bones won't bounce back off the ground like they used to," Crow said.

"I'll bet every one of you five bucks I can ride them all for eight seconds before I eat dirt," Ben said, not looking at the men but admiring the horses.

The men glanced at each other, walked off a few yards, and talked to themselves for a few minutes. They came back and Mac said, "You're on, Ben, but we all want you to know we'll feel bad about taking your money. Riding six horses without a spill is one thing, but riding ten would be a miracle."

"I know," Ben smiled. "If you win you'll lose sleep over it."

"But there's one condition," Dave said.

Ben eyed him suspiciously.

"We're going to invite all the other ranchers over next Saturday to watch you ride and have a party. We haven't had a good party in years. But you can't practice on any of the horses and you have to stay on each horse for ten seconds not eight."

"That's more than one condition," Ben said, but he agreed, saying to Dave with a smile, "You keep honest time if you bet against me."

"Party will start at noon. You ride about three," Dave said.

Late that afternoon Ben was about ready to ride back to the cabin when Peggy came over to him. "You have the boys counting their money already," Peggy

said.

"They'd better not count it too quickly," Ben replied, but he really figured he would lose.

"It will be a good party," Peggy said. "We all need a party."

Without thinking or knowing why, Ben replied, "I hope there are a few single women coming."

Peggy smiled and walked away.

"Peggy," Ben called.

Peggy turned around.

"I want to thank you for coming up to the cabin when you did."

"You ride your sadness out, Ben. It will never go away, but you can beat it."

"I hope so," Ben said.

"For the party you wear your American flag fringed chaps, those fancy silver spurs with the big rowels, and that buckle you won in Pueblo. Give them a show, Ben. We all need a show."

******

"The next Saturday was a little chilly but there was not a cloud in the sky, Ben said to Meathead. "There were over two hundred people at the ranch. Some people had to park more than half a mile away. People came from town and from ranches as far away as fifty miles. Dave had phoned a few people and told them to invite everybody they knew. Word had then spread like a wildfire that I had taken a bet I could ride ten broncs in a row for ten seconds before getting bucked off. People brought guitars, banjos, harmonicas, and fiddles. Others were cooking hamburgers, and steaks, and hot dogs, and there were pies, and potato salad, and cold slaw, and cold beer and whiskey - all for the taking. Even Duke was having a good time - probably because he didn't have to cook. People were laughing and making small talk but they'd all come to see me ride."

"Everybody was making side bets."

"I did what Peggy asked. I had on my American flag colored fringed chaps, and fancy spurs, and my big buckle from Pueblo. I was wearing a bright blue shirt with long white fringe on the yoke and a white hat. I'd also tied a yellow bandana around my throat and had even gone to town and bought a pair of leather gloves."

"Whoopee shit did I look like a dandy!"

"Everybody shook hands with me and introduced me to friends."

"'I hope you land on your ass,' some men would laugh."

"'I'm betting on you,' others would say."

"I didn't eat. I didn't want to throw up in front of a lot of people if my guts got all shook up. But I did drink a few beers."

"The night before, I couldn't sleep. It was like the first rodeo in Pueblo when my stomach was filled with spiders and scorpions and I was filled with doubt."

"But seeing the people who had come only to see me, I lost all my fear. I felt special. I was taking the people away from all their fears, and wants, and worries over life. For a few minutes or hours they were thinking only about me and I swore I'd ride every one of those horses."

"After awhile I wanted to be alone and I went and sat by a tree close to the chuck house. For the first time since the war there were no bad thoughts in my mind. There was no remorse or sadness."

"You help me ride Lisa, I said to the sky."

"You be with me, I said to Barbara."

"Lazun, this cowboy isn't going to get bucked off."

"Then it came to me that it really didn't matter if I rode all ten of those wild horses or not. It didn't matter if I rode one or two or three. The people were going to have a good time no matter what I did."

"I looked back at the sky and there was Lisa. She was smiling so big her smile made me smile. 'Don't worry about my bones resting next to Ma and Pa, she said to me. 'Bones don't mean anything.'"

"I felt Barbara's lips on my neck. 'Find love Ben, find love, and ride those horses for me.'"

"I shut my eyes and sighed."

"When I opened my eyes there was a young lady looking at me. In an instant I saw she had long black hair, eyes the color of rich black dirt, and a figure that no man could ignore. Her pants and shirt were so tight on her they looked like they'd been painted on. She smiled and two dimples appeared on her face. Not little girl nice dimples but dimples with a touch of naughty in them."

"'I don't want to be rude, she said to me, 'but I saw you and I thought maybe before the night is over you would like to dance.'"

"I'd love to dance, I said."

"'You'll find me,' she said. 'My name is Rose.'"

******

Thirty minutes before he was due to ride, Ben stood by the holding pen where the wild horses were. Unlike the first time he'd ridden a bronc he felt sorry for them. He pictured them getting captured and he knew they were both angry and afraid. "You will never know freedom again," he said to the horses. "I'm sorry for that but there is nothing I can do."

By five minutes to three people were crowded around the corral five and six deep and Whitey and Mac had the first horse saddled.

Dave was in the middle of the corral. "Ladies and gentlemen, I would like to introduce Mr. Ben Sharps," Dave hollered.

Ben walked into the center of the corral, took off his hat and waved. The people clapped and whistled as Ben and Dave shook hands. "Good luck," Dave said, and walked away.

Ben slowly turned in a circle and looked at all the people. He saw Rose and he walked over and gave her his bandana. "I'll get this back when we dance," he said.

All the men in the crowd whistled. Some of the women smiled and some of them frowned.

******

"I tell you Meathead as I started to walk to that first horse I don't remember my boots hitting the ground. Suddenly I was so afraid I didn't really know where I was. The faces of the people circling the corral blurred and started spinning around like I was the center of a spinning top. Their cheers and hoots and whistles were louder than an avalanche in my head. My stomach knotted up so tight I had to fight to not bend over.

When I got to the horse, Whitey looked me straight in the eyes and said, 'Ben Sharps, I'd just as soon lose my five dollars.'"

"Thanks Whitey, I mumbled."

"I put my foot in the stirrup, took the reins, grabbed the saddle horn and suddenly the crowd grew as quiet as if they were in church. I looked up at the sky and there was one little powder puff cloud and it seemed to smile at me. Then I was in the saddle."

******

Ben stopped Meathead and drank a shot of whiskey and rolled a smoke and lit it.

He looked at the pinion trees and the dry rock-strewn ground. He looked at the sky. There wasn't even a rabbit's hair of wind or the chirp of a bird to disturb the silence. He rubbed his chin. He took a drag on the smoke and inhaled deeply, pulling the smoke into the very bottom of his lungs and exhaled slowly.

"I rode seven horses in a row without a hitch," Ben said. "Not even coming close to a fall."

"Dave gave me five minutes between rides to rest up."

"The eighth horse knocked me off but I'd already been on ten seconds. But I landed hard and it knocked the wind out of me. Mac and Whitey had to help me up.”

“The ninth horse also knocked me off a hair past ten seconds.”

“But a hair is enough. If a bullet misses a person by a hair it might as well have been a mile.”

“But I landed on the shoulder I’d broken and been shot through and it felt like somebody had run a red hot sword through my shoulder.”

“Mac and Whitey half drug me to the edge of the corral. Mac was concerned. ‘Maybe you should just let this one go,’ he said.”

“I shook my head.”

“The tenth horse was the biggest and meanest. He was blacker than midnight, his eyes were spooked out and his mouth was foaming. Whitey and Mac could hardly hold him down. He was prancing around, kicking, and throwing his head, and was so agitated he’d broken into a sweat.”

“Looking back, my head had been rattled around so much I think I was unconscious on my feet.”

“I half stumbled to the horse and pulled myself into the saddle, barely able to move my left arm.”

“Not one person in the crowd was making any noise and I could feel that they were nervous and feared for me.”

"When Mac and Whitey let go, the horse bolted higher into the air than I'd ever been. I slipped to the left and almost went off but I caught myself just as he shot up again. I almost went off again but managed more out of luck than skill to stay on."

"Then the horse went crazy. He bucked and twisted left and right, but suddenly I felt hands holding onto me. Lazun's hands, and sister's hands, and Barbara's hands, and I knew they would not let me fall."

"I spurred the horse hard and took off my hat and waved it above my head."

"I didn't give a damn if my shoulder hurt or not."

"When Dave signaled ten seconds, Lazun, and Lisa, and Barbara, let go of me and that horse bucked me so high in the air I swear I was higher than the trees. I saw every face in the crowd look at me and just before I hit the ground I heard the crowd moan in unison."

"When I woke up, I was stretched out underneath a tree with my hat beside me. Peggy was wiping my face with a wet towel and Dave was pressing on my ribs. People were all around me looking worried and talking in whispers."

"Dave had checked all my bones. 'You're not busted up,' he said."

"I sat up slowly and my vision came in and out of focus."

"Did I ride him? I asked Peggy."

"'You sure did,' Peggy beamed, and kissed me on the forehead."

"I put my hat on and stood and ran to the trees and threw up my guts."

"The people started hollering and laughing."

"Whitey and Mac and Crow and Moose let me puke and then they picked me up by my arms and legs and carried me to a stock tank and tossed me in."

"I sputtered and spit and kept putting my head underneath the water until all the cobwebs were gone."

"When I clambered out of the stock tank, more beers were shoved in my face than I could count. I started drinking. People were pounding me on the back, shaking my hand, and talking so fast I didn't know what in the hell they were saying. But it didn't matter, I'd ridden all ten."

"Whoopee shit!"

"Ridden all ten."

"Then the guitar players, and the harmonica players, and the fiddle players were playing and I was dancing with Rose."

"I could have been dancing with her grandmother

and had a great time."

Ben butted the smoke, dismounted, and holding onto the reins he started to walk. He didn't look around him but he looked at the ground. "Glory is a small thing in life," he said.

"Glory and fame really don't mean too much. It's like it happens to a few people to give other's something to strive for or want to be. It's like a good party. When the party is over all that's left to do is clean up the mess."

"I sure enjoyed the glory of that day though, even if I did puke in front of several hundred people."

"I was proud and people were proud of me and for me."

"I learned later on, fame and glory have a way of drawing a lot of bad people to it. People who only want to use others."

"So it is, Meathead."

"So it is."

"I don't know how I got to my cabin after the party. I don't remember getting there or going to bed. I woke up in the morning feeling like a ton or rocks had been dumped on my body and lying next to me was Rose. We were both naked. She got out of bed and got dressed, kissed me on the cheek and left."

"It's a sad thing in life to make love to a beautiful

woman and not be able to remember it."

"I never saw Rose again. I heard she had been passing through town and heard about the party and decided to come out to the ranch."

"I do know whatever man latched onto her might have had a rough road. A woman who paints on her clothes and has naughty dimples should make a man wary."

"After the party I was fine for awhile," Ben said.

"I didn't think about Barbara or the war. I didn't have any bad dreams and I slept good."

"I didn't feel complete but I didn't feel empty."

"In early May I went to Colorado Springs to a rodeo and took second place and then I went to Durango and got third. When I got back to the ranch, Peggy told me Reno had been killed. He was pulling sweeps and fell off the tractor and the sweeps had cut him almost in half. He might have fallen asleep or he might have had a heart attack. Nobody knew. She was sorry I had missed the funeral but they had buried Reno next to his wife and daughter."

"Peggy said Reno doing something he loved was a good way for her brother to die, and even though he had left her the farm, she was going to sell it."

"I didn't tell her about Reno's dream of owning a fishing boat in Alaska."

"That night at the cabin I sat on the porch drinking whiskey. There was no moon and thin wispy clouds drifted listlessly through the sky. I thanked Reno for the hand up on his horse when I was a boy and letting me wipe my tears on his woolly coat. I thanked Reno for letting me sit by his wife and daughter's graves. I thanked him for taking me to Colorado. I hoped there was a place after death for people who had never realized a dream. I hoped Reno was somewhere on a fishing boat with his wife and daughter, and the nets were so full of salmon they could barely lift them into the boat. I hoped the saltwater smell was so strong it was all Reno could smell. I hoped there were so many seagulls in the sky he couldn't see the sun."

CHAPTER SEVENTEEN

For a reason that Ben did not understand Reno's death made Ben feel isolated and confused by the world more than he ever had been.

He started drinking heavier than he ever had, beginning each day with a shot of whiskey and always ending the day drunk. He smoked cigarette after cigarette until the fingers he held the cigarettes with were stained yellow. The men started to avoid him and Dave was thinking about firing Ben - a drunk cowboy would only end up getting hurt or hurting someone.

When Ben left the ranch for the next rodeo he saw in Peggy's eyes a great disappointment and he knew he should not come back to the ranch until he could work things out within himself. It was not right to weigh people down with a burden that was not theirs. When he was leaving, the men shook hands with him differently - more a farewell than a good luck.

Ben went from rodeo to rodeo with a grimness that verged on hate. What exactly the hate was centered on, he did not really know - but hate kept him going. He also stopped reading - reading was just another useless endeavor in life. After a rodeo in Casper, Wyoming, Ben wrote Dave and told him thank you for all he had done for him but it was best if he did not come back to the ranch. He said to tell the men hello for him and to divvy up between them the tack from his rodeo winnings he had left behind. He also said to tell Peggy he was sorry.

After he mailed the letter he felt relieved. There was nobody in his life he could let down.

Now when Ben rode a bronc he was ruthless, spurring the horse as hard as he could, secretly wishing that one of the broncs would throw him and break his neck. But even with his emptiness and hate, his fame grew. Ben Sharps, who had ridden ten broncs in a row two seconds past time. Ben Sharps, who rode like a man possessed. Ben Sharps, the fearless veteran of World War II. In 1947, Ben never placed worse than third in any rodeo he entered.

In the cowboy world, Ben was becoming a household name. The magazines and newspapers were always showing photographs of him waving his hat and spurring the bronc on. They didn't mention that half of the time he was so drunk he couldn't speak without slurring his words, and he was surly to reporters. They didn't mention he had a reputation of getting in fist fights in bars and didn't really care if he won or lost - hitting or getting hit had the same grim satisfaction to Ben.

They also didn't mention that he didn't have any friends on the circuit. The other cowboys respected his ability but they thought he was crazy and dangerous. Ben rode, got drunk, rode, got drunk, and then went on to the next rodeo. He didn't care if he had any friends or not. What were friends but something that could be lost?

With his fame also came women.

******

"You know Meathead I really don't know what went on in my head back then. I think I embraced sadness. I was too stupid to look at all the good things life was giving me. There has to be a reason some people live and some people die. Who knows what the reason is, but there has to be a reason."

"I struck out at life like life was my enemy, and

besides being a drunk, I used people - mainly women."

"People shouldn't use people."

"It is a great transgression and only causes regrets."

"Regrets for the user and pain for the used."

"At every rodeo there were always women who wanted to go out with me. At first I ignored them. I didn't have any interest in women. I didn't have any interest in anything except riding a bronc. But then I started picking up a woman at the beginning of the rodeo. From rodeo to rodeo it was the same thing. Pick up a woman, go to a bar, drink, end up in my camper, and then, when the rodeo was over, saying goodbye with a promise to write or call. But as soon as I was on the highway I forgot all about them."

"I imagine a few of them really did like me and weren't taking their clothes off only because I was Ben Sharps. But none of them made me feel warm or needed - they just made me feel emptier."

"I spent four years on the road without ever going back to the ranch. I did rodeos in every western state and three provinces in Canada. When the last rodeo was over for the season, I'd stop in a town and rent a room for the winter. I had tons of money and had signed with an agent named Phil Stephens out of Reno. He managed several cowboys on the circuit and seemed to be honest. He did all my bookings, got me endorsements, and he received ten percent of everything. I even joined the Pro Rodeo Association. Why, I don't know. Organizations of any kind have never set right with me. All organizations are comprised of people who think the same and like to pat each other on the back."

"I did ads in magazines for saddles, bits, chewing tobacco, trucks, and cigarettes."

"I did ads for western shirts, Levi's, belt buckles, hats, and even one for dog food. Like a dog gives a shit about some dumb-ass saddle bronc rider."

"Phil was handling all my finances and was supposedly depositing my money into various accounts and investing some for when I was old. Whenever I called him he would send me whatever money I needed and statements as to how much I had.

There was one point I had close to fifteen thousand dollars. But I spent money like it was water, never looking ahead or thinking my rodeo career would ever end."

"People tell you to live each day like it will be your last."

"That works unless you live too long."

"It works if you have money."

"I had a new truck with my name in big fancy

letters on the door and a new trailer with all the company logos that sponsored me stuck all over it. The trailer was big enough for six people. I had new clothes, boots, hats, and more shirts than I could wear."

"All the buckles and saddles and tack I won I sold and blew the money on booze and women."

"During those years, Lisa never appeared to me. It was like she was tired of seeing me drunk and lost and had given up on me."

"Hell, people have to give up on a person if they have given up on themselves."

"Several times I wanted to go visit Dave and Peggy and see the men, but I didn't.

Even with my fame, I knew I was a disappointment to them."

"But I missed the cabin. I missed the nights sitting on the porch alone and looking at the stars. I missed the mountains and the freshness of them. I missed talking to the men and eating in the chuck house."

"At times, half-drunk out of my mind, I would no longer feel empty or hateful but I would feel a terrible loneliness - a loneliness that wasn't all for me. The world seemed lonely and no matter what, it would always be lonely. I knew there was nothing I could do about it - or anybody could do about it."

"Meathead, I needed love."

"I didn't know it then, but it was true."

"But you can't buy love."

"You can't even look for it. It has to find you."

"Through it all I still dreamed of the war. The dreams were as vivid as the real experience and they left me weary and full of questions."

******

In May of 1951 Ben was in Boise, Idaho. It is a pretty town with the Boise River running right through the center of town. He'd arrived at the rodeo grounds three days before the rodeo was to start. He had spent the winter in Spokane, Washington, and he had cut back on his drinking and smoking. He had somewhat enjoyed the winter, finding at times he was not haunted by memories of the war or Barbara or Reno's death. It could have been the snow or the images of the distant mountains or it could have been merely time. Whatever the reason, Ben felt better than he had in years. He had written Dave and Peggy and told them he missed the ranch and thanked them for all they had done for him.

Peggy wrote back saying they followed his career and he was handsome in all the advertisements he was doing. All the men were fine, a little slower, but still fine, and Duke was still quiet and a bit crankier.

Dave was getting arthritis in his hands and the cold bothered him a lot. She was doing well and was trying to talk Dave into taking her to Mexico the next winter. She had always wanted to go to Mexico. In all the years they had been together they had never been on a vacation, unless a weekend in Denver was a vacation. She had also sold Reno's land. She ended the letter with - now you write, we all miss you, you know you always have a home here.

She did not ask about his drinking.

The letter made Ben smile and he put it in a cardboard box where he kept the clippings and photographs of himself.

It was late in the afternoon, and Ben was sitting on the steps to his trailer, when, for the first time in his life he felt the rush of time. He was thirty-three years old. If he was thirty-three Dave and Peggy had to be in their sixties and the men at the ranch had to be close to sixty.

******

"Meathead, I was sitting on the steps of my trailer and it was like a light bulb went on in my head. The last years of hating and drinking and loneliness seemed to evaporate with the flash of light. I saw what was around me for the first time in years. It wasn't like the flash that had entered my head during the war that left me feeling empty. I was still empty, but I could control it."

"Lisa appeared in the sky. She was still young and beautiful and she smiled at me - a caring smile - not a gleeful or happy smile - more a smile a mother gives an older child when they have gone off on their own and done well."

"I've missed you, Lisa," I said.

"'You can really treat yourself badly over things you have no control over,' she told me."

"I'm kind of a sorry person."

"'Ben, you have to let the world be what it is going to be. You can't change it and you can't change what has happened.'"

"I know, but I don't seem to have any power over how I react."

"'You are going to meet a lady soon and fall in love.'"

"That would be nice. I'm tired of being alone."

"'You're not alone, Ben. There are thousands of people all over the country who know who you are. You're Ben Sharps, the best saddle bronc rider the rodeo has ever seen. You made your dream, Ben.'"

"I need a new dream. I didn't live up to my potential."

"Lisa smiled at me again. 'You keep forgetting to look at the sky and think about me,' she said and was gone."

"I sat on the steps for about another hour, not thinking about anything when a truck towing a horse trailer pulled into the rodeo area and stopped next to my trailer. A lady got out of the truck, smiled a fleeting smile at me like she really wanted to be alone, but she felt like she had to be polite. Then, without looking at me again, she unloaded a bay quarter horse from the trailer that was already saddled and bridled and led him into the arena and started riding."

"Meathead, my heart flipped over about six times and my throat went dry."

"I walked over to the fence that circled the arena and watched the lady ride. She was a good horsewoman, not the best, but good. She was not beautiful in a striking way, but she was pretty. She had an oval face, big round eyes that I could not see the color of, shoulder-length auburn hair, and strong almost manly shoulders and arms. She did not have any makeup on and she was wearing black Levi's, scuffed cowboy boots, and a white sleeveless western shirt. Every time she rode by me she did not look at me."

"I waved twice but I might as well have been waving at the wind."

"I went back to the trailer and sat on the steps, figuring I'd try to talk to her when she came back."

"About an hour later she walked her horse back and loaded him. I stood and said in my most friendly voice, 'Hello, I'm Ben Sharps.' She looked at me like I was invisible and replied, 'hello,' like the last thing she wanted to do in the world was say hello to me. She got in her truck and drove off."

"I was dumbfounded, Meathead."

"Some women have good sense," Meathead said.

"I did notice she was not wearing an engagement ring or a wedding ring."

"That night all I could think about was the lady."

"The next day all I could think about was the lady."

"During the rodeo parade I hoped to see her in the crowd but she wasn't there."

"The evening of the rodeo, as the bleachers were filling, I looked and looked for her but she was not there or I'd missed her."

"The first night when I rode I was thinking of the lady so much I had a terrible ride and was in fifth place after the evening was done. But I really didn't care."

"The second night the lady wasn't there again and once again I had a bad ride, but I moved up to fourth place.

"In my trailer that night I remembered how I felt

when I first met Barbara. I didn't feel the same way thinking about this lady, but how it was different I didn't know. I only knew I wanted to meet her, and if I did meet her, I wanted to marry her."

"Love at first sight is a great thing."

"Love is a great thing."

"I was about to get in bed when I felt a warm hand on my face and Barbara whispered to me. 'You will find love Ben, but don't throw it away by being stupid. Love doesn't take, it gives.'"

"For the first time I realized that even with my love for Barbara I never really thought about how she felt. I wanted to be the best saddle bronc rider in the rodeo and I had never really thought about what she needed."

"Maybe she needed you to be the best saddle bronc rider in the rodeo," Meathead said.

"Maybe she needed a friend more, Meathead."

"The last night of the rodeo I looked at every seat in the grandstands. The lady was not there but I told myself if I did not see her I would go all over Boise, Idaho the next day until I found her."

"I drew a horse called Midnight Sin and I had no sooner gotten out of the gate than the horse sent me flying over his head like I was nothing more than a piece of popcorn. The last thing I remember was trying to spin in midair so I didn't land on my back."

******

Ben rode out of the pinion trees and stopped. In front of him were dusty brown rolling hills that looked like they belonged in a different country. On the edge of a hill less than a half mile away was a windmill. There was no wind and the windmill blades were not moving. Ben figured they couldn't care less if they ever did.

Ben rolled a smoke, lit it, smoked leisurely until the cigarette was gone, and then nudged Meathead. "We'll go get you a drink," he said, feeling thirsty himself.

He thought about his daughter and hoped she received the letter that was in his pocket.

******

"When I woke up after being bucked off Midnight Sin, I didn't know where I was," Ben said.

"I couldn't focus my eyes, everything was fuzzy and gray. But there was a smell that at first I couldn't identify. Then it dawned on me. It was the smell of medicine. My eyes came into focus and I was in a hospital bed with an IV stuck in my arm. My head throbbed so bad I felt like my eyeballs would pop out. The sunshine was coming through the window. I had been out all night. A strange thought came to me. I could have been killed and wouldn't have even known it. It was like men blown up by bombs or shot in the head during the war. All their wants and desires were gone in a mere instant – dreams and desires all for nothing."

"But maybe that's all life really is – all for nothing.

"I was looking out the window when I heard a person walk into the room. I smiled at the nurse. I want to marry you, I said."

"'You dumb-ass cowboy. All you want to marry is a horse,' she said, but with a slight grin. 'Now roll over. I need to give you a shot where your brain is.'"

******

Meathead drank deeply from the stock tank by the windmill. Ben went to the other side of the tank and drank, tossed water on his face and then soaked his hat in the water, wrung it out, and put it back on.

He took a shot of whiskey and then dipped the whiskey bottle in the stock tank, filling it close to two thirds full and put it back in the saddle bag.

A sudden gust of wind made the windmill blades turn one revolution and then the wind was gone - letting the windmill know it didn't give a damn about its function or about water.

Six doves sailed toward the tank, saw Ben, and veered north.

Ben thought about the ranch he had worked on in southern, Arizona. In the fall he would sit by a stock tank and shoot twenty to thirty doves an evening. One day he shot a dove and the puff of feathers as the shot ripped into the dove seemed to magnify in Ben's mind and freeze in that one instant - the feathers did not float to the ground and the dove hung in midair - one more breath between life and death. Then the dove thudded to the ground and the feathers drifted off with the breeze. Ben felt sorry for the dove - sorry for the feathers. The dove only needed water and Ben had shot it.

Ben never shot another dove although he liked them fried in bacon grease when other people shot them. Even eating was a riddle of life.

Ben mounted Meathead and headed north toward a series of tree-studded hills where the doves had flown.

******

"Her name was Nancy Cook. Her eyes were so green everything green on the face of the earth paled compared to them. When she was happy, they seemed to sway like tall green grass when the wind hits it. When she was mad, they shot green darts that were so intense they scorched a person."

"The doctor told me I had received a serious

concussion when Midnight Sin tossed me and that I should not ride for at least six months, if even then. It dawned on me then that even though I was only thirty-three years old I was getting old for a saddle bronc rider. The thought of it scared me and I could see myself like Duke, cooking at some ranch, too old and washed up to do anything else, or being like Mac and the men working for a couple of hundred bucks a month."

"But even with the fear I knew I would not stop riding until I had to or it killed me."

"Stubborn and hardheaded are no way to be in life."

"Brains aren't your strong suit," Meathead said.

"That's why you and I get along," Ben replied. "Stupidity suits us."

Meathead snorted.

"I was in the hospital for three weeks. Phil Stephens, my agent, called me once telling me tough luck and to call him when I got better and could get back on the circuit."

"For three weeks, Nancy ignored me. She was friendly like a nurse should be but I was no more than a patient. I had flowers sent to her at the hospital and all I got for it was the remark, 'Thank you.'"

"As I got better I could walk around the hospital

and eat in the cafeteria. I asked Nancy to eat lunch with me - no. I asked her to go for a walk with me - no. I asked her if she would play cards - no. I asked her if she had a boyfriend - no, which was a great relief. I wanted to ask her if she would come to my room, take her clothes off, dance for me, then jump in my bed and give me another concussion but I knew the answer."

Ben chuckled with the thought.

"I asked all the other nurses about her and found out Nancy had been engaged once but he had left town with another woman. All I could find out about the guy was that he was a worthless cowboy - which didn't do my cause any good. I did find out Nancy lived in a house with a little acreage for her horse. Her only love was riding."

"The more Nancy ignored me the more I ached inside."

"But it was a good ache."

"For all my time in the hospital I didn't drink or smoke and I didn't miss either one. I also started to read again and found out how much I missed reading. But I also found out what a mess the world was in, and the news about Europe, Russia, and Korea bothered me. Every time I read about a war in the world it always rekindled my thoughts of the war and Lazun."

"I did not think about my sister or Barbara or Reno."

"Why, I don't know? But for that period of time they never entered my mind.

It's a strange thing in life what haunts people at times and not others. It's like the demons just bide their time waiting for that weak moment and then they rip into a person's heart and guts."

"The doctor told me I would be released from the hospital in two days. I called my agent, Phil Stephens, but he was never in his office and did not return my phone calls. At the time it did not bother me. I had close to $800 in my pocket so money wasn't an issue."

"The day before I was to be released, Nancy came to my room. 'Well cowboy,' she said. 'I guess you can get back in your truck and in a few weeks jump on another horse until you finally draw one that will kill you.'"

"It's all I know what to do, I told her."

"'That's the problem,' she replied sadly, looking at me with those big greener- than- grass eyes."

"I knew then she liked me. It was just that I was a dumb-ass cowboy."

"I'd stop being a cowboy for you, I said."

"'Maybe for awhile you would, but it wouldn't last. I know it wouldn't.'"

"Would you please go out to dinner with me tomorrow tonight? I asked, trying not to sound like I was begging."

"Nancy looked out the window, looked at me, and looked out the window again."

"I was as nervous as a kid going to his first day of school."

'I'll meet you at Ruth's Steakhouse tomorrow night at eight,' she said and left the room."

"My God, Meathead, if there was a heaven I felt like I had died and gone to the promised land."

"Whoopee shit!"

"But I should have known I was nothing but a liar."

"I also wondered why the women I have ever been serious about in my life were nurses."

******

The next afternoon, and out of the hospital, Ben got a haircut. He put on his best boots, best white cowboy shirt, and his biggest belt buckle. He drove by Ruth's Steakhouse twice to make sure he knew how to get there. He drove past a bar but did not go in. Although the urge was great, he did not think Nancy would like him drinking and smoking. He then spent from four until seven pacing back and forth in his trailer like a convict who was about to be released from prison. At seven thirty he was standing in front of the restaurant nervously wondering if Nancy would show up. The nervousness made him feel guilty, thinking back on all the women he had gone out with and then completely forgotten after he left town.

By five till eight Nancy had not shown up.

At eight Nancy had not shown up.

At eight fifteen she had still not shown up and Ben figured it was what he really deserved. He started to leave when Nancy parked across the street, got out of her truck, waved merrily at him and said with no apology for being late, "I hope you're hungry."

"You are pretty smart," Ben said with a smile.

"Ben Sharps," she said. "I'm smarter than you will ever be and don't you ever forget it."

******

Ben and Meathead reached the hills where the doves had flown. Ben stopped and looked up at the hills, decided he didn't want to ride uphill, and turned Meathead south along the base of the hills. "You know Meathead, if a person was born on top of a hill then life would always have been downhill. I think most of us poor bastards are born at the bottom of a canyon and life is always uphill."

"Learn to live in a canyon then and don't reach for what you can't get," Meathead said.

"Sometimes I don't like your answers," Ben said.

Ben stopped and dismounted by a boulder at least ten feet tall and as big around. He took a shot of whiskey and rolled a smoke and sat down by the boulder. Meathead did not move away from him but dropped her head and shut her eyes. A dozen vultures spiraled effortlessly through the sky. Ben smoked and watched them for several minutes.

Ben butted his smoke.

"I know you're not listening Meathead, but watching Nancy walk from her truck toward me in front of Ruth's Steakhouse was like the first light of day hitting my face after a cold night. Only my night had been years long."

"She had on a red pleated skirt, a white blouse, and was wearing two large silver loop earrings that made her look like a gypsy. Later on that's what I called her - Gypsy."

"That night she wove a spell on me, Meathead."

"Whoopee shit did she weave a spell."

"Damn love anyway."

CHAPTER EIGHTEEN

"Love is a strange thing, Meathead. It's not like hate. A person knows why they dislike someone or hate them. But ask a person why they love a certain person, most of the time they have no idea - they just know they do. Go figure."

"I don't know why I loved Nancy. I don't really know if she really ever loved me."

******

Ben mounted Meathead and continued along the base of the hills. A covey of scaled quail darted off to his left and was gone from view in an instant. A red-tailed hawk following the contour of the hills did not see the quail - the hawk would stay hungry - the quail safe for another moment of time - but always hiding

- always on the alert - life nothing but running from cover to cover.

"God, if you are up there, you set this world up viciously," Ben said.

Ben thought about the belief that after a person dies they keep coming back to earth until they had figured it all out and became good. Some people it might take ten lifetimes - others fifty.

"Shit, maybe we only come back worse," Ben muttered.

"Maybe the road to rest is when all the bad things in life have come back so many times they finally become so bad that everything will end up in a place that is only darkness. A place so dark not one molecule of light can enter - a place of no feelings, no nothing, supreme eternal evil."

"Maybe evil has to defeat itself. Love sure as hell can't do it."

Ben came to a stacked pile of rocks over five feet tall and three feet at the base that at one time somebody had made for a marker. He stopped and examined the rocks. "I wonder what they were marking?" he asked, perplexed by the rocks.

"Maybe it was a boundary marker put up by Indians as a warning to stay off of their land?"

"Maybe a Mexican made it for the same reason."

"Cowboys have barbed wire, the biggest marker of them all."

"Boundaries are only things that the next group in power changes anyway."

Ben nudged Meathead. Ben looked up and the sun seemed to be about three o'clock high. It would not start getting dark until around seven.

"I'm going to have to find that special tree soon," Ben said.

He patted the letter in his pocket.

******

After Ben and Nancy had dinner at Ruth's Steak House Ben went back to his trailer at the rodeo grounds. He had not asked her to come to his trailer. She had not asked him to come home with her. The evening had been fun and Ben had felt comfortable. Their conversation had been light, no politics, no lost loves, not even one word about the rodeo. Nancy talked about her younger life and Ben listened, not telling her about his.

Nancy had been born in Boise and was thirty years old. She was an only child who had never known her father. He had run off with a woman from Spokane when Nancy was three years old and her mother had never remarried. Not knowing her father, she had never really missed him. Her mother was now bedridden in an old folk's home in town and did not know anybody around her - not even Nancy. It saddened Nancy but she accepted it. By her conversation, and the way she told her life story, Ben knew Nancy was pragmatic and accepted life the way it was. He also knew that if he was ever going to marry her he would have to live by her rules. Nancy having said, "I made my own way. I don't need a man who wants to take care of me."

Nancy had gotten good grades in school and put herself through nursing school. She started working when she was fourteen, saving most of her money. By the end of college she had worked in grocery stores, a cleaners, bars, restaurants, cleaned houses, and worked for a rancher outside of town where she fell in love with horses. Her mother had never been more than a waitress and, although they had never been hungry, Nancy wanted more. She now owned her own house and had her horse and enjoyed her life. She also enjoyed her job at the hospital even though many times it was sad. She told Ben, "My job helps people and gives me a deep satisfaction."

The statement had made Ben feel uneasy knowing he had never really helped anybody in his life.

Nancy told Ben she had had several boyfriends, but her choice of men was always suspect at best, and she really wasn't looking for any long-term relationship.

They talked until closing time, parting with a handshake and agreeing to meet for lunch the next day.

In the trailer, Ben did not really know what to do. The doctors had told him he should not ride for at least six months but he had a great urge to do it anyway. But he also knew, without a doubt, he wanted to marry Nancy. Why, he did not really know? But he knew he loved her. He also felt she would never marry him unless he settled down and got a job that did not keep him on the road. He knew she couldn't care less about any famous saddle bronc rider from the rodeo.

Ben did not sleep well that night trying to figure a way out of his predicament.

Dawn found him without an answer but he had figured out he didn't love the rodeo anymore - a bronc wouldn't keep him warm in bed or cook him breakfast.

In the morning, Ben once again tried to call Phil Stephens but there still was no answer. Checking his schedule he knew he was scheduled to be in a rodeo in Salt Lake City. He called the promoter who told him he'd heard about his misfortune and hoped he would see him - Ben drew a good crowd.

In mid-morning Ben tried to call Phil Stephens but again there was no answer and he started to feel apprehensive.

When Ben met Nancy for lunch she was in her nurse's uniform.

******

"The first thing Nancy said to me after we sat down was, 'Ben Sharps, I know you have been a womanizer for years but I want you to know for some reason I really like you. I don't know if I love you, but I like you. I also know I don't trust you but I would like to try to love you. I know if you stay on the circuit it won't work and you know as well as I do what the doctor told you.'"

"I have to go to Reno and see my agent, I told her and then I could come back."

"'You write me,'" she said, and wrote her address and phone number on a napkin."

"After lunch we hugged outside and I watched her walk to her truck."

"Seeing her walk away I felt sad."

"As I was driving away from Boise I almost wished I had not met Nancy. I could just go to the next rodeo, ride, maybe get messed up enough I could never ride again and then work on some ranch until I died. I'd spend my off time sitting in some bar and telling people about when I was famous."

"With about seven hundred dollars left in my pocket, I decided to not follow the doctor's advice and I entered the rodeo in Salt Lake City. I placed second but each ride made my head feel like it was about to explode. I was eating aspirin ten at a time.

Every night I wrote Nancy. I missed her and I wanted her but I did not ache for her. I knew if she would not have me, it would not be the end of the world."

"After the rodeo in Salt Lake and many calls to Phil Stephens with no answer, I headed for Reno. When I got there it was no great surprise his office was empty. I should have been angry, but I wasn't. My money was gone but I'd never really been in the rodeo for the money anyway."

"It made it easy for me to decide to head back to Boise. I had my truck and trailer and fourteen hundred dollars and I really didn't give a damn if I ever saw another rodeo again."

"Several years later I heard that Phil Stephens had shot himself in the head in Sacramento, but he didn't leave a note behind. I don't think he felt guilty about stealing my money."

"I think he was broke and didn't want to get a real job."

"Poor bastard, nobody likes a thief. Not even another thief."

******

Driving from Reno toward Boise, Ben took his time. He called Nancy and told her he was on the way back. She said it would be nice to see him and for some reason she missed him and told him, "You be careful."

"You love me," Ben replied.

She laughed.

Ben knew he was about to start a new phase in his life. He did not feel lonely or out of touch with the world, although he had no idea what he would do. The first night he pulled into a rest area and for most of the evening he went through his cardboard box of articles and photographs of himself. Looking at pictures was like looking at a different person - a person he could no longer relate to - a person who had really never existed. He held his purple heart in his hand. It was merely a piece of metal - a worthless prize for not getting killed - something that did nothing for his life or others. He felt like throwing it away, went to the garbage can, hesitated, and then placed it back into the box.

"The box is a coffin for memories," he told himself as he put the box of articles and photographs away.

Later in the evening he wrote Dave and Peggy. He told them he had fallen in love and that his rodeo days were over. He did not tell them Phil Stephens had taken all his money or about his concussion. He told them when he got settled he would like to come and visit and that he hoped all was well.

In early June of 1950, Ben's trailer was parked on Nancy's land. He stayed in his trailer and she stayed in her house. They did not sleep together, but took long walks and talked - although they never spoke of marriage. They did not hold hands when they walked, or show a great amount of emotion toward each other, but both of them were growing closer with each passing day. Ben took a job at the feed store unloading trucks and delivering feed to ranchers. He fell in with people easily and was the talk of the town, being a famous saddle bronc rider, but he kept his distance. He only wanted to do his job and then go back to his trailer and wait for Nancy to come home from the hospital. He still had not had a drink or smoked - although at times the urge was strong.

Nancy knew she loved Ben, and like Ben, she did not know why. Even though she loved him, she was wary of him. There were times his eyes went to a distant place that no one would ever see but himself. She would watch him from her window as he did small things around the place - fixing a corral fence or pulling weeds, and it was like his body was real but it was only a shell - there was nothing inside the body - no heart or soul. There was also something terrible inside of him that he kept caged, but she feared the cage was weak and at any moment whatever he kept caged would escape.

Nancy had heard many stories about Ben's rodeo days. She knew he had fought a lot and drank and that he really didn't associate with anybody. She also knew people could change but most didn't.

One evening they were sitting on Nancy's porch steps. The sun had been down for awhile and the western sky was a dried-blood purple - all the red had been absorbed by the earth. There was a slight breeze - making the evening comfortable. A few crickets were chirping. Ben had never told Nancy the story of his life and Nancy had never egged him on for information. For some reason Ben told her his story - starting from the beginning with his parents, to his sister trying to fly, and he hitting his father with a shovel. He told her about Reno, and the ranch, and Maria, and the time he rode ten broncs in a row two seconds over time. He did not tell her about Barbara and how Barbara died. He told her he had been in the war and got shot but he did not go into details or bring up Lazun. He told her about Phil Stephens taking all his money.

When he was done, Nancy was silent for a long time. The stars had come out and there was no moon. Several bats flew through the sky - mosquitoes to them a bounty. "Ben," Nancy finally said. "I think you are going to be one of those people who never really get a grip on life. You might have been better off to have been born a hundred years ago when you could get on a horse and ride with no real set direction. You could have been a scout or a trader or a trapper. You could have married an Indian woman who all she wanted was a nice tent and deer meat and one day you would have died and nobody would have really known if you had lived or not."

Ben did not have an answer.

"All you cowboys are only living a dream now," Nancy went on. "One day there will not be any big ranches. They will be dude ranches, and hunting clubs, and fishing clubs where people can dress like cowboys and live the myth. That's all the rodeo really is, is a myth. Big men trying to stay boys and trying to think the world will never change."

"I never liked cattle or fences," Ben said. "I ended up on a ranch by pure luck."

Nancy smiled. "All life is luck."

"Right now I'm lucky I found you," Ben said.

"Time will tell," Nancy said, not looking Ben in the eyes.

******

"Nancy and I got married on June 28, 1950," Ben said.

"We bought two gold rings at J.C. Penny's for $85 and went to the Justice of the Peace, his wife was the witness and we got married."

Ben smiled.

"That night we went to Ruth's Steakhouse and on the way home we bought a six pack of beer. It was the first drink I'd had in months."

"We sat on the porch, drank beer, and looked at the stars."

"We didn't talk about the future, or what our plans were, but I did tell Nancy I did not want any children. All she said was that she understood. After we drank all the beer we went to her bedroom and made love. It wasn't passionate or lustful. It was more like it was what we were supposed to do, part of the contract between a man and a wife."

"The next day Nancy told me she would just as soon I stayed in my trailer and she stayed in her house. We could eat together but after we made love she liked to sleep alone. I wasn't offended at all. It was fine with me."

"It went well until July."

"Damn July."

"The Korean War started."

"Damn war."

"Damn July – damn Korean War."

******

Ben was delivering a load of salt blocks to a rancher ten miles from town. It was almost one hundred degrees and even with the air coming through the window the day was oppressive. Mr. Bowmen and two of his four sons, James and Ron, were waiting for Ben when he pulled into the headquarters. The first thing Mr. Bowmen said as Ben got out of the truck was, "yellow bastards, we're in another war."

"I'm going," James said, filled with pride.

"Me too," Ron said.

Ben looked at the two boys and he could see himself getting on the train for boot camp. He could feel the ache from missing Barbara during the long years in Italy and France. He could see the German boy crying beneath the tree. He could see Lazun's body - the eyes lifeless and looking at the sky. He could see himself killing and killing and killing. He could smell smoke and seared flesh and hear the cries of wounded men.

Ben fell back against the truck and everything overwhelmed him – Lisa dying - Maria dying - Lazun dying - Barbara dying - Reno dying.

Mr. Bowmen grabbed Ben's shoulder. "Ben, you okay?" he asked, his voice filled with concern.

The two boys came in and out of focus to Ben and then he hollered at the boys. "Even if you don't get killed you'll die. It's their war, you let them fight it.

Listen to me. It will eat your guts out. You stay home and work for your father."

Ben drove back to town without unloading the salt blocks and went to the bar.

It was ten o'clock at night and Ben was drunk when Nancy found him. She was not mad. She walked up to him, took the glass of whiskey out of his hand and said quietly. "We're going home, Ben. The war has nothing to do with you. But you must promise me you will not get drunk anymore. You can have a few drinks but you can't get drunk."

Ben did not protest as she helped him out of the bar. But Ben knew his demons had escaped their cage. He did not know it, but Nancy knew also.

******

Without stopping Meathead, Ben reached back and got the bottle of whiskey and took a long pull and then another one. He put the bottle back and rolled a smoke.

"I don't remember what all I told Nancy that night I got drunk," Ben said. "I think I told her all about Barbara and the war. I think I told her about killing Germans who wanted to surrender. I think I told her about Lazun. I think I told her I almost jumped off the ship rail and I think I even told her about seeing my sister at times."

"Nancy held me while I talked and then I fell asleep. But I dreamed dreams that were more vivid than life. I saw my sister flying through the sky and she suddenly burst into flames and vanished. I saw Lazun crying. I saw Barbara, but her back was too me and she would not turn around. I saw Maria lighting her candles with all the saints on the glass containers, but the wicks would not catch. I saw her crucifix with Jesus, and blood was pouring out of his eyes - a river of tears."

"When I woke up Nancy was gone and I felt like I did not belong."

"I went back to Mr. Bowman's ranch and he and I unloaded the salt blocks.

When we were done he looked at me seriously and said, 'Ben, I think it is my sons' duty to fight for their country.'"

"All I could think of to say was I suppose you're right, when I knew it was not right. Korea was not invading America."

"I went back to my job, told them I was sick, and went to the bar."

"After several drinks I remembered Nancy telling me not to get drunk and I got in my truck and headed out of town. I just drove. I wished I could drive forever and never really be a part of the world. I would see everything through the truck window but never be a part of it. About twenty miles outside of town I stopped and turned around and headed for home. Standing by my trailer I looked at Nancy's house. It was a nice house, a small two-bedroom frame that was painted white. The front porch had potted flowers scattered on it and there were two chairs. The small front yard was trimmed neatly. Her horse in the corral looked at me nonchalantly then looked away."

"I went inside and walked from room to room. Everything in the house was Nancy's. There were pictures of her mother - pictures of her with friends. There were flowers in vases. It was her safe haven - her dream - her place of rest - her place to ignore the world and say this is my world. There was a picture of her and me after the wedding, but we were not smiling. We were looking into the camera independently."

"I knew there would never really be much of me in the house."

"The thought made me sad, but I knew there was nothing I could do about it."

"I went to my trailer. The trailer was sterile - a metal shell that surrounded nothing. I had a box of pictures and articles and a box of silver belt buckles - all my other rodeo things I had sold or given away. I didn't have pictures on the walls or mementos from life that people keep and give to their children or loved ones."

"I went back outside and looked at my name on the truck and the sponsor emblems on the trailer and I thought, Ben Sharps, the saddle bronc rider - Ben Sharps, the busted out saddle bronc rider - Ben Sharps, the feed truck driver."

"I felt empty and useless and even though I had Nancy I could not see a future. All I could see were kids going off to war and knowing there would be another war, and another war, and another war."

"I went to Nancy's house and sat on the porch steps and looked towards town. There were houses, and people, and stores, and all the people had different dreams and different wants - very few of them would ever reach a dream or a want - a brotherhood of futility."

"I wondered what is it in man that makes us want to go on when we know it will never really get better. Life merely stays the same, generation to generation, war to war, crisis to crisis. But I didn't know the answer."

"God, to some, is the answer."

"They are the lucky ones I suppose."

"I still don't know the answer."

"When Nancy came home she kissed me on the forehead and said simply. 'Ben, you have to control whatever is eating at your insides or it will destroy you. Can you do it?'"

"For you I can, I replied."

"I should have said, for you I will try."

******

Ben rented a sander and sanded his name and sponsors off his trailer and truck. He did not have the truck repainted. He didn't care if it rusted or not.

Unknowing to Ben, Nancy now felt he really did not love her, although he was good to her and gentle. It was like he was not really with her, even when they were talking or making love. He was somewhere in the past - caught so deeply in the darkness he created he would never really see a new day. Her feelings made her sad but did not weigh her down - it was merely how it was and maybe one day he would love her.

Nancy and Ben did not talk about the war. Ben avoided TV, and the radio, and newspapers, but he started to read again. Nancy and he would eat dinner, sit on the porch, and he would go to his trailer to read while she watched TV.

Ben bought a twelve-year-old quarter horse and he and Nancy started riding together. Ben enjoyed riding with Nancy. It was nice to ride for fun.

Ben hid his thoughts about the war to Nancy and the people he worked with. But at night, in his trailer, Ben could see the faces of the men as they walked into battle as vividly as if he was there once again.

Several times, even though he did not believe in the war, he wanted to go to the recruiter and reenlist in the army. There might be a few boys he could save. But each time, he thought about Nancy, and he did not want to make her worry like he had over Barbara or Barbara over him. He did not consider that, busted up the way he was, the army would not take him.

Over the next year, Ben wrote Dave and Peggy several times and sent them a photograph of Nancy and him. He told them he was doing fine and did not miss the rodeo. Peggy wrote back. The ranch was doing well and it would be nice if he and Nancy would visit one day. Moose had quit and the last thing they heard he was headed for Montana. Mac had busted his leg but it healed nicely. Barbara's parents had moved to Denver. Ben figured they reached a point they had to leave the ghosts behind.

Ben went to work everyday although he did not enjoy it. It was merely a dead-end job - a job that would never go anywhere, but it gave Nancy and him a little spending money. He enjoyed talking to the ranchers when he made deliveries but he did not miss a ranch.

One thing that Ben did miss at times was the cabin he had lived in when he got back from the war. There had been no inner peace in the solitude but there had been nothing he could hurt. At times, he felt one day he would hurt Nancy, and the thought bothered him.

******

Meathead was ambling along and Ben was not paying any attention to the trail. Meathead stumbled slightly and Ben jerked. "Watch where you're going," he growled.

"You're the one supposed to know where we are going," Meathead said.

Ben stopped the horse and got off. Not far away he saw two ground owls standing by their burrow. The brown and white owls were only about six inches tall and their big eyes, with their golden centers, stared right at Ben.

Ben smiled. One of the owls turned his head almost completely around in a complete circle before looking back at Ben.

"You can see where you've been and can see where you're going," Ben said.

The two owls, tired of Ben, hopped into their burrow.

Ben rolled a smoke and lit it.

"The Korean War was over in September of 1953," he said to Meathead.

"It didn't do a damn thing."

"The day it was over Nancy and I went to the bar and had a few drinks and then we went home, and just for a change of pace, we made love in my trailer. I felt good, but I knew some of the boys coming home would never be the same, and the families of those who had been killed would never be the same, but at least it was over."

"The government tried to make up reasons why the war had been necessary but most of the people in the country didn't really care. Nothing had been won. There were no spoils and without spoils there is no glory."

"Hell, most people don't even know where Korea is."

"Most people now don't even care about the boys who fought in Korea."

Ben butted the smoke and got back on Meathead.

"Looking back, the three years were pretty uneventful. I wasn't happy. I wasn't sad. I just kind of was. If that makes any sense?

"I guess in life we all need labels to substantiate what we are - teacher - clerk - secretary - CEO - maid - laborer - truck driver - cowboy - king - queen - peon - soldier. I wonder what ever happened to human being, or mankind, or person."

"We're all in the military and just don't want to admit it."

"We all have our own uniform."

"Even old age is a uniform - a uniform life gives you for living too long."

"I went with Nancy to visit her mother in the old folk's home. I had never been to a rest home. I had never really been around old people. It was strange and I didn't know how to act or what to say. All I really felt was a great loneliness emitting from them. For growing old they were in a fancy prison. Her mother was bedridden - her mind lost to some dream that would not let her return to the real world. I looked at her and wondered what god she had offended that his wrath would be so great. After we left the home, I did not tell Nancy, but I vowed to myself that when it came to the point I could no longer take care of myself I would kill myself before I went to a rest home."

"I never went back to that place again."

"There are some religions that believe suicide is evil and those who commit suicide cannot enter heaven."

"It would be ironic if there is no relief in heaven."

"Only another test of faith."

"A test one can never pass."

CHAPTER NINETEEN

In October of 1954, Nancy and Ben drove to Colorado to visit Dave and Peggy.

It had been eight years since Ben had been back to the ranch. They left early one morning going in Ben's truck and trailer and were not in a great hurry. Nancy wanted to camp in the mountains each night. Ben felt both elated and apprehensive about going to the ranch.

Ben enjoyed the ride. Every night was clear and beautiful with the stars in their full glory. They stopped in Denver, drove up Pikes Peak and tossed pennies on Kit Carson's grave, Nancy telling Ben, "Now you can't tell me your wish."

Ben didn't tell her he did not have a wish. He said

his wish was a secret.

That night they rented a room and Ben called Dave and Peggy informing them they would be in the next day. For some reason Peggy's voice sounded strained to Ben, and it worried him, but he didn't say anything to Nancy.

Nancy was bubbly and excited during the trip. She had never been out of Boise and all the sights were invigorating. She was even more exuberant in her love making.

Sitting in the truck as Ben drove, Nancy thought back on the previous years with Ben. They had been good years although Ben was not the man she thought she would marry. She still did not know if she loved him in the true sense of the word. But Ben made her comfortable and played to the nurse side of her - there was something in her that needed to help people - and she knew Ben needed help. He was like a little kid who could not control his feelings, or his emotions, so most of the time he was stoic, afraid to show happiness or sadness. But he had controlled his drinking and had never been drunk since the first day of the Korean War. She did wonder at times if he missed the rodeo circuit, but she never brought it up.

As they got close to the ranch, Ben saw places that he and Barbara had been to.

They passed the point in the river where they had gone back into the trees and made love for the first time and the feelings of the day flooded over Ben. As they drove up the dirt road that lead to the ranch headquarters, Ben remembered how anxious he was waiting for Barbara to come out to the ranch the first time, and how embarrassed he felt picking flowers for her with the men watching. "The country is so beautiful," Nancy said.

Ben also remembered riding into the ranch with Reno and how excited he was about becoming a cowboy.

Driving into the headquarters nothing had really changed except the buildings were a little more aged.

Ben stopped the truck and he and Nancy got out just as Peggy stepped out onto the front porch. Peggy's hair was almost completely white, but still long and pulled back into a ponytail. She had gained some weight and even from a distance she looked tired. Peggy ran toward them and embraced Ben. "Oh Ben, oh Ben, it's been so long," she cried.

Ben held her but he did not know what to say although his heart was overflowing.

Peggy stepped away from Ben and looked at Nancy. "So you are the lucky one who finally lassoed Ben Sharps," she smiled, dabbing at the tears in her eyes.

"I don't know if luck had anything to do with it," Nancy replied, returning Peggy's smile.

Ben saw a deep sadness in Peggy's eyes.

Duke came out onto the porch of the chuck house, waved, and then went back inside. "I see Duke is still about as social as an old goat," Ben said.

"He hides his caring," Peggy said. "Why don't you go say hello to him and Nancy and I will go to the house."

"Where are the men?" Ben asked.

"They went up to clean the cabin. We figured you and Nancy would like to stay there."

Ben headed for the chuck house. Duke was sitting at the table drinking a cup of coffee. Time had not been bad to him although his hair was thinning and his eyes still had the dull look of a thinker who knew he would never have any answers. "Coffee is where it always was," Duke said to Ben.

Ben poured himself a cup of coffee. "It's good to see you," he said as he sat down.

"Good to see you also," Duke said in a rare moment that anything ever pleased him.

Ben looked around the chuck house. For an instant he saw Maria's candles and her Jesus on the wall. "When I came here I worked for Maria," Ben said. "It doesn't seem like so many years ago."

"Time is sneaky," Duke said.

"I wonder how much different my life would have been if after the war I would have stayed on the ranch?" Ben asked himself more than Duke.

"You would have spent your time dreaming about being in the rodeo," Duke said.

Ben smiled wryly and sipped his coffee. "Guess most of life is wishing for something else than what a man has," he said.

"Without wishing for something we'd all jump off some cliff," Duke said.

"What do you wish for, Duke?" Ben asked.

Duke looked out the window and did not answer for a few moments then he said, "I wish that someday man will get along and there won't be any more wars."

"You know that will never happen," Ben replied.

"It's a wish that keeps me from jumping off a cliff," Duke said and laughed satirically.

Ben sipped his coffee.

"What do you wish for now that you are no longer riding in the rodeo?" Duke asked.

"I wish I didn't feel empty at times," Ben said truthfully.

"That's the curse of people who feel," Duke said.

Ben stood, shook hands with Duke, and said simply. "It's good seeing you, Duke."

As Ben opened the door Duke said to him, "Remember one thing Ben, we're all empty in one way or another."

Ben went to the graveyard. The toys on top of the children's graves had faded more but there were shiny yellow and red plastic flowers on Maria's grave. "I hope you have found rest and your people," Ben said to her grave.

Ben knocked on the door to the main house. When Peggy let him in he was surprised to see Dave sitting in an arm chair in the living room. Nancy was sitting on a sofa and gave Ben a worried look. Dave was gaunt and pale and had lost a lot of weight. His clothes hung on him like a death shroud but his eyes were still blazing. A pair of crutches lay on the floor by the chair. Ben was so shocked he suddenly felt weak and did not know what to say. "I ate some of Duke's food," Dave smiled thinly.

Ben shook hands with Dave.

"He's got cancer all over his body," Peggy said. "They give him a few months at the best."

She did not cry.

"I've had a good life," Dave said. "No big complaints." Then he smiled at Ben. "I only wish I could have seen you ride in one of those big fancy rodeos and heard the crowd cheer. You made a name for yourself Ben."

"It doesn't mean much," Ben said.

"Maybe not to you, but to a lot of people from around here you're a hero."

Ben sat down by Nancy.

"At least you didn't marry one of those buckle shiners that follow the rodeos," Dave grinned, referring to rodeo hookers.

"Dave," Peggy scolded.

Nancy smiled.

"She married me because she knew I was busted out, and being a nurse she wants to help people," Ben said jokingly, but seriously to himself.

"Nancy told us she is a nurse. It's a great job and takes a person with a lot of heart and caring," Dave said and leaned his head back on the chair and closed his eyes.

"We should go outside," Peggy said. "He gets tired easily."

Nancy and Peggy and Ben sat on the porch. "Dave doesn't want anyone's sympathy," Peggy said looking Ben straight in the eyes.

"Of course not, but it doesn't seem right," Ben said.

"Ben, you're still trying to make sense of things when there really is no sense to anything. You just have to accept life," Peggy said.

Ben looked at the road that came into the ranch

between the narrow cliffs. "I remember first coming in here with Reno and looking back at those cliffs and it was like this ranch was not a part of the world. You drove in and you left the outside world behind."

"Dave spent his whole life here. He has been very fortunate," Peggy said, adding, "Dave wanted you to come and to see you one more time. He never really showed it, but you were like a son to him. He bragged on you Ben. Ben Sharps, the best saddle bronc rider the rodeo has ever seen."

Ben smiled.

"He also bet on you that you would ride those ten horses," Peggy said.

"I will come back to the funeral," Ben said.

"There won't be one or any kind of ceremony. He wants to be cremated and I will scatter his ashes on the ranch."

"What will you do, Peggy?" Ben almost cried.

"The men will keep the ranch going. I have always done the books and when the time comes I can't hang onto it, I will sell out and move to town. This has been a great place, but I've always wanted a little house in town with a small garden, and a front porch with a rocking chair. I can sit in the chair and think back on my life with its sadness and its beauty and wilt slowly away like a fading flower."

Peggy stood. "Now you two walk around. Duke wants you both to eat at the chuck house tonight with the men and then you can ride to the cabin."

Ben hugged Peggy.

Peggy smiled at Nancy. "He's a good man but a hard keeper," she said and went into the house.

Ben and Nancy walked off the porch and after a few steps they held hands. They did not see Peggy watching them through the window with tears in her eyes.

******

Ben stopped Meathead and looked south. Not far away were three volcanic cones that were over a hundred yards tall and less than fifty yards apart. From their tops, the black volcanic rock snaked off in different directions - rivers stuck in time to never flow again. Carved into the twisted, pockmarked and tortured black rocks, were many Indian pictographs. Scattered around the cones were red cinders, some more than twenty feet tall and ten feet around - given a resting place when the cones had blown their tops. A few prickly pear cacti grew in the lava flows.

Ben turned toward the cones and picked his way through the lava flows and cinders. He looked at the pictographs of deer and antelope but he didn't pay them much mind. They were a history that was long forgotten - dreams carved into rocks that had lost their true meaning with the passage of time - a reminder that nothing was permanent and nothing could be relied on - not even rock.

"Nancy and I ate with Whitey and Mac and Crow at the chuck house that first night," Ben said to Meathead.

"The men told her stories about me and laughed and joked at my expense. Duke had fried chicken and gravy, corn and biscuits and a cherry pie. We did not talk about Dave, but I suppose the men accepted death more than I ever did. I knew they would take care of Peggy and not slack in their work."

"They had not heard from Moose."

"Nancy seemed to enjoy the men and the attention and she kidded back with them."

"After dinner Nancy and I rode to the cabin. The cabin was spotless. The men had hauled in a double bed, put on clean sheets, and there was a cooler with bacon and eggs and two six packs of beer in it."

"The cabin had not changed. It sat up in the mountains and let the world go on around it. It made me smile and remember the many nights I sat on the porch and listened to the sounds of the mountains."

"It was that night sitting on the porch with Nancy and drinking a few beers that I knew one day in my life I would be living alone. I didn't know why? But looking at Nancy in the fading light I knew it would not last and I also knew after her, I would never be with another woman."

"Nancy went inside and went to bed and I stayed on the porch. It had been several years since I had really looked at the stars, or heard crickets, or the wind going through the trees. I felt badly for Dave and sad for Peggy but I also felt calm - not at peace with myself but calm - calm like when a person finally accepts death or the insanity of life."

"The half moon appeared over the trees. Its battle-worn surface was as vivid as if I was holding the moon in my hand. My sister appeared. The moonbeams shining through her made her shimmer and made her eyes as bright as the stars. 'I told you, you would find love,' she said to me."

"It's been a long time since I've seen you,' I said."

"'Time means nothing to me now, Ben,' she smiled."

"I don't know if I am in love."

"'I know, but it will be ok if you let it. Nancy is a wonderful woman and she only wants to help you.'"

"At times I feel like I am in a glass box and I watch the world go on around me but I can't get out of the box to join the rest of the world. But it's strange because I really don't want to be part of the world. I don't believe in anything most people believe in. I don't see any pertinence in life or a reason to really be alive."

"'I can't give you any answers, Ben. I don't know if there are any.'"

"Have you ever seen Ma and Pa? I asked."

"Lisa shook her head."

"I was just wondering if they ever found rest?"

"'I hope so,' Lisa said. 'They had a terrible life.'"

"Have you ever seen Barbara?" I asked. "I still feel her with me at times."

"Lisa shook her head again."

"What are you anyway, Lisa? Are you a ghost? Are you a spirit? Do I see you only in my mind?"

"'I don't know, Ben. I know I can feel your needs and longings. I know I don't need anything. I have no wants or desires except for you to be happy. I have never seen a god, but I feel like I'm a part of everything. I'm a part of the stars and the trees and the earth and the sky. I'm a part of places in the universe I have never seen. I'm a part of worlds and universes yet to be born. I know for all time I will always be a part of something.'"

"I wonder if when I die I will be able to fly? I asked."

"'If you can ride ten broncs two seconds over time you should be able to fly she said with a starlit smile, and vanished.'"

"I went into the cabin. Nancy had left one kerosene lamp burning. She was asleep on the bed and the shadows lay on her like a light blanket. She slept peacefully and deeply. Her eyelids did not flutter in dreams and her breathing was slow and methodical."

"I sat down in a chair and looked at her and it was the first time I had ever really seen her. I saw the soft creases in her face that were not from worry. I saw the way her eyebrows arched slightly as if they were smiling. I saw the thin line to her lips. I saw a tiny scar on the left side of her nose. I noticed how gentle her hands looked and how graceful they were - the hands of a nurse. The hands that would hold a stranger's hand and tell them it would be ok, or that they were going to die, but that dying was ok."

"For those brief moments, I truly loved Nancy. For those brief moments there was nothing else in the world except her peaceful sleep and the sound of her contented breathing. She opened her eyes and smiled at me, more asleep than awake, and then closed her eyes again."

"I sat looking at her for at least another hour, but

the deep feeling of love never returned."

******

Ben stopped Meathead at the base of one of the volcanic cones and took a shot of whiskey. He thought about the center of the earth filled with molten rock - churning cauldrons of pent-up force and destruction. "Maybe because our home is so violent, man can only be violent," Ben thought.

He then thought about primitive people he had read about that tossed humans into volcanoes to appease them - like their god of molten rock really gave a damn.

Ben took another shot of whiskey and rolled a smoke and lit it. "Can you imagine years ago Meathead? Maybe some poor bastard was picking seeds or hunting not far from here and suddenly the earth shuddered and this cone shot out of the ground spewing fire and molten rock. That poor son-of-a-bitch would have thought he'd really screwed up. He would have become a priest and roamed the earth telling everybody he met that the end was near and they had better repent."

"Poor dumb bastard - wrong place at the wrong time."

Ben turned west, back towards an area where many pinion trees grew on the ranch. "It's getting close to time Meathead."

******

Ben and Nancy spent two more days at the cabin - each night making love. During the day they would hike or ride and then eat lunch with Dave and Peggy. Ben did not talk to the men much. They were busy working and there really wasn't much to say.

The men were gone the morning Ben and Nancy left. Duke was in town getting supplies. Ben shook hands with Dave, who was too weak to get out of his chair. Outside, he hugged Peggy and for the first time since knowing her he kissed her on the forehead. Both Peggy and Ben knew he would never be back.

Peggy hugged Nancy, telling her. "Ben's not too bad for a cur dog."

Ben headed south on the paved road instead of north. He drove through town and looked at the feed store, and the river, and the cafe, and then he turned around and headed north.

All during the day Ben was quiet and Nancy did not invade his silence, but inside of her she felt him slipping away - slipping to a place she could never follow, nor did she really want to follow.

Two months after their return to Boise, Nancy nervously told Ben she was pregnant.

Ben did his best to sound excited and happy but

inside the thought scared him. Although he thought he did a good job with his deceit, Nancy saw through him like he was a single pane window.

******

"When Nancy told me she was pregnant, my first reaction was I wanted to get in the truck and leave. I couldn't understand bringing children into this world - cursing them with our mistakes so most of their lives would be filled with questions and pain. That night I couldn't sleep. All I could think about was what our child would have to live through and how any child could go through life and not become embittered or insane. There was only one way. A person would have to ignore the world."

"You can't ignore the world."

"Bringing life into the world is not a joy."

"How can you tell a child I am sorry for giving you life?"

"How can you tell a child you were a mistake?"

"Maybe life is all a mistake."

******

Ben rode into the pinion trees and stopped. The day was beginning to cool and there was a steady breeze from the south. Ben figured it was close to four o'clock. Birds darted through the trees looking for bugs and seeds. From horizon to horizon there were over a half dozen hawks in the sky hoping to not spend a hungry night.

"It's been a fairly nice day," Ben said to Meathead.

"For you, you're riding," Meathead said.

"Two sides to everything I suppose," Ben replied, but his answer was perplexing.

******

Ben fought his emotions during Nancy's pregnancy but he never let on his true feelings. He was attentive to Nancy. He cooked breakfast, cleaned the house, and even did the laundry. Nancy's pregnancy was not a good one. As the months passed she gained over forty pounds. Her back hurt. Her legs and ankles were swollen twice their normal size and she was plagued by headaches. Her morning sickness was excruciating. But Nancy never complained. She knitted booties and gloves and little hats. She bought a crib. "As much pain as I am going through, this baby has to be a boy," she told Ben.

Ben worried over Nancy but he dreaded the thought of the child and secretly hoped the baby was a girl. If it was a girl, he would not have as much responsibility like raising a boy.

Ben began secretly drinking at night after Nancy had gone to bed. He bought a bottle of whiskey and hid it behind the horse corrals. He never got drunk but he began to have two or three shots a night - hiding his breath with breath mints. The drinking made him feel guilty but it did not stop him.

Even with Ben's attentiveness, Nancy saw the fear and apprehension in his eyes over the baby. She knew he was deeply troubled but she could not think of anything to say that would take it away. She hoped Ben would get over it. But deep inside of her, she knew Ben would never be able to accept the child.

With her feelings Nancy began to separate herself from Ben. Without really knowing it she began to be short with him and criticized most things he did. With the criticism Ben began to drink more, even at times stopping at the bar after work.

During Nancy's sixth month, Ben received a letter from Peggy that Dave had died. She was happy his suffering was over. They had scattered his ashes on the ranch. That night Ben went to the bar and got drunk and got into a fight for no good reason. He was arrested and tossed in jail. Waiting at home Nancy was worried to death. After many phone calls she found out what had happened and in an instant most of the good feelings she had for Ben vanished. Her responsibility was her child, not a man who could not face the realities of life, and even though it was sad, she knew in time she would leave Ben.

******

"I don't even know why I got in a fight that night," Ben said to Meathead.

"I was drinking and I started to argue with a man I didn't know. I suddenly hit him on the side of the head and knocked him off the barstool. He'd no sooner hit the floor than I jumped on him and kept punching him. When two men pulled me off, I wanted to kill the son-of-a-bitch and I didn't even know him. I'd broken the poor bastard's nose and his face looked like red Jell-O."

"When the cops tossed me in the drunk tank I puked my guts out and then I lay on the metal bunk with no mattress and felt lower than dog shit."

"What a mess I am, I said to the ceiling."

"The next day I was officially charged with aggravated assault and they released me. When I got home, I saw pity and disdain in Nancy's eyes and I could not blame her.

'I won't have any drunken brawler be a father to my child,' she told me coldly."

"I could not return her glare and just stood there looking at the floor."

"That night I wrote Peggy and told her how sorry I was for her loss but I did not mention that Nancy was pregnant."

"The next day I apologized to Nancy and told her I would not do it again. But even to me, my words sounded false and I knew Nancy did not believe me."

"When Jenny Sparks was born I was doing ninety days in jail for beating a man unconscious."

"When I got out of jail and went home, Nancy would not let me in the house and she told me to haul my trailer off her property and that she had filed for a divorce."

"I asked her if I could see the baby."

"She nodded her head, shut the door, and came back holding the baby."

"Jenny was sleeping. Her little face was peaceful and carefree. I ran my finger gently over her forehead and I felt a love for her I had never felt before."

******

Ben rode and looked at the hangman's noose. "The tree I am looking for is close by," he said to Meathead.

CHAPTER TWENTY

Ben sold his horse, pulled his trailer to the back of the feed lot and continued working. He gave Nancy a hundred dollars a month to help with Jenny. When the divorce was finalized, Nancy told Ben she did not want him coming over and seeing the baby. It would be better for Jenny if she never knew her father but she would always keep Ben up to date on Jenny's life. All he had to do was write or call. She also said she did not need any money from him - she did not want to feel obligated. Nancy also told him she would tell Jenny, when she was old enough, her father was Ben Sharps, one of the best saddle bronc riders the rodeo had ever seen, and although Ben loved her deeply he could not settle down.

Nancy did not cry when they hugged and said goodbye.

In March of 1954, Ben hooked up to his trailer and headed toward Montana. On the way out of town, he closed out his bank account and mailed a check for one thousand dollars to Nancy with a note that said - I am sorry but I hope you know I love you and Jenny.

He had twelve hundred dollars to his name and had no idea why he was going to Montana.

******

Ben stopped Meathead and reached back and got the bottle of whiskey and took a long pull. He dismounted and stuck the bottle in the crook of a tree limb. "Some cowboy who needs a shot of watered-down whiskey will find that one day and be happy," Ben said as he got back on Meathead.

Ben rolled a smoke and lit it and dismounted again and got his whiskey back.

"Let some poor dumb son-of-a-bitch find his own whiskey," he said as he got back on Meathead and took another swallow. He finished his smoke before he moved on.

Ben rode slowly, closely examining each pinion tree as he passed them. He wanted the perfect branch to sling the rope over, the perfect branch for an imperfect life.

"Where does time go?" Ben asked Meathead.

Meathead did not answer.

"Here I am eighty-seven years old."

"Everybody I really knew in my life except Nancy and Jenny are dead. Peggy sold the ranch, bought her little house in town, and died in nineteen sixty-one from a heart attack while doing dishes. I was working on a ranch in Wyoming and happened to run into Whitey in town. Whitey was driving a truck."

"A year later Whitey died in a crash in Seattle. Moose got stomped to death by a bull in Montana. Duke died in his sleep living in a cheap hotel in Denver. Crow drowned when he fell out of a boat while fishing."

"I never knew a cowboy who could swim."

"After I left Boise I never took the time to get close to any people. I never tried to get close to another woman."

"I'd write Peggy occasionally."

"I worked on ranches all over the west for honest but low pay work. I built and fixed fences, branded cattle, broke horses, froze in the winter, dried up like a prune in the summer, you name it, what ever was to be done on a ranch I did."

"But staying on one ranch for long never suited

me. I'd grow restless, draw my wages, and head for another part of the west."

"Whenever I quit a ranch the boss would always say that I was a good hand and could always come back. People dumb enough to work for lousy wages are always welcomed back."

"I never did go back to the rodeo. I probably could have done a few more years and made some good money. But what was I going to do with the money? There was nothing I wanted to do."

"I sent money to Nancy after each of my checks even though she had told me she did not want my money. Occasionally she would write me back and tell me how Jenny was doing. The letters always made me feel sad and guilty, but I knew Jenny was better off without me even though I felt a deep love for her that I could not explain."

"When Jenny was eight years old Nancy married a man from Oregon who owned dry cleaners all over the state and had a small horse farm. He'd been fishing close to Boise and got sick and had to go to the hospital. Nancy and he fell in love and they moved to his place outside of Bend, Oregon. Nancy sold her home in Boise."

"Nancy wrote and said Jenny was a most blessed little girl."

"I was happy for Nancy and happy Jenny would have such a wonderful home."

"The years went by and I went from ranch to ranch. I worked in Wyoming, Washington, Idaho, Montana, Arizona, Nevada, and even California. I wasn't chasing anything or didn't want anything. I didn't even think about much or look up at the sky for my sister. I didn't drink that much either, although I smoked a lot."

"At the beginning of the Vietnam War, I was working on a ranch in Nebraska and like the Korean War, the war brought back all the memories and guilt. I didn't believe in the war but I wasn't like the hippies who thought they could stop all wars. I respected the hippies though - they wanted a simpler life. Most of them are getting old now and understand they really didn't change much in the world. Power pulls the strings."

"As the war dragged on it bothered me more. Our boys were fighting in a country far from home in a war that we had no business being in. It was another war with no honor. A war we could never win."

"During those years there was never a day that went by without me thinking about Jenny, but I never told anybody I had a daughter, or that I had ever been married. I really didn't talk to people."

"Several years into the war, I received a letter from Nancy. Jenny wanted desperately to meet her real father and if I did not have enough money Nancy would pay for my way to Bend, Oregon."

"Jenny was a teenager. The thought of seeing her scared me to death. I had never seen her except when she was a baby. Nancy had sent me several photographs throughout the years but I did not keep them. Looking at them my sadness and guilt were too much and it is hard to look at your own child when she is a stranger. I had never written, keeping with Nancy's wishes, even though I always wanted to."

"After several weeks of agonizing, I finally wrote Nancy and said I would come to Bend and see Jenny."

"A week letter I received a letter from Jenny. She told me she was happy I was coming to see her. She signed the letter...Love...Jenny. She had drawn a picture of a cowboy riding a bronc and written under it - My Daddy."

"The letter made me feel happy."

******

Ben bought several sets of new clothes, a new cowboy hat, and polished his buckle. He bought a train ticket from Lincoln, Nebraska, to Bend, Oregon. He did not want to fly - being above the ground seemed alien to him.

Watching the world go by on the train reminded Ben of his life - he could see life around him but he could not really touch it - he only went through it - watching but never being a part of it.

Ben tried to figure out what he would say to Jenny when he met her. But he could not really think of anything that sounded appropriate. "I'm sorry for leaving when you were a baby. I've missed you and even though I have never seen you, I love you."

The words seemed hollow and devoid of any feeling, although they were not lies.

Ben did understand there was nothing in life that could be redone. There was no way to erase transgression or guilt. He had to live with them - battle them every day.

The first night on the train Ben fought going to the club car for a few drinks. But his will was not strong enough. There were several couples in the club car seemingly having a good time. Ben sat alone and drank two whiskeys. Ben's reflection stared back at him from the window glass. It was strange, although he shaved every day, he had not really looked at himself in a mirror for years. He noticed his hair was graying and there were many creases in his weathered face. He looked at his nicked and beaten hands and noticed his knuckles were starting to swell.

He ordered another whiskey and rolled a cigarette. The people in the club car stared at him. He felt uneasy, realizing most people bought cigarettes. A lady asked Ben, "Are you a real cowboy?"

At first Ben did not know what to say then he answered, "Yes ma'am, I suppose I am."

"It must be a wonderful life," she said with admiration.

"It's all I know," Ben replied.

******

Ben stopped Meathead by a large ancient pinion tree. The tree grew by itself on top of a small hill and overlooked hundreds of other trees that surrounded it. It was like the tree was the ruler of the forest. One of the lower branches of the large pinion was at least ten feet above the ground and grew parallel with the ground for over six feet. The base of the branch was well over two feet around. "Here it is," Ben said, admiring the tree.

Ben dismounted, but instead of letting Meathead roam he tied her to another branch of the tree.

Meathead gave him a dirty look.

Ben took his whiskey and walked around the tree several times. "I bet you never knew you'd be a hanging tree," he said to the tree.

A sudden brisk breeze shook the tree as if it answered,

"No."

Ben sat down beneath the tree and took off his hat. He took a long shot of whiskey, set the bottle down, and slowly rolled a smoke and lit it.

Ben inhaled the smoke deeply and exhaled loudly like a deep sigh. Looking out over the tops of the other trees was like looking at a vast green ocean and he remembered the way the sun set on the ocean when he was coming back from England. For the first time in years he wondered how Betsy was doing or if she was still alive. He wondered if she had the large family she wanted.

He wished he had tried to find out where she lived - taken the effort and told her how nice their one night had been together and that he had never in his life had more fun dancing.

Ben took another deep pull on the smoke and butted it.

"When the train was a few hours out of Bend I wanted to jump off," Ben said to Meathead.

"The thought of seeing Jenny scared me more than the war. I couldn't think of anything to say to her and I hadn't even bought her a gift."

"What kind of a father is that?"

"You gave her life," Meathead said.

"It was an accident."

"All life is an accident."

"Shit," Ben said.

"Shit," Meathead said.

"As the train was coming to a stop in Bend I saw Nancy and Jenny. Nancy didn't look a day older and she looked content. There was a peacefulness that emitted from her. Jenny was beautiful - a young girl beginning to bud into a woman. She was taller than Nancy, had long black hair that was braided, and she was thin like me."

"Her eyes were happy and she had delicate hands like Nancy's."

"A lump formed in my throat and I almost decided to not get off the train when Nancy saw me and with a big smile she waved and pointed at me."

"Jenny looked directly at me, looked hesitant for a moment, and then she waved and jumped up and down like a little kid."

"I stepped off the train and Jenny ran to me, jumped into my arms, and cried out happily, "Oh daddy, daddy, I'm so happy you came to see me.""

"It was an embrace I will never forget."

******

Ben rented a room and every morning Nancy would bring Jenny by and drop her off. Ben rented a car and spent four days with Jenny. They went out to eat. They went to the movies. They fed the ducks in the park. Jenny was bubbly and happy and told Ben all about her life. She loved her step-father and he was very good to her. She had her own horse and she was taking dressage lessons. She even told Ben she understood that he could not take on the responsibility of a child - some people were not supposed to have children, but he was her real father and she would always love him.

She had even dug up old articles about Ben when he was riding broncs.

Ben could never tell her how he felt, but he really did not have to, as Jenny did most of the talking.

Ben refused an invitation to come over and have dinner with Nancy and her husband. It did not seem right and he did not want to interfere or cast a shadow on Nancy's or her husband's life.

Nancy told him he would always be an old red neck but it was ok, she understood.

******

"It was a nice four days, Meathead. Maybe the best four days I ever spent in my life."

"I was nervous and felt out of place but Jenny made me feel good, and even though I had nothing to do with it, she was living a good life."

"It was nice to see a young person who was not

raised like I was - getting whipped and berated all the time. It was nice to see the glow of young life."

"Jenny asked me about my life. I didn't tell her about the war or Barbara. I told her about my sister dying young but not that she had tried to fly. I didn't tell her how I was raised. I mostly told her about the ranch and my rodeo days. She was proud that I was a cowboy."

"Didn't seem right, Nancy and her step-father had made everything possible for her and she was proud I was a cowboy."

"I never could tell her how much I loved her and missed her. At times I got close but then I could not force the words out."

"As I was about to board the train back to Nebraska, I gave her a single yellow rose. You are the rose of my life I told her."

"She hugged me and kissed me and with a tear in her eye she told me she loved me and we should try and see each other at least once a year."

"I told her that would be nice."

"I hugged Nancy, couldn't say anything and got on the train."

"The last time I saw either one of them was from a train window waving good-bye."

"I can still see them in my mind like it was yesterday.

Nancy had her arm around Jenny. Jenny was happily waving but Nancy looked sad - sad for maybe what could have been, or what might have been, or sad for me."

"I went to the club car and had a few drinks. Sitting in my seat that night all I could think about was the fact I had given up the only thing in my life that was truly a part of me."

"I'd cut out what little heart I had."

"At some stop that night a young soldier in uniform got on the train and sat in the seat across the aisle from me. 'I'm headed to Advanced Infantry Training,' he told me proudly."

"I wanted to tell him, son, there won't be any parades for you and there is no glory."

"Instead I said with a heavy heart, I wish you the best and I hope it doesn't steal your heart."

"I've never seen Jenny again. I figured I would only get in the way of her life and the sorrow I felt after seeing her the first time was not worth the joy of seeing her again. We wrote a lot for awhile, but with time it slowed down. She went to college and married a nice man. She has three children. The children are grown now and have good jobs and as of yet have no children - none of them have had to join the military and get involved with the mess the country is in. Jenny and her husband live near Portland. Over the last ten years we've written a few times. Her letters are polite and newsy and she always signs them - you are my favorite cowboy, Love, Jenny - with a P.S., visit any time."

"I was never able to tell her how I really felt about her and how not knowing her left a hole in me."

"The letter in my pocket will."

"I never wrote Nancy again. There was no need to interfere with her life."

"Her husband died a few years ago and she is living in an old folk's home and has all her senses. She has had a good life - some power has blessed her for being a nurse."

"Lisa loved me. Barbara loved me. Nancy loved me in her own way. But Jenny loves me because of blood - only because of blood. She never knew me. Blood is blood.

Blood can be filled with hate. Blood can be filled with love."

"My child loves."

"Despite me, she loves."

******

Ben took another shot of whiskey and put his hat back on. There was not a cloud in the sky. A lone crow landed on the top of a tree a few trees from Ben and looked at Ben like he was examining him from the inside out.

"God send you for my soul?" Ben asked the crow.

The crow tilted his head like he could not understand Ben.

"God send you for my soul?" Ben asked louder.

The crow cawed three times.

"You go tell God I don't have a soul."

The crow did not move.

"Get out of here," Ben ordered.

The crow sailed off, not looking back.

Ben took another shot of whiskey and rolled a smoke and lit it. He smoked half the cigarette, butted it, stood and took the rope off the saddle.

He slid the hangman's noose up and down a few times and satisfied, he unrolled the rope and tossed the loop over the large branch. Holding the loop and the rope he lifted his weight off the ground. The rope supported him without stretching.

He left the rope hanging from the branch, sat back down, took another shot of whiskey and rolled another smoke and lit it.

"The rope won't break my neck but it will only take a few seconds for me to pass out," Ben said.

Ben tried to make his mind go blank - to not think about anything - for the first time in years his sister appeared in front of him. Ben smiled. "Oh Lisa, it's good to see you," he said.

"I've never left you, Ben," his sister said, looking at him with concern.

"I'll be flying with you soon," Ben said.

"It's not time for you to fly," his sister said.

"I'm tired of life. I'm tired of being only a shell. In a few years I won't be able to walk. If I live much longer I'll have to go to a home and in time they will have to feed me and I won't be able to even wipe my own ass."

"There are no broncs to ride in the sky, Ben."

"I haven't been on a bronc in years."

"What is life but a bronc?" his sister asked.

Ben smiled and took another shot of whiskey and a pull on the smoke. "You were always smarter than I was. You always had a good heart."

"No, Ben. I couldn't take life. You're the one who has endured. You're the one with a good heart," his sister said and vanished.

"I have a heart like a rock," Ben said.

The crow flew back and landed on the top of the tree and looked at Ben.

"I told you I don't have a soul," Ben said to the crow, slightly perturbed.

The crow flew over and landed on the branch

with the rope hanging from it. It looked at Ben, then hopped over and pecked at the rope several times.

"Noose is too big for your skinny neck," Ben said.

The crow cawed three times like it was laughing, hopped up in the air several times like it was doing a jig, and then flew off again.

"Wonder what that dumb son-of-a-bitch is up to?" Ben pondered. "What's funny about a hangman's rope?"

Ben butted the smoke and took another shot of whiskey.

"Well Meathead, I wonder how you will spend the rest of your life," Ben said.

"Don't know," Meathead replied, "Never really thought about it too much."

"I guess we just live and die whether we think about life or not," Ben said.

"It took you eighty-seven years to figure that out," Meathead scoffed.

"I guess I let life overwhelm me," Ben said.

"How can you say that when you have lived this long?" Meathead asked.

"I haven't enjoyed much of my life," Ben said.

"I think you have enjoyed more than you really know. You've been in love. You've had good friends and at one time in your life you were the best saddle bronc rider the rodeo has ever seen."

"I just don't understand," Ben said.

"Shit, try being a horse," Meathead said.

Ben poured the rest of the whiskey on the ground, stood, and put the empty bottle in the saddlebag.

"When I'm gone you won't have anybody to talk to," Ben said to Meathead.

"You're the one who always wants to talk," Meathead said.

"I suppose we humans are full of ourselves even if there is nothing to be full of," Ben said.

"You people are just hung up thinking you're better than any other living thing in the world, when in all truth I think man might be the worst thing that has happened to the world."

"I can't argue with that," Ben said.

Ben sat underneath the tree again and looked at the hangman's rope dangling from the branch. "You've always been my destiny," he said to the rope.

He shut his eyes.

******

After Ben's visit to Jenny he continued moving from ranch to ranch all over the west, never staying on any one ranch for more than two seasons. There were no highs or lows to his life, just a lingering sadness that he could never shake. There was nothing in life that seemed to have any meaning and nothing he could do about it. His only enjoyment was reading and even reading held no solace to Ben. Ben figured his life as being stuck somewhere in-between, he just couldn't figure out what the in-between was.

Ben had been healthy for many years, but then in his early sixties, little things started to go wrong. He lost his teeth and he started to feel tired and sluggish and at times he was short of breath. He went to a VA hospital in Wyoming and the doctor told him he had high blood pressure and his lungs and liver were about shot from drinking and smoking for all of his life. The doctor warned Ben to stop drinking and smoking and tried to put him on heart medicine. Ben did not fill the prescription and did not give up drinking or smoking.

When Ben was seventy, he told himself if drinking and smoking or a heart attack didn't kill him, when the time came he would kill himself.

But it was strange to Ben. The older he got he started to fear death. After the war he had never really feared death, but in later life there were times a sudden intense fear overcame him when he thought about dying. Life had been a bunch of shit but the thought of there being nothing after death frightened him. He had only prayed a few times in his life. But now, at times, he would think about God, and although he could not truly believe in God, he could not get the thought out of his mind that there might be a God. With his fear he cut back more on his drinking and smoking.

"If there is a God, I am truly in some deep shit," he would say.

Ben would lay awake at night thinking about excuses he could give to God on why he had screwed up his life so much, but he never came up with a good one. How could he pull the wool over the eyes of something that knew everything? But, he did decide he had only broken a few of God's commandments. He had never stolen. He had never committed adultery. He had coveted a few wives in his time but never let it go past a thought. There was no commandment against drinking, or fighting, or smoking, or wasting one's life. There were two that bothered him the most though, "Thou Shall Not Kill." He had killed and killed in hate. There could be no forgiveness for taking another life - even in a war. And, "Thou Shall Honor Thy Father and Mother." Even though he had forgiven them, he could not honor them.

Ben was eighty-four years old when Mr. Kutler hired him on. The last three years had been good years to Ben. Even the United States sending forces to Afghanistan and Iraq did not bother him like earlier wars - he figured everything in life was futile anyway and nothing would ever really change. He spent most of his time reading books and feeding birds, fixing a little fence, bringing in strays and messing with windmills. When he went to town, he did not go to bars but got his supplies, went to the liquor store, got his books, and headed home. Town was alien to him - there was nothing there he wanted. The only thing town did to him was make him sad for all the young people who were speeding their lives away trying to catch a dream that was not really their own.

******

"Looking back I guess there was nothing else in life I could have really been," Ben said to Meathead.

"Could you see me as a doctor or a lawyer or a teacher?" Ben laughed.

"Guess we are born into what we are going to be and it's like we really have no control over it. It controls us."

"If I would have been born in a big city I'd be a bum."

"Now I'm a cowboy bum."

"Cowboy's about the only job that one can be poor, not be worth a damn, but people still respect."

"Lord help us Jesus."

Meathead looked at Ben like he was boring.

Ben stood and carefully brushed off his pants. He took several deep breaths and looked out over the trees. The sun had just hit the tops of the trees and a steady breeze kicked up from the east.

He took the letter out of his pocket he'd written to Jenny, reread it, and put it back.

He took the remaining tobacco pouches, opened them, and turning in a circle he scattered the tobacco to the wind but he did not pray.

He took the free end of the rope, circled the tree trunk with it several times, tied a square knot, which left the noose hanging down about three feet from the branch. When Meathead walked out from underneath him, his feet would still be several feet above the ground.

Ben took off his hat and hung it from a small branch, mounted Meathead and moved underneath the noose. "You've been a good old horse," Ben said.

Meathead did not answer.

Ben slipped the noose over his head and tightened it around his neck. The rope was scratchy but not offensive and strangely soothing.

He looked up through the branches of the tree. It was like the branches of the tree divided the sky into pieces of a puzzle - each piece a world of its own.

His mother's face appeared in one of the patches of sky. She did not look worn or haggard. "I loved you in the only way I knew how," she said to Ben.

"I know," Ben replied.

"Your sister dying took what little of my heart I had left," she said.

"Sis can fly Ma," Ben said. "She got her dream."

His mother smiled and then vanished.

In another patch of sky Ben's father's face appeared. He had not changed. He looked mean and resentful - filled with hate. "I gave you my mark," he said to Ben. "I'm sorry."

"I did to myself all that has happened in my life," Ben said. "It is not your mark."

"Can you forgive me?" his father asked.

Ben nodded but could not reply.

The face vanished.

Barbara appeared in a patch of the sky. She was wearing the outfit she wore the last time Ben saw her, and had on bright red lipstick - lipstick the color of blood. "We had a great love, Ben," she said.

Tears filled Ben's eyes. "It's a love that never really left me," Ben said.

"It might have been a curse to you," Barbara said sadly.

"Love is never a curse," Ben said.

"You should not do what you are about to do," Barbara said. "You should go and see Jenny and visit your grandchildren."

"It's been too many years."

"Blood is blood, you said it yourself Ben."

"I wish so you had not been killed," Ben said.

"I died serving people, Ben. It was not a bad death."

Ben smiled and wiped the tears from his eyes. Barbara vanished.

Lazun appeared in a patch of the sky. "Well cowboy, I guess you never saw the error of your ways," he said with a big grin on his face.

"Oh, I saw it," Ben said. "But I was never strong enough to do anything about it."

"Did you ever eat a calzone?" Lazun asked.

"No, but I ate a lot of canned spaghetti."

Lazun smiled again.

"You were the best friend I ever had," Ben said.

"War can make some good friends," Lazun said.

"I wish it would have been me that was killed and not you," Ben said just as Lazun vanished.

Reno appeared in another patch of sky with a woman and a child. "I helped you up on a horse when you were a boy. Now let me help you down from a horse," Reno said and held out his hand.

Ben started to hold out his hand but withdrew it.

"No shame in asking for help," Reno said. "It is never too late to make amends."

"Have you seen the ocean and been on a fishing boat?" Ben asked.

"I no longer need dreams," Reno said.

Reno and the woman and the child vanished.

Mac and Moose and Crow and Whitey appeared in the sky. "Never thought you'd give up," Whitey said.

"I don't want to die being taken care of like a baby," Ben said.

"Every day is a gift of life," Mac said, and they all vanished.

Maria appeared in the sky. She pointed a lit candle in a glass container with a Saint painted on it at Ben. "I have found my rest," she said and vanished.

Dave and Peggy appeared but they did not look at Ben. They were only looking at each other. Three young children, holding hands and laughing, circled them. They vanished.

Duke appeared in the sky. "You and me are the same," Duke said. "Some people enjoy their misery."

"I never enjoyed it," Ben said.

"Then give it up," Duke said and vanished.

Then all the German soldiers Ben had killed in the war paraded by Ben. They did not look at Ben, but looked through him. They looked lost and disillusioned. One of the soldiers muttered, "We did not have a chance at life like you did. Do not end yours." They slowly faded away, like their spirits did not want to go back to where they had come from.

In a patch of sky, an old man appeared that Ben did not recognize. "You gave me a good life Ben Sharps," he said.

"Who are you?" Ben asked.

"I am the young German soldier who was crying by the tree that you did not shoot. I went on to be a doctor and devoted my life to the poor."

"I'm glad I didn't kill you," Ben said.

No more images appeared. Ben lowered his head.

"Forgive me my trespasses," Ben prayed, and spurred Meathead hard.

CHAPTER TWENTY-ONE

After Ben spurred Meathead she did not move an inch.

"Come on and get, you cantankerous old hunk of dog meat," Ben swore and spurred Meathead harder.

Meathead did not move but flicked at him with her tail.

Ben kicked Meathead as hard as he could.

Meathead lowered her head and shut her eyes like she was going to take a nap.

Ben yanked on the reins and pounded his heels into the horse's sides. Meathead held her position.

Ben yanked on the reins as hard as he could and kicked until he was out of breath.

"You son-of-a-bitch," he gasped. "You don't move and I'll take my shotgun and blow my brains out."

Meathead did not move.

Ben pulled the shotgun out of its scabbard.

"A person who blows his brains out only wants sympathy," Meathead said.

"What do you mean?" Ben asked angrily.

"Somebody has to clean up the mess. But I guess for you there wouldn't be much mess. Your brain is about the size of a peanut."

Holding the stock of the shotgun with both hands, Ben put the shotgun barrel on his forehead and rested his thumb on the trigger.

The crow that had landed on the treetops flew down and landed on Meathead's head, looked at Ben seriously, and then bowed his head like he was ashamed of Ben. "I told you I don't have a damn soul," Ben cursed at the crow.

The crow cawed three times.

Ben lowered the shotgun and swatted at the crow, that, just as he was about to be hit, flew and landed on the top of the tree and cawed three more times.

Ben pointed the shotgun once again at his head, hesitated for a moment and then slipped the shotgun back in the scabbard.

"A man trying to die and what gets in the way but a damn horse that won't move and a bullshit crow," Ben stormed. "What the hell is going on?"

Ben kicked Meathead several more times but she still would not move.

"I'll jump off by myself," Ben swore and tried to slide out of the saddle to the left, but Meathead moved left and Ben couldn't get his leg over the saddle horn.

Ben tried to get off to the right but Meathead moved to the right.

He tried to slide off the horse's rump but Meathead moved backwards.

Ben kicked Meathead over a dozen times until he couldn't move his legs anymore and could hardly take a breath.

"Have another smoke," Meathead said.

"I can't, I'm out of tobacco," Ben sputtered breathlessly.

The crow cawed three times at Ben.

"There's nothing in life more aggravating than something that talks too much," Ben said to the crow.

The crow cawed three more times.

Ben's shoulders slumped and he sagged in the saddle. He shut his eyes. Ben thought about all the ranches he had worked on. He thought about the miles of fence he had fixed, the cattle he had roped, and all the horses he had ridden. He thought about all the rodeos he had ridden in and the cheers and whistles and smiles of the people as they saw him ride. He remembered little boys coming up to him and shaking his hand and telling him they wanted to be just like him - one of the best saddle bronc riders in the rodeo. He remembered riding in the rodeo parades with the flags flying, and the bands playing, and how proud he was to be what he was. He saw Jenny smiling as he handed her the yellow rose.

Ben opened his eyes and his sister appeared. "After this time I will never appear to you again," she said, but she was not sad, she was smiling.

"Is the sky heaven?" Ben asked.

"That's for you to find out Ben, but not today."

"I'm worn out and I've lived too long."

"There must be something else for you to do in life," his sister said, "Or you wouldn't have lived this long. You go see your daughter, Ben. You tell her how much you missed her and how not seeing her throughout her life put a hole in your heart. You tell her you always loved her."

"I said that in the note in my pocket," Ben said.

"So you want to kill yourself because you failed her? How would that make her feel?"

"I want to die because I am tired of life. I want to die because all the good people I have known are dead and I'm still alive. I want to die because I don't understand anything. I suppose the main reason I want to die myself is I feel like a failure, not just to my daughter, but how I lived my life."

The noose around Ben's neck was starting to itch and he moved it to a different position.

"Every life in one way or another is a failure," his sister said. "No one in his own mind ever lives up to his potential."

"I'm a worthless old cowboy," Ben sighed.

"What's wrong with that?" his sister asked.

Ben looked at the crow on top of the tree and then at the back of Meathead's head. Her ears were pointed back listening.

"What else could you have been, Ben?" his sister prodded.

"I suppose there was nothing else I could have been," he answered reluctantly.

"Finish your life out, Ben," his sister said.

With a smile and a wave, she vanished.

"Be one with the sky and the stars," Ben said. "I'll miss you."

The crow on the top of the tree flew off.

Meathead took a deep breath.

Ben moved his legs away from Meathead's side to kick her again but he stopped.

Ben slipped the noose off his head, let go of it, and looked at it hanging from the branch. "It's an ugly thing isn't it, Meathead?" he said.

Meathead moved several steps away from the rope.

Ben dismounted, got his hat, and put it on. The sun had dipped below the trees and a few blue-gray hazy clouds lay on the horizon like smoke.

Ben took the letter out of his pocket he had written to his daughter but he did not read it. He lit the Zippo and started the letter on fire – holding it until the flames almost burned his fingers. Then he dropped it to the ground. When it was nothing but a folded gray-white ash he ground the ash into the dirt.

Ben looked at the hangman's noose once again. He took the empty whiskey bottle out of the saddle bags, stuck the neck of the bottle into the noose. and pulled the noose tightly around it. A gust of wind moved the rope and bottle slightly from east to west.

At the base of the tree Ben dug a hole and placed the Zippo lighter at the bottom of the hole and covered it. He found a large rock and placed it gently on top.

The sun went completely below the horizon - the sky grew darker - the North Star appeared - alone and proud.

Ben remounted Meathead. Without a nudge Meathead turned in the direction of the trailer. "Take me home old friend," Ben said.

In the dark Meathead picked her way through the trees and rocks and cactus. "I think in a few days you and I will drive to Oregon," Ben said to Meathead.

"I can rent us a little place not far from where my daughter lives and you can live out your days eating good grass."

"The hay will be so good and sweet you'll shit a river for at least a week," Ben laughed.

"I'll get to know my daughter and grandkids," Ben smiled. "I might even live to see a great grandchild."

"I'll tell them about being a cowboy and how at one time I was the best damn saddle bronc rider the rodeo had ever seen."

They rode in silence for awhile. Darkness enveloped the land. Ben looked up at the Big Dipper. A shooting star flashed through the middle of it. "Thanks, Lisa," Ben said. "It took you a long time to teach me how to fly."

"Thanks Ma and Pa. Thanks Reno. Thanks Dave and Peggy. Thanks Maria. Thanks Crow and Whitey and Moose and Mac. Thanks Duke. Thanks Lazun. Thanks Nancy. Love you Barbara. Thank you for your forgiveness Jenny."

"I'm sorry for those who I've hurt."

Meathead started down a hill. "I ever tell you Meathead about the time I rode ten broncs two seconds over time?" Ben asked.

"About a hundred times," Meathead said.

"Well I'm going to tell you again. At your age you might have forgotten some of it."

Meathead shook her head.

"It wasn't long after the war and it was the biggest party I had ever seen," Ben started. "There must have been at least a thousand people. People came from all over Colorado as well as Nebraska and Wyoming to see if Ben Sharps could ride ten broncs in a row without eating dirt. There were people playing guitars and banjoes and fiddles and harmonicas. Every way you looked there was a pretty girl who only had eyes for me. I took every bet I could, even though I didn't have any money. Those boys were just giving me their money. There was no way I wasn't going to ride those ten broncs even though they were the meanest toughest broncs I'd ever seen."

"Whoopee shit!

"You should have heard the people applaud after I rode the last one. You would have thought I was the president or something."

"Son-of-a-bitch Meathead, it was a great day."

"Whoopee shit!"

Meathead crow-hopped twice making Ben grab the saddle horn and almost knocking his false teeth out.

"Whoa up," Ben ordered. "You're too old to get frisky." Meathead snorted.

Not far away, Ben saw the starlight reflect off the roof of his trailer. "Oregon will be a good place to die," Ben said.

Ben unsaddled Meathead by the shed, took the tack in, and came back with the curry comb. He curried Meathead and then led her to the corral where her hay and sweet feed waited.

He patted her twice on the neck and she butted him playfully. Ben then closed the gate. Leaning on the rail he looked at the shadowed form of Meathead contentedly eating. "I want to thank you for not letting me die," Ben said to Meathead.

Meathead turned her head and looked at him - bits of hay were hanging out of her mouth but she didn't say anything.

"You wouldn't happen to have any whiskey or tobacco? Ben asked.

"It's bad for your health," Meathead said.

Ben smiled.

The End